EVERY DAY

EVERY DAY

ELIZABETH RICHARDS

CENTURY

Published by Century Books in 1996

13579108642

Copyright © Elizabeth Richards 1996

Elizabeth Richards has asserted her right under the Copyright, Designs and Patents Act,
1988 to be identified as the author of this work

First published in the United Kingdom by Century Books,
Random House UK Limited
20 Vauxhall Bridge Road, London, SW1V 2SA

Random House Australia (Pty) Limited
16 Dalmore Drive, Scoresby,
Victoria 3179, Australia

Random House New Zealand Limited
18 Poland Road, Glenfield
Auckland 10, New Zealand

Random House South Africa (Pty) Limited
PO Box 2263, Rosebank 2121,
South Africa

Random House UK Limited Reg. No. 954009

A CIP catalogue record for this book is available from the British Library

Papers used by Random House UK Limited are natural, recyclable products made from
wood grown in sustainable forests. The manufacturing processes conform to the
environmental regulations of the country of origin

ISBN 0 71 2677216

Printed and bound in Great Britain by
Mackays of Chatham PLC, Chatham, Kent

FOR MY FATHER

My special thanks to Caron K., for spreading the word, to Ron Bernstein, for finding *Every Day* a home on the West Coast, and to my editor, Emily Bestler, for her perseverance and enthusiasm.

I am also grateful to my teachers Ron, Michael and Shelby and indebted to E.G., Mitchell, Sarah and the Cordelias for their love and good humor throughout the years.

Finally, I want to thank my agent, Ann Rittenberg, for years of brilliant work, faith and friendship.

ONE

The card was postmarked Kanab, Utah, and it said he was coming today, that he'd call, that he needed to see me. All morning, between things, I've been looking for it, drifting through rooms with my eyes on stacks of papers, wastebaskets, piles of laundry, wondering how on earth I could have mislaid something so important. At one point, in the baby's room, I said aloud, 'Now what could I have done with it?' My voice was lifted, girlish. I wasn't loud, so the baby didn't wake. She stirred, brought her feet up to meet her velvety hands, then sighed. Jane, my eight-year-old, was downstairs with the TV on, so I know she didn't hear. Earlier, though, she had remarked upon my short fuse, advising therapy once again, which they seem to be teaching children about in the third grade now. Isaac, fourteen, is at baseball practice. As far as he's concerned, I don't have an awareness of men, have no connection to or need for them, and if he even suspected I was crazed because I couldn't find a postcard written to me by a man who happens to be his father but has made no attempt to see him in fourteen years, he'd never stop gagging.

The man's name is Fowler. At the time of my knowing him I was a wreck, but I could have stayed that way and not noticed. We made a truckload of plans, the old story, and he went on to fulfill them without me. We had a son with whom he fell in love but to whom he had the same trouble committing himself. I was seventeen when he left, but thanks to Isaac and my mother, I didn't have time to bottom out. The three of us lived in the apartment where I grew up while I earned the credits for an equivalency diploma and eventually a BA from Hunter. My father, who had gotten his own place downtown while I was still in grade school, gave us money and had us to lunch on Saturdays. He still does the lunch thing when we can coordinate schedules. But I know that my mother goes every Saturday. They are devoted grandparents, and they're devoted to each other. They just don't live in the same house. From them I have learned that living arrangements can be just that: living arrangements.

For fourteen years I've had no direct news of Fowler. I've seen his name listed as visiting lecturer for some of

New York's film series. I know when a film of his is playing or up for an award. I know he's moved out of the antisocial underground commentary he was first famous for into grander issues of progressive social import. I suspect him of having lost his humor, which seems just deserts for a man who once considered the world his playground.

After my current boss, Gillette, rescued me from certain doom as a temp, I met Simon playing tennis in Central Park. He was lithe, older, keen on just about anything. Gillette said he had 'Just Divorced' stamped all over him, but I didn't care. We got married at the boat pond eight months after we met, a district judge officiating at what my mother still refers to as 'that no-frills affair'. It was the best party I ever attended. We have our three extraordinary children (Isaac knows Simon isn't his father, but he'll take no part in a discussion about his real father), our debts and our loud, uproarious life. Admitted: it is inconceivable that a postcard from Fowler should land anywhere but on the cutting room floor. But I stopped breathing for a minute when it came. I stopped the million things I do per hour. We have unfinished business.

I began an involved primping session: nail care, a facial over the spaghetti pot, for which Jane has still not forgiven me, and now, a bubble bath. Attending to body matters mortifies me, as I've become aware of serious changes. My backside, for instance, used to be a rather firm and perky area. Now it responds only to food and gravity. My arms hang. Bubbles are nice because it's possible to reinvent a younger body, the one Fowler knew, the one I was so eager to show him when I was fifteen. Of course it would be unconscionable for me to be making an effort like this if it was intended to encourage a tryst. But that isn't my purpose. I certainly don't mind the idea of his wanting to see me, but I mean to be even more self-serving here. I will take great delight in any discomfort I can cause him after these fourteen years of raising a child who may never live his father's deficiency down. Fowler once told me, during a lecturing junket, that I'd be the one to leave him. We were at the Wursthaus in Cambridge after one of his Eastern Seaboard screenings. (We went up the coast, from Maryland to Maine, showing his first film at colleges, one that I'd helped him edit.) I had four-week-old Isaac in the Snugli. Fowler looked wan, although the film, about wealthy women living in their cars, had been well received. He said, 'You'll leave me. Just wait.' Stupidly, I waited.

All sorts of excuses were given when he cut out: I

was bound to Isaac now, I'd have to return to school, his career as a film-maker was being stifled by the academic life, we were too much with each other and not enough out in the world that would feed our geniuses. I could have better managed the admission that he was bored.

I hug my steaming knees, then stretch. It is still morning, minutes shy of noon. A Saturday. Sunlight refracts in the water where the bubbles have vanished. I am a housewife. I live an hour outside of Manhattan, and I have work I can do at home and be paid for. My husband has never so much as uttered a cruel word to me, he is a fine father, and any bill I can't manage he takes on even if it means a third job. He isn't the humorless dolt I once imagined I'd end up with if I couldn't have Fowler.

'Mom, I have to *go*!' Jane bellows from the living room. Our downstairs toilet is broken. I told Simon I'd get it taken care of today.

I hurry, creating a tidal wave of bathwater. The cordless rings atop the hamper. I freeze, knee-deep in suds, my skin goosebumpy. My throat is full. I clear, answer, wait.

'Well.' The twang, earned in Southern roots and upbringing. Sun in the voice. 'You've got a cold.'

'No.'

'It is you, isn't it?'

'Yes.'

He laughs. 'Meet me. I'm standing on Fifth Avenue, across from the Sherry Netherland. Can you get here?'

I hear Jane's heavy tread, her whining diphthong. 'Mo-om.' I consider his invitation, pull at the plug chain with my toes. The drain sucks the water out in greedy, loud gulps. 'In an hour,' I say. I'll take the girls to Kirsten's. She's home Saturdays with her two. Jane loves it there because of Adrienne, eleven, the local expert on AIDS.

'I'll have one drink while I wait,' he says. 'I'll calm down. This city gets to me. Fabulous.' He clicks off.

Still holding the phone, I let Jane in.

'A towel would do wonders,' she says. 'And try not to drop the phone. You'll be a crispy critter.'

She beams at this. I pull my blue wrapper around me. 'OK, Mom,' I tell her. My daughter, the forty-year-old. She knows more now than I'll ever know.

'Mom, are you losing weight?'

Jane asks me this from time to time because she knows it makes me feel good because I am not losing weight. I haven't gained, but I haven't overthrown a few pounds left me from having Daisy, my glorious ten-pounder. Some days it gets to me, although today isn't one of them.

She sits down. Peeing is not a private event for the girls in this family. Simon and Isaac close the door, but we can always hear. 'Who was that anyway?'

'A friend. I'm taking you over to Kirsten's for the afternoon.'

'But Dad said he'd take us to the pool.' Her mouth does the thing all her friends' mouths do to display disgust, upper lip raised on one side, and her eyes roll.

'Kirsten has a pool.'

'It's above ground!'

I'm about to call up my don't-give-me-that-yuppie-private-school-me-generation backtalk speech when I catch myself. In light of the criminal I've decided to have lunch with, I let her have her protest.

'Put your bathing suit in a bag.'

'Fine,' she says, huffing, and flushes.

I think about underwear for the first time in a while, choosing a Victoria's Secret print set. Over this, jeans and a black silk blouse, all of it reminiscent of younger days when Fowler and I went to downtown bars to meet his friends. Jane comes in with her neon beach bag and scowls. 'Mom, are you going to a concert?'

'Yes. The Stones are playing Central Park.'

'Very funny, Mom. Daisy's up, you know.' There are so many ways in which I am a bad mother today. I can't get past Jane with a thing.

I can hear Daisy, my serene child, cooing and laughing in the little room next to mine. With her I felt I'd finally perfected baby-making: she slept through at three months, she nursed for twelve, she's been sick three times in eighteen months, and she hasn't lost her fat yet. I'm still in love the way I was when they were rolling her in to me at the hospital in her plastic tray. Of course I adore my older ones, but Daisy lets me breathe. Isaac is so angry, so protective of all of us, so ready for the shadow that is his absent father to come in and ruin things, that he never enjoys anything except, occasionally, baseball practice. Jane runs our home. Daisy doesn't seem to need me at all, and so I need her every minute.

'Can I take her out of her crib?' Jane asks, sure of my answer.

'Yes. Put her suit in too. I'll get some crackers and juice.'

We travel well, as a family. We're usually prepared with snacks and tapes for the car and car games that can drag on for hours. The children have always liked going places, even if it's two minutes to Kirsten's or six hours to see friends in Vermont. In the front seat Jane empties the glove compartment in search of the 10,000 Maniacs tape, which I know Isaac took to listen to in the Mustard Bomb, our expiring second car meant for local outings.

'Isaac's such a shmuck,' she says.

'Jane, must you?' I plead. It's not entirely her fault she has such a vocabulary. Both brother and father have been known to cast such an aspersion on whomever from time to time.

'He takes everything.' She slams the compartment and crosses her arms.

'Aouff,' Daisy keeps saying, which I take as an indication that I should hand her something to eat.

'When are you going to be home?' Jane whines. 'I want to go out and get my own Maniacs tape.'

'This afternoon,' I promise. 'We'll go to Sam Goody and get you one, and maybe something for Daisy to listen to.'

'OK.'

I can't bear to see my kids unhappy, and I often promise them things we can ill afford. The two older ones are aware of this defect in my parenting, but it isn't often that they try for an upper hand. I don't know how we've done it, but we've gotten them to believe in limits.

Kirsten's on her knees in front of the peonies, pruning.

'Can I dump them?' I call from the car.

She stands up, her gardening clothes wrinkly and smeared here and there with topsoil, her highlit hair falling out of its back clip. 'Do they have suits?'

'Natch.' We smile at each other, squinting. Kirsten is the only friend I have to whom I can safely say 'natch', the only one who knows this is a leftover word and that I'm not from somewhere people would generally die to be from. I do have some names in my ancestry, but if there was ever any money it's been spent.

Jane hands me her beach bag and streaks into the house to find Adrienne. I gather Daisy from her car seat, let her straddle my waist and take up fistfuls of my hair.

'Monkey!' Kirsten says to her, trying to ease the transition, failing, as Daisy starts to howl because she knows she's about to be mommyless.

'She'll eat everything you have,' I say. 'You're a better friend than I am.'

'I'll get you back,' Kirsten counters. 'Ted's away all of next week. If you think I'm staying here alone, you're wrong. There was another "blackout" yesterday.'

She refers to a new gang agenda, about which we've been warned by the papers, the talk radio and local news stations. It involves too much horror to describe in rational terms, but it has the suburban folk as wide-eyed as the city folk.

'I'll call you. I left Simon a note. I'm going into the city for lunch, and he'll probably pick them up before I get home.'

I squeeze Daisy, try to urge the last sob out. 'Love you, Muffin,' I whisper. I give her to Kirsten, and then I turn, unable to watch her face registering the tragedy of my leaving. Not until I get on the parkway do I dare think of anything but her and how I should never let her out of my sight. Not until I'm safely through the toll do I let go enough to enjoy being sleek, or as sleek as I get under the circumstances, in my fleur-de-lis lingerie, in my worn jeans and platform sandals. I am thirty-one years old. At this moment I might look assured, I might look ridiculous, but I know one thing: this visit with Fowler is an act of will on my part. I'm driving south to where Fowler is. No music. No news. Just the brain thudding with heart's messages, telling me to claim from him what he owes Isaac, what he owes me.

My friend Pam told someone about the pregnancy a few days before our unmodel behavior, mine and Fowler's, was made public by Hastings Prep administrators. I remember a very early morning, how I sensed that other people knew, students, some teachers, even a woman on the kitchen staff who looked at my face probingly when she handed me my second plate of hash browns. Fowler and I had driven over the Massachusetts state line into New York where, he suggested, we could talk about the predicament more rationally, without distraction. He had tried to coerce me into an abortion. Sometimes I think of that effort as generous of him, and indicative of his knowing that he'd never follow through on fatherhood. At the time it struck me as outrageously selfish. I refused. I thought that a baby couldn't be a happier idea, especially if it were Fowler's. I remember shouting at him, invoking Thoreau, twisting his words to make him sound like a hypocrite. He did nothing. He hung on the steering wheel, silent.

When we got back to campus, it was dawn. A green smell emanated from the leaves where the water hung, restive and full, before the April wind pulled it to the ground. The combination of that fresh smell and the one of Fowler's poncho, medicinal, having been packed away in a box with camphor balls for a season, is one I can still recall. I was enshrouded, hidden, under the poncho, and he guided me to the dorm. I imagined witnesses in the landscape, in windows, doorframes, peering out from behind hedges. I knew Pam had told someone. My idyllic boarding-school world, complete with secret older lover, had changed. It had become a place in which something I had thought could happen only to the lazy, husky-voiced girls I envied, girls like Pam, had happened to me.

'Like something out of a movie,' my mother said after she received the letter from the headmaster announcing the 'unfortunate – for all concerned – circumstance'. Every family of every Hastings student, past and present, barring only the deceased graduates, received a copy of this letter detailing the reasons for Fowler's being fired and my expulsion, 'sadly, two months prior to graduation'. My mother thought the public announcement galling, and she only questioned me one time about why I'd chosen not to have an abortion. She was with me the day Isaac was born. She wept tears of joy on seeing him in my arms. After Fowler left and I went to live with her, she communicated her trouble with the situation only through an earlier bedtime, one she's kept for all the fourteen years we've known Isaac. 'He's a divine boy,' she often says, shrugging, which I take to mean that she can't imagine how he could have had such a father, and perhaps that she could have seen Fowler coming for a million miles, so why hadn't I?

My father, circumspect to the last, said the school

authorities wouldn't have done anything like this unless they'd decided it was absolutely necessary. He was at a philosophers' conference in Chicago when Isaac was born, but he too wept when they met. Neither of my parents, despite their bohemianism, was able to understand how anyone could up and leave a child of his own in the manner that Fowler did.

After all this time he couldn't have sounded more like himself: charged, definite. I can't imagine what he knows of me now, other than my address and phone number. I don't even know how he got those. We were never married, so when he left I had nothing on him, couldn't sue for divorce or freeze his assets or take out judgments so someone could collar him in an airport. And I'm not sure I'd have done all that anyway. It would have made the fact of his leaving even uglier, more unspeakable. At the time I had Isaac, I was taken in a way I never anticipated, and it softened the blow. Now that I lead the kind of life Fowler and I agreed we'd never live because it would deaden the sensibilities we made such careers of having, I can say I don't hate him. I could not pity him, but I don't hate him. I didn't want it, the misadventure, the friends in vogue, the *faux artistes* or the real ones, all in black leather, their hair spoiled with dye, sculpted, or simply shaved off.

'Fucking lost souls,' I say aloud, in the vernacular of that other time. I mean to include myself. It's what we were. Lost and trying to capitalize on that fact. So sure of ourselves in a nihilistic way. So arrogant.

'What do you need *me* for?' I remember asking him shortly before Isaac was born. We'd established ourselves in a cavernous room above a Korean market in the East Village. 'You'd have done this anyway. You'd be here anyway.'

'Oh, Leigh,' he said. 'Let's not do "need" tonight. "Need" is so schmaltzy. Need'll kill you. You don't want to be *needed*, for God's sake.'

Although stung, I understood what he meant. But I had no choice at that point, with a baby coming. I was going to be needed, whether I liked it or not.

But for a long time I did capitalize on the double vision. On the one hand, I was needed (by Isaac), stable (in my goals, in staying in New York where my parents were). On the other, I was an unwed mother with atheistic, separated parents. I was bored unless something outrageous was going on. I liked it, when I met Simon's father, that he'd spent nights in white-collar prison for extortion. I liked it that his various wives had undone themselves in one way or another (plastic surgery, dangerous dieting, excommunication from their children

with previous husbands) in order to accommodate him,
only to lose him. I just liked the possibility of him, the
alternative he offered as a human being. The message
that just beyond where we're looking, something wild is
preparing to enter and shake us up, make us account for
what we're doing, still moves me. I was, in many ways,
reminded of Fowler when I met him, the first time, on
Fire Island. He was coming off the tennis court,
perspiring, bronzed beyond decency. 'Tatskela!' he
shouted when he saw me, and I felt instantly adored.
For a second I could see why women dropped their lives
for him.

He came to our wedding in a leather tux, his wife of
the minute dressed as a cabaret performer.

'Could you *believe*?' Simon said, when we got to the
hotel. 'A gangster and his moll.'

I told him I sort of liked their effrontery, their proud
transience. 'What does it matter anyway?' I hooted.
'That's the way he is! He'll always have one foot in the
door, one out.'

Simon stood there, his arms long, helpless against me
and his father.

'You two will get along very well, in that case. You
both trade on that.'

He is a kind and careful man, and he doesn't believe

in being in two places at once. The fact that I do, that I can't help this, is my biggest failing.

'I won't be pigeon-holed,' I added, with the seriousness he required at the time. 'You are what you are.'

'Dishrag,' I say, in reference to my time with Fowler. 'I was a dishrag.'

I cross to the East Side at 57th Street and take a chance on a parking garage off Fifth Avenue. Simon and I don't go in for this kind of expedience when we come into Manhattan; we plan parking ahead of time. But a person on a mission such as mine shouldn't get bogged down in too much banality.

The parking attendant sneers at our downscale wagon. He points out a dent and some scratches on the passenger side to make sure I am aware of their previous incurrence.

'Don't worry,' I say. 'I'm not going to sue you.'

He smiles stingily. I have always wanted to say that to someone. Now I have.

I walk over to Fifth and toward the hotel. It is hard to imagine that there are others with similar stories going to meet prior loves to try to make sense of the damage, but there must be. You hear it all the time on the news, estranged fathers and children and the mothers of those children convening, come what will. Most of the stories I hear are gory, occurring in projects and outside city schools, places where gunfire is the rule rather than the exception.

I stop on 60th Street, sickened, as I'd always predicted I would be if the chance to see Fowler again, to present him with the fact of his son's existence and mine, ever arose. I have neglected to mention shame. Shame, as I know it, is a chameleon. It appears in your children's faces when what you have done mortifies them. It reaches you in snippets of others' conversations: hospital staff, your parents' friends, your new husband's business associates. It is inescapable, and it doesn't transmogrify or dissipate the way that anger and love do. I clutch my bag and step out into the street. I am ashamed, not for what I'm about to do, but for what I've done. My son's fierce granite eyes bore into me from everywhere.

I was at Hastings a whole year before I even connected Fowler's face with his name. Pam and I were dancing in our room in ski boots. He came roaring in, bellowing about noise and unearned senses of entitlement. He'd been trying to hold an advisee meeting in the common room below ours, could we possibly save it for the slopes?

'I don't ski,' I told him.

'That's of no consequence,' he said.

Pam and I happened to be drunk, and Fowler's rage thrilled and amused us. He was insufferably handsome, with finger-combed streaky blond hair and dark eyes, a combination that continues to be compelling for any girl who lays eyes on Isaac. I expected sarcasm and meanness from a guy like Fowler, but I was taken in by something else: a business, a rush to be done with this interview so he could get to the next thing, a total denial of weariness. An energy. He had energy, what were the senior boys saying that year, *out the wazoo*. You couldn't keep up with him. Yes, he was handsome. Yes, purported to be brilliant. But he didn't have time to devote to his appearance or his brilliance. He had things to do, people to advise, places to go. You could hop aboard, see if you could stomach the ride, or just sit back and watch his dust.

'I'll see you two Monday morning at 7.30 in the Hall of Languages. You can tell me and the acting disciplinary synod what you've been drinking that makes you think you can ski indoors.'

He picked up a glass that said New York Rangers. (Pam had a car; we were forever filling up the tank for our AWOL runs to the liquor store and being awarded

free glasses featuring sports teams we had no interest in.)
He sniffed. 'Forget rum. It ruins the taste of the Coke.'

He was gone. Some people just leave. Fowler was
able to vanish. Extreme, he was. A big deal. He made
me tired, and he hadn't been in our room but four
minutes.

'What was that?' I said to Pam, who'd begun her
unbuckling.

'Fuck him,' Pam said. 'Man's got the biggest chip on
his shoulder since Richard the Third.'

I laughed and fell back on my messy bed. But I
thought Pam was wrong. There was no chip. Fowler
didn't give a damn about who had money and ski boots.
He just didn't want them to get in his way, to waste his
time with extravagant excuses. I closed my eyes. I
thought about seeing him up close again, getting a
chance to say something, stopping him dead in his blurry
tracks.

For English my first year at Hastings I'd been the only
girl in the class of Mr Inslee Brinkman. 'Some names
you just don't know what to do with,' my father had
said when I told him. There were various unkind
nicknames, ranging in their aptness. I went with 'Pinky'
or 'Sprinkles', which seemed the most fitting. Brinkman

was a bachelor close to retirement who knew grammar as one does one's own face. He could be seen of a Saturday afternoon in the fields beyond the athletic buildings, his back bent, in search of rare breeds of mushrooms. Everyone in his class learned the word 'myxomycophyte'. I actually liked him in the end, and I even saw reason in his giving me a C.

My second year, the year of the ski-boot incident, I had Chip Greenaway for English. He had a Dartmouth smile and a thick neck. He was also the varsity football coach. He spent more time stamping on the desktops than he did with his feet on the floor. He was emphatic, but no one seemed to know about what. I didn't learn a thing from him except to shield my head whenever I perceived an overhead shadow. He did fall once, toppled by passion over some abstruse literary conceit. A lot of people got As in his class, evidence, we felt sure, that Greenaway was of a lower order.

Then I was put in Fowler's class. Advanced Placement. This is what my A in Greenaway's class earned me. I knew I had no business in AP anything, but by this time I was enamored of the notion of collecting experience for experience's sake, no matter how painful it promised to be. I'd learned this not from the Lake Poets, but from Pam, my roommate of all three years.

Pam had schooled me in the thrills of marijuana, alcohol and shoplifting. I still didn't believe her on the sex issue. I went into Fowler's hardball English class in the fall believing that he could teach me about that at the very least, and maybe I'd learn something about poetry too.

I'd been on Martha's Vineyard all summer, staying with Pam in her family's lavish compound, by day earning minimum wage for shoveling French fries into waxpaper-lined baskets that also contained gourmet burgers and by night testing the limits of my tolerance for vodka and gin. We'd been sharing the house with an endless battery of male guests: bartenders, sailing and tennis instructors, the odd college grad enrolled in a business training program at a bank sent up by Pam's real-estate broker mother. No night was predictable. There were no set sleeping arrangements. One morning I woke up in Pam's arms. 'He left,' Pam muttered, and then rolled over and slept until I got home from work. By Labor Day I thought I'd seen it all. My father, a Polish Jew who wouldn't have been allowed to play tennis where Pam and I went to hit in the late afternoons, couldn't understand why I'd wanted to sling hash instead of come with the family to Fire Island for the four hundredth summer in a row. My mother said, 'Let her go. It's a nice place. She'll have fun there.' She knew. She used to summer there until she married my father.

'Nice bracelet,' Fowler said, tapping the grey rope bracelet on my wrist. 'Let me guess: summer on an island, lots of people, you don't remember a single name. Great stuff. You must be tired. Time to get down to brass tacks.'

He handed out a reading list no elderly person with time on his or her hands could have tackled in five years: The Book of Job, *Tristram Shandy*, *The Divine Comedy*, *Middlemarch*, *Ulysses*, *Moby Dick*, *War and Peace*. I looked up with glazed, tired eyes that begged to be impressed.

He was smiling at all of us, waiting for us to look up in horror. I steeled myself. No way. I'd drop the course in the afternoon. I'd laugh my way back to the dorm. As Pam had said so often, 'Fuck him.' Mr Nowhere doing his Nowhere thing in the middle of Nowhere, Massachusetts. Getting over his brilliance. Fuck him.

He took the roll, making checks as each student responded grimly to the reality of being present. Again he looked up, victorious.

'You're here. Get ready. This is going to break all of your backs. But it'll be good. You'll all be as tired as Lisa over here.'

'Leigh,' I corrected.

'You should be as tired as Adelman over here. Don't worry. She can handle it. So can you.'

I swallowed. My last name still rang out like the shofar in this bleak wilderness of pristine Waspdom. I watched him sift through a pile of dittos, decide which to hand out first, start them around, give no instructions, assume everything of us, assume I hadn't taken offense. And, oddly enough, I hadn't.

'It was great,' I told Pam, who seemed eager to know. 'You know, the kind of class everyone who has no life should take.'

We were in the snack bar, smoking, waiting for our group to assemble: Bill, Murph and Todd, I could have died of boredom, were buying food. It was amazing what they could put away, not so amazing to me now that I see how much Isaac needs to sustain him for a mere morning. 'Totally repulsive,' Pam had said the night before. She'd never met people who actually ate.

'You call *this* a life?' she said, indicating the panorama of students in booths stuffing their faces with grease and sugar.

'I know,' I said, my voice sliding like Pam's. 'I'd much rather be in the dorm reading Job.'

'Look,' Pam warned, 'at least he's fun to look at. All I do in English is stare at Greenaway's nose and try to figure out how many times it's been broken.'

Todd and Murph slid their burgers onto the table. 'Scoot over,' Murph told me. He hip-checked me. He was tall and beefy, like most of the boys at Hastings. He made a show of wanting me, but he always had to get to bed early because of a game the next day, thank God. He was from a town outside of Hartford. Todd, from Greenwich, was in the daily habit of pressing Pam to accompany him to the woods for drugs.

'Hopeless,' she called him.

Our intolerance for these boys had magnified since I'd begun Fowler's class and our discussions about him had become regular. I thought Pam might have been miffed that she didn't have a daily crack at getting his attention.

'Hey, Nymphette, where are your wings?' Todd said to Pam in between bites of burger.

Pam sucked hard on a Parliament. She spoke before exhaling. 'Come again?'

Todd chuckled to himself, and Murph waited respectfully for the other shoe to fall. Bill, our wrestler, was unwrapping a Hostess fruit pie.

'I thought all angels had wings.' Todd smiled, his eyes red, dopey slits.

'I can't deal,' Pam said. She looked at her watch, which was intricate enough. 'Time for my enema. Bye, fuzzy-wuzzies.'

She got up. She waited for me to get up. I stubbed out my cigarette on the top of a Coke can.

'This is so where I don't want to be,' Pam said as we walked across the golf course, knee-deep in mist, the lake, still and silver, to our right. To our left, the library lights were being shut off, window by window. Ahead, downhill, was our dorm. My sandals were wet from the grass, and I was sliding a bit as I walked.

'Have an affair with the guy, would you?' Pam said.

'You have an affair with him.' Of course I didn't mean this. I was close. I'd been going for extra tuition. He'd suggested Saturday morning coffee elsewhere. He'd probably never met a girl who was half-Jewish.

'No can do,' Pam said.

'Why not? You've got a better shot at him than I do.'

Pam was languorous, blond, ready. I was thinner, more nervous, smaller in almost every way. She dropped a whole, burning cigarette into the grass and laughed self-consciously.

'I don't want to get near the guy. He might find out how dumb I am.'

'So?' We laughed.

'It's not like it's a government secret,' Pam said. 'All you have to do for people to figure out you're brainless is to get yourself sent to a school where at least one building bears your family name.'

We stopped at some trees near the north entrance.

'Fucking amazing moon,' Pam said.

'God, will you look at it? I might puke,' I said. I was referring to a dorm meeting I could see taking place in the common room. A lot of the girls were already in sleepwear. Pam and I wore T-shirts to sleep, even if it was below zero out.

'Could I have a camera over here?' Pam yelled loud enough to be heard through the open window. 'Is this an ad for Lanz nightgowns?'

I stayed under the trees. I watched Pam, for once not envying her, thinking there was something sad and off-balance about this beautiful rich girl yelling to no purpose in the New England wilderness, and wondering what my connection, a girl of very different social and economic bearing, who was actually in love and not just playing at it, to her really was.

That my truancy, and not Pam's, became public has left me very sour on the subject of her. Although I have no cause to see or speak to her now, and the only news I have of her is that she lives in Newport with her husband and a pair of stunning twin daughters (their picture was featured in an alumni bulletin, which amazed me, as the Pam I knew would have torched such mail before responding to enclosed questionnaires), I sometimes imagine a reunion. We have lunch somewhere ludicrous for my budget, cheap for hers, and she tells me how bored she is and that she's having her house redone at great expense. I show her my children's pictures, one of Isaac in his sky-blue baseball jersey ready to swing, a young Fowler with his eyes typically narrowed to focus on any place other than where you stand beholding him. One of Jane ready for a birthday party on the front steps, looking ever so pleased with herself. One of Daisy in a sunhat, a wondering smile directed at our tiny garden. She shows me a clipping of her twin beauties, each holding up a tennis trophy. We eat, laugh a bit, and then I tell her I haven't forgiven her for telling whomever it was that I was pregnant, for forcing me into hiding, for making a fiasco out of what could simply have been seen as a misfortune. Of course, I was the obstinate one, wanting to go through with Isaac. But I can't think of anything without him in focus, and Pam is only guilty of having a bigger mouth than I thought she had.

She was out cold, not even under the covers of her twin iron bed, after a brutal field hockey scrimmage, the night Fowler knocked once and blew into our room. I was at my desk, my bible open to Job, my mind on Fowler as an undergraduate at his Southern college. I'd been reading up on him in the orientation handbook for the fiftieth time, mulling over his credentials and trying to picture him in a pair of ripped jeans and sandals, fine hair to his shoulders, in the middle of some campus-wide protest. Impossible. He didn't waste time on politics. He probably tore around that campus as he did ours, white shirtsleeves rolled to his elbows, tie loosened to accommodate his whirlwind, leaving trails of people dazed or irritated or swooning or all three. He probably hadn't even waited around to attend his own graduation.

'Come on,' he said. 'We're going to the movies.'

I didn't say a word. I turned off the desk light, grabbed my school sweatshirt and some loose dollars from the bureau and followed him out.

We drove into New York State and saw a double feature of *Jules and Jim* and *The Four Hundred Blows*. I tried not to read the subtitles. He sat with his elbows on the armrests and his hands pressed together under his chin as if in prayer. Occasionally he'd turn and whisper,

'Watch', then 'See?' as if there was something more of note than the characters' expressions or gestures could communicate and I'd be privileged to pick up on it. I'd seen both movies before, could have lived without *The Four Hundred Blows*, but I didn't mind seeing *Jules and Jim* again, which has always struck me as the happiest possible portrait of a *ménage à trois*.

'Can I ask you why we just did that?' I said when we left the theater.

'You may,' he said. 'But first, I think, a hot beverage.'

We drank coffee at a diner, three cups each. He wasn't eating anything, so I didn't push for food. He said, 'So?'

I felt like saying 'Noo?', which is what my father would have said.

'What about those movies?'

'What about them?' Truffaut would have been disgusted.

'They're the first movies I ever saw. My mother took me. I was nine. We lived in Boston.'

I did the prayer thing with my hands that he'd been doing as we watched the movies. 'Are we doing sob stories? Because if we are I'll have to remember my first movie too, and I'm not sure I can.'

He laughed. 'You're tough. You're not used to being up this late, are you?'

I sprayed coffee all over the table, some on his shirt. 'You can't be serious.'

'I wasn't,' he said. 'I know you and Tillinghast' (that was Pam's last name) 'never go to bed. Thus the coma when I came in to get you.'

Pam did have a way of looking terminal when she slept, as if she'd never snap out of it.

He went on, despite my sarcasm. He said he'd been writing for the movies, between four and six every morning. 'I start just about the time you and Tillinghast come oozing up from the lake after the night's dissipation. You look wonderful at that hour, like some undiscovered species, slow but undeniable.'

It seemed he never stopped, never let his guard down, always saw and knew everything, was never without his arsenal of commentary and prediction.

'Why are you telling me this?' I said, trying to sound bored.

'Because you want to know what I do.'

'Like fun.' I smiled. I'd given myself away.

We talked about movies. I told him about seeing *The Sound of Music* three times in three days, first with my grandmother Liza, who somehow earned the nickname

Pussy, then with my mother, then with a friend of Liza's, Holly Butterfield, who loved taking me places because she had no grandchildren of her own. I told him about leaving the theater after the first time, spellbound, on a late fall afternoon, during the season he and I were in now. It was cold. Somehow the excitement continued, I said. I tried to describe the clarity of color, of happening, in the movie as I saw it that day, how these seemed extendable to the sharp beauty of an early winter night, how this was a kind of love I hadn't known before, this love for a movie, for all movies. He watched me. He put money on the table, then stood, and reached for my hand.

'Where are we going now?' I asked, giving it. My questions had sounded unforgivably childish to me all evening.

'Driving,' he said. 'Continue the excitement.'

We drove through towns whose main streets were pitch black, reminders that we were out at the wrong time, had we no shame. We rattled through some covered bridges. He talked about ideas for movies, reasons to make them, what they meant, in terms of livelihood, for him.

'Some teacher,' I said, too tired to care what I was saying.

'It's possible, Adelman, to do more than one thing at a time.'

I didn't like his instructional tone just then. 'Good,' I said. 'Take me back to campus, in that case, because I'd like to continue this conversation while I'm sleeping.' I had given up on sex for the evening.

He stopped the car just shy of the two brick pillars that marked the front entrance to Hastings Prep. He was staring straight through the windshield at the brightening sky.

'Two things,' he said, 'that matter. Movies and you.'

I sighed. I was exhausted.

'And anything you're thinking,' he corrected himself. 'Now go. Go in through the back door. It's open, as you know.'

Again, I did as he said. I stole over the wet grass and up through the metal staircasing to my room where Pam was still comatose, seeming not to have moved. I lay down on my bed, and when I woke two hours later I wasn't even tired. I felt charged, on top of things, ready for him and anything he was planning to dish out.

It is important, for my own sake and for Isaac's, that I

remind myself from time to time of Fowler's less salient features, the ones that kept me watching for his car lights on Thursdays when we went driving over state lines to see movies we'd already seen, to have coffee and, finally, sex. We made love in the car, and this was what ultimately bound me to him: a sadness. He didn't gear up for the act in the obvious ways the guys on Martha's Vineyard had (aided by drink, music, urging from peers). He didn't struggle with it. He was careful. At times I thought I was too much for him, that he'd weep or cry out for help. It was the only time I could imagine him as a child, grabbing at the world, seeking help when it became too much. On the rare, sweet occasion when Isaac comes to me in tears I see Fowler in him.

I expect to see him at the bar, downing the drink of the day and talking up the employees, but he isn't there. He's at a table beyond, staring into the middle distance, missing my entrance from the left. The hair at his temples has gone beyond grey to white. Leaning against the table is a walking stick. This year he turned forty-seven.

I stop and wave. An absurd gesture, really, given our history. From his post at the table he opens his arms. He

smiles without constraint, with relief I think. I put my
bag on the seat and reach for the hand he's offering me.

'Leigh,' he says, softly, tapering, like the final word in
a poem or a prayer. He tightens his grip on my hand,
and I shut my eyes to the heartbreak of his face because
I know, without his saying another word, that he's
dying.

TWO

There's a line prudence begs you not to cross in love. It makes a distinction between your perceptions of the one you love and what is actual about him. Once you cross this line you abandon the truth that both of you are fallible and that whatever is between you is volatile and fragile. As a teenager I crossed this line, and once I had, it wasn't visible. I fed my idea of me and Fowler as lasting and invincible with details of the attention he paid me. I embellished our evenings together with promise, and when he wasn't with me I imagined he was. I invented irresistible postures for him, charming comments, an undeniable allure. The line I crossed allowed me to wallow in his very existence, and only when he was finally gone, when he'd found a place for himself that had no place for me, did I realize what I'd done.

'You look wonderful,' he says. Instead of railing

against all the years he stole from Isaac, I want to weep.
He's got my hand, both hands. In his grip there's a faint
tremble. His long fingers are softened by weather and
years. His hair is so fine, to the collar, the length it
always was.

'Sit,' he says. 'Let's take the afternoon.'

I slide in. It's not a crime, this line I cross in love. I
do remember moments when Fowler had me completely
in mind, would come to find me wherever I happened
to be in my series of grim jobs before Isaac was born.
He'd have a triumph to share or a film idea for us to
work on, or an exotic dinner in a bag. 'Sweet girl,' he'd
say. 'My sweet, sweet girl.' It's not a crime to believe
such words, to believe you'll hear them again and again.
It's something people innocently do.

'Tell me,' he says.

Eight years with a man who speaks directly hasn't
kept me in practice for this. I used to consider myself a
repartee queen. Now I'm tongue-tied.

'You first.'

He smiles into his glass. I haven't been able to deduce
what the drink *du jour* is.

'I'll be in New York for a while. I wanted you to
know about it. Or: you've been on my mind.'

It could never be 'I've missed you', 'I made a terrible

mistake', 'I was cruel', 'Thank you for not having me killed.' It has to be some either/or circumstance, some choice that demands thought or commitment. Which would I prefer: that we're colliding, as of this moment, or that I've never left his heart?

'I'll pretend I've been on your mind,' I decide.

'Fair enough. All right. Let's get two of something and I'll tell you the rest.'

We order Scotch. We never went in for prissy drinks. Now that I don't drink the hard stuff any more, a Scotch will knock me into the state required to handle this man.

'I've done these movies,' he says, 'but you know all that. Soon a teaching post comes up at NYU. So I'm back in the East Village, wandering those avenues.'

He stops, deals with a cough, one hand fluttering up with a handkerchief, not reaching a destination, accepts our drinks from the waiter, who for some reason will not look either of us in the face.

'And you thought I should know.'

He sips, pats the table. 'Indeed.'

I wanted it to be more tender, more wrenching, torrid in some way. Not adversarial. If I pulled out Isaac's baseball photograph now, the tone would surely turn hostile.

I taste the Scotch. Fire water. What I seem to crave. Anything to turn this interview into the kind of raw afternoon we'd have had as younger people. To turn me to him, move us to the floor, the back seat, any bed, to make him say, 'I'm going in', to make me tighten around him.

'No,' I say.

'No?' He looks strange, almost offended.

'No. That isn't why you wrote. You didn't write to me because you're in New York for a spell. You've been in New York a lot in recent years, and this is my first postcard. My first phone call. Let's not waste time. Tell me about the cane.'

He leans back in his chair, eyes narrowed at my powers of deduction, which are not extraordinary but which he once told me were. He nurses the Scotch with the offense.

He speaks slowly, as if I'm disabled, not he. 'Why stop at the cane? Notice my hands. They shake. And it isn't because I'm nervous, although that's usually true.'

'I'm sorry.' I want to apologize for searching for lesions, protruding bones, death in the eyes, the telltale signs Jane's friend Adrienne can list at will.

'Don't be,' he continues. 'I've been well most of my life. I've been criticized, as has my work, for being

unsympathetic to a world that moves at a slower pace.
So I'm going to wind down for a while, teach this
course and finish working on something. I'm told I have
the winter. Or, in a best-case scenario, I could linger on
horribly until the weather gets warm.'

'It isn't −' I begin.

'*No*,' he says firmly. 'That would be too boring.
What's chosen me is far less usual. I remain, as ever, an
open invitation to drama.'

I swallow. Now the Scotch is a friend, a buffer. 'Who
told you?'

'Some demi-god at a clinic. A man with more winters
ahead of him than you and I have combined.' He shakes
the ice and drains the color from the glass. 'An expert,
in a word.'

It's an impossible moment, but I take heart in the fact
that we've stared at each other over tables before.
We've arrived at impasses, redirected ourselves or just
borne them.

'I want *your* news,' he says. 'I want to celebrate.'

It isn't going to be what I thought, this day. It's not
going to be about claiming things, about rights.

'Do you want to do photographs, career switches or
marital news?' I'm getting it back, the trick of being
with him.

'Your choice.'

I waste no time. 'I write things for a glamorous, lonely person named Gillette. She has too much money and a theory that when there's too much money people fall from grace. She's straight out of one of your movies. Right now I'm researching the decline of manners in Western Civilization during times of economic glut. Otherwise, I live in a house. I have three kids, one of whom you know.'

'Let me see *you*,' he says. 'Your eyes, your mouth. Your wrists. Just let me see you.'

Forget sleek, I'm sticking to my clothes. I've worn the wrong thing, as always. A sundress would have been more representational, more honest, perhaps less of a come hither. The Scotch sings in my head, tells me I *can* be two people. I can be Simon's wife, the mother of my three. And I can be Fowler's for a few hours. There's no harm in it. Perhaps I should thank the Lord I can still be swayed like this, can still get overwhelmed. Perhaps this meeting is meant to test my sexual and romantic mettle. Perhaps I *can* afford to expand.

'I'm right here,' I say. 'Just look.'

Imagine a life that works solely on this premise: unforeseeable things do happen, and it is possible to be shaken by them. You have considered yourself a happily married woman for some time, have even boasted to those closest to you that this is the case, and then you spend an hour with a man whose words and touch do the same things to you that you remember happening when you were a teenager falling in love for the first time. Imagine this man is the same one you loved back then. You didn't think you'd ever be inclined toward him again, but now you suddenly wonder what you'd do without his attention. You begin to behave uncharacteristically, and yet you feel oddly yourself. It's a fierce shame to your current life, this falling, but you've come alive in a way you haven't since your teens. Your temperature is running one degree higher than usual; your heart beats fast. You remember feeling beautiful in profile walking beside this man years ago, just hours after he'd first kissed you. It could be that, in friendly light, you are now as beautiful as you were then. It seems you and he are moving at a different speed from the rest of humanity, slower, more careful, less angry. You are so full you can't imagine being antagonized by anything, and yet you know that this very admission, that you're in love again, with the wrong person, will break hearts. It's shocking to you that love is this way, that love was ever this way, so demanding of you, so wrenching, but here it is. You didn't intend for this to happen.

Fowler and I are back downtown, crossing over the Bowery from Great Jones Street in frightful heat neither of us seems to mind. I've called Kirsten, who thinks I'm with Gillette, lunching. It's not an unusual scenario, my getting caught up in business with Gillette after a boozy lunch. I've told Kirsten Gillette is an eternal wreck over men and that working for her entails buoying her up during the worst squalls. On occasion Gillette will ask me to handle the runoff when she's betwixt and between. I have found myself eating lunch at Lutece with a dumpee, ordering drink after drink for him so he'll go home painless and unaware of my mission to let him down for her. Simon thinks I should seek new employment, but I've grown fond of Gillette. What I'm doing with Fowler wouldn't faze her in the least. Whenever I suggest a less hectic relationship schedule to her, Gillette reminds me that there are many women – Georges Sand, Camille Claudel, to name two – who were not lesbians and made conscious choices against marriage because they had to. Marriage would have killed them, she says, as it would kill her. 'You can handle it,' she tells me. 'You thrive on detail work. I'm after vision. I'm impossible, and every man who gets

near me finds that out. Because that's what men are
after — vision — and they don't like to compete with
women over it.'

I thought of Simon's vision, if he has one, being
thwarted by his first marriage to a surgeon. How could
he compete with her, setting up computer systems for
small businesses and schools while she went out to save
lives every day? He was in constant eclipse. It is no
wonder he finds me a comfort: I rarely discuss my
work, as I am dubious about what will come of it and I
fear being dull. Furthermore, 'vision' is a word I
wouldn't dare utter seriously, particularly in current
company.

Fowler is a tall man, not large, so the walking stick
doesn't diminish him. There is no limp, no stiffness,
only a gingerly favoring of the stronger leg. I both want
and don't want to know the exact diagnosis of his
illness, as I both want and don't want what we're
heading for.

At a stoplight he turns to me. 'I want to be sure of
one thing,' he says.

I could make a comment about uncertainty, its
prevalence over certitude, but in his eyes there is
pleading.

'Shoot.'

'That you don't feel pity,' he says. 'That your best interest doesn't get messy with altruism or pity.'

I'm insulted, but I've read about defensiveness in people who are ailing, who know that ultimately no one can help them. I tell him I don't feel pity, which is true. I'm too wrapped up in being wanted.

We cross to a street where almost every building is abandoned, then arrive at the one, Fowler's, that has a proper door and other signs of life: garbage awaiting pickup on the curb, some flowerboxes, shades, air conditioners on several floors. It's a walkup, which seems cruel, but we turn after the row of mailboxes into a small foyer where he unlocks several locks. The apartment is bright and airy, the one with the flowerboxes full of geraniums and impatiens, red, white and violet. The walls are bone white, the wood floors polished to perfection. Sparse furnishings give the place a handy, easy, south-western flavor. Bookshelves and stacks of labeled moving boxes take up the corners. I remember this about him: a fondness for some order in the house, even when life was complete chaos.

'Nice,' I say, dopey with the heat and drink.

'Nice with you in it,' he says. He tosses his seersucker jacket onto a chair in the big living room. 'Let me get you something.'

'I think I may have had enough,' I tease, knowing we'll have more, wishing we didn't have to get destroyed to get to bed.

He brings two cans of Tecate and sits on the sand-colored sofa. I join him there, not close enough, willing him to pull me to him when the mood strikes. The beer is freezing. I hold the bottle to each side of my face and let the water drip off.

'You're the one I've thought about,' he says, 'since I've known about this illness thing. The minute I knew I wanted to call you. But you've got so much now, a world, don't you know, and I couldn't imagine the phone ringing in it and me being on the other end. I'd get your husband, I thought. Or my son. I didn't think I had the right.'

I remember Fowler saying 'my son' into Isaac's minute ear on the nights none of us slept. He'd say it over and over to calm Isaac at his colicky worst, and once in a while it worked.

All the years I've spent adding tarnish to Fowler's image, I never once suspected he cared about rights. And I certainly couldn't imagine him thinking of me at a crucial juncture, only in passing, or if he were drunkenly detailing his past to a woman who had asked about it.

'You were my friend,' he says, focused on the wood

grain of the sea chest that works as a coffee table. 'You were a wonderful friend, and Isaac was a miracle. I couldn't bear the weight of it, you see. I was unable.'

I had rather hoped we'd get into this later, afterwards, in bed, talking lazily after sex.

'What weight,' I say quietly. 'What do you mean?'

He clasps his hands behind my head and looks hard into my face. 'I thought I would burst from it, from what I felt, so responsible, so panicked from his absolute perfection, so sorry I wasn't going to manage to stay. When I saw him, I knew nothing would ever be the same.'

Having had three children, this doesn't strike me as a new or unmanageable state of mind and heart. 'That's what happens when you have babies,' I say. 'You have to move over. You have to not mind things getting different.'

'I'm telling you,' he says. 'I couldn't. I was unable.'

'How did you know I'd be able?' I ask. 'How did you know I'd stay and see things through? I could have chosen to come apart at the seams and leave Isaac in a dumpster. How did you know I'd manage when you couldn't?'

Tears are on their way, and my voice shakes. He

slides his palms over my shoulders and down my arms.
This time, his hands are steady.

'Because I knew you could. We're different. Look at
where we are now.'

'And where *are* you?' I shout at him. 'Other than ill
and established in Alphabetland, where *are* you?' I can't
believe I'm angry at him for being sick. I can't believe
I'm capable of such cruelty.

He looks into his lap. 'I'm where I've always been,'
he says. 'On the periphery. Peering in. Basically, I'm
nowhere. It's not a place you were comfortable with. I
knew that, but I wanted to give you what you wanted. I
tried, and I failed. End of story.'

I'm not satisfied. I'm hot and drunk and crying and
not the bottomless pit of love I thought I was an hour
ago. *'End of story?'*

'Mine, not yours.'

I pull his arms back around my waist. For some
reason I cannot bear for this afternoon to turn sour.
'No,' I say, easing us back onto the cushions.

'Is this what you want?' he whispers into my neck.

I don't answer, just concentrate on the task at hand,
his shirt buttons, belt buckle, his weight on me.

*

I call home from the outdoor lot where Fowler and I parked. 'The girls are going crazy,' Simon says, exasperated. 'Where are you?'

'Downtown,' I tell him. 'I'm on my way.'

'Hurry. Jane's got plans for you.'

'I'll take her out when I get home.' I spaced out on the trip to Sam Goody. She's probably seething. I don't know how I'll achieve all this travel today. In traffic it will take me an hour and a half to get home, but I will take her to get that tape, by God.

'Isaac got on base three times,' he says. 'He's gone down to Burger King for a victory dinner.'

'I'll be home soon.'

'Love you,' Simon says. It's our way of signing off. I echo, fretting that I may sound hollow.

Fowler is over paying the parking fee. He unfolds singles from a clip, then turns to locate me. We're disheveled, but then everybody is in the heat. Even the parking attendants aren't ready for it. They swab their brows with their forearms. They open and close car doors with unnecessary force.

'I won't call you,' he promises as I get in the car. I can't look him in the eye. It's as if I've just had my first orgasm. I'm embarrassed, shocked, and overjoyed. And now that I've heard Simon's voice again, I've begun to panic. Not that he'll find out, because I don't see how he could, but that I can have good sex with two men. I thought there was some law of exclusion. I thought if I ever veered off from Simon for a second, I'd pay in part for my sin with the shame and frustration of not coming. This time, however, despite my nerves, it happened twice for me, the second time slowly, Fowler telling me where he was in it all the while. I didn't mind his whispering, keeping me posted. He was calling me back, in a way, from the far-off place he used to suggest I disappeared into during sex.

He leans in and kisses me, his smile fading into the work of the kiss, which makes me want to start up again, as I'm sure he does, to show me, finish things off in a more memorable way. I can't help but compare them: Simon, a muffled cry, as if he were still in the army barracks he is so loath to talk about, and Fowler, wordy, noisy, then out for the count. We must have slept forty-five minutes. I woke in a sweat, from out of somewhere deep, as if I'd had anesthesia.

'I want to come back,' I say, praying, *Lord, don't let this back up on me.*

'Please,' Fowler says, his eyes pleased, hopeful. 'Please.'

I go into my bag and give him the photograph of Isaac. Then I pull out of the parking lot. I catch him in the rearview mirror staring down at it, then looking up and exhaling deeply. It's a moment that strikes me as more intimate than any other of this afternoon, more so than his obvious appraisal of me, *élongée*, on his couch, than any touch. As I make my way through the unaccommodating Village streets to 14th and West, I try to see his face, hear him exactly as he must have sounded just minutes ago, but there is no precision in the image. This has happened to me before: when I become taken with someone I can't envision the face or recall the voice in the way I thought I heard it. I know there was a fierceness, a power about this afternoon that is unusual. I know that at present I do not regret what I've done. And I know that not once did either of us utter the word 'love'.

On 79th and Columbus I park at a meter, race to Gillette's building and ask the doorman to ring up and see if she's home. After she answers he hands me the phone.

'I've got Pasquale here. He doesn't mind if you don't.'

Pasquale is the soccer player she mentioned at our last lunch, eight years her junior. 'Great.' I hand the house phone back to the doorman, who stows it in a drawer.

'17B,' he says, grinning. I feel his gaze all over me as I wait, my back to him, at the elevator bank. He knows. He knows and wouldn't mind a little of my generosity himself. He's probably an old hand at this. He obviously thinks I am.

'You look *fabulous*!' Gillette says, turning me around to face Pasquale, a compact, leering man with Byronic hair. He's got on running shorts and nothing else and she's in her tailored skirt for the office and a tank top. Even he seems to know I've cheated. He says 'Yes' a lot, and he keeps both hands on Gillette at all times.

I finally ask her for the shower.

After telling him to wait, she does an about-face down the hall to the linen closet and then leads me, bearing plush lavender towels, into the guest bathroom. I pull off my terrible clothes.

'I'm sorry. I'm in an awful rush. I was supposed to be home three hours ago.'

She searches my face. 'What have we been up to, Leigh?'

'Please,' I tell her. 'Just please.' I turn on the water and get in. She holds the curtain open to finish her thought.

'I see,' she says. 'I'll get you something to wear. Relax.'

I wash reluctantly, resenting the duty of having to erase this afternoon that has charged me so. Gillette knocks and enters with a frosted glass containing iced tea with a mint sprig and a long-stemmed silver spoon. She holds up a floral shift from Laura Ashley, tag still on.

'I hate this. Keep it. It'll look great on. Leave your clothes here.'

'Anything,' I say, absorbing the insult. I suck down the iced tea, slip on the dress, my sandals, and my watch. I comb my wet hair in the mirror. 'You're the same,' I tell it after Gillette goes out.

She and Pasquale are waiting in the den, eager to get to something, it looks like. 'Thank you,' I say generally. 'I'm sorry for disturbing you.'

'You'll call me,' Gillette says at the door. 'We owe Barry the chapter on Louis Quatorze before he goes to the Vineyard. That's August *one*.'

Gillette often uses the plural pronoun when discussing dealings with Barry, her editor, although he doesn't know I'm researching and writing this book for her. 'I get so many assignments,' she has said, 'he must know I'm farming some of it out.'

'I'll call you,' I assure her. I do the continental double kiss with each of them. 'Bye.'

'*Bellissima*,' Pasquale says behind her, his eyes giving

me a happy world where this sort of thing, married folk dropping in for showers after trysts, goes on all the time.

We bought our house, the smallest of four on a woodsy cul-de-sac in Ardsley, on a lifetime plan in the early eighties, when it was still possible for families that didn't contain at least one doctor or lawyer to do so. Compared to our neighbors, all of whom drive cars with 'MD' plates, we are shabby but respectable. Simon's educational past is less checkered than mine: he has two advanced degrees, M.Phil. and MBA, which he earned while his ex-wife interned in Manhattan's best private hospitals. We aren't academic-stickers-on-the-station-wagon types (who knows what we'll become if Isaac lands up at Harvard), but somehow established New York suburbanites can sniff out erudition once they've discounted the possibility of any substantial cash flow. Something distinctive has to be on the résumé in order for dinner invitations or club memberships to occur. A friend of Simon's offered to sponsor us for the country club, but we declined. We couldn't afford it. 'So we attach ourselves to people who have pools,' Simon suggested when Jane and Isaac were feeling the sting from that lost opportunity. 'And tennis courts,' he added, as an enticement.

It's a split-level white ranch with a two-car garage under the master bedroom and a basketball hoop that Simon and Isaac make a show of using on the weekends. The front lawn is too steep to do anything with except mow. Simon has managed to cultivate a small vegetable garden in the back where, he brags, he grows three two-hundred-dollar tomatoes per year. It's too shady back there for much volume. But gardening has become a family entertainment. Isaac checks on the plants every morning before he leaves for his counseling job at a local day camp. Jane digs around in there with her baking utensils, and Daisy squawks and points and begs to be let free in the dirt. This is where I find them all when I arrive at the house at ten to seven.

'Mom!' Jane shouts from the hosta bed, seeming to have forgotten my broken promise to her. Isaac surveys me silently, one hand gripping a stake, a figure straight out of Norman Rockwell. Simon has Daisy working beside him at the weeding. He stands up and smiles proudly.

'She's got the idea,' he says. 'Now I just have to stop her from eating them.'

I hurry to my youngest to make sure, yes, it's true,

she's been eating dirt, fistfuls of it. 'Oh Lord,' I sigh, so normal, so typical-mom, as Jane would say.

'She eats worms,' Jane says menacingly, now at my side, waiting for her moments of attention from me.

'Let me pick her up,' Simon says. 'You'll get your dress dirty.'

He doesn't usually notice if I have on a new dress, so this isn't worrisome until Jane says she likes my dress, where did I get it?

'Gillette,' I tell her. 'She hates it.'

'Wow,' Jane says, meaning it, fingering the fabric.

'Mama,' Daisy says, pleased.

'You look pretty, Mom,' Jane says. And Isaac, who hardly ever looks at me any more, says, 'Yeah, Mom, you do.'

'I've got two steaks, Isaac already ate, the girls can have chicken nuggets, and I can have it all ready by the time you get back from Goody's if you take the kids with you,' Simon says, begging me with his eyes.

It's instant, shedding the self for the others. I'm used to it. 'Let me grab a Coke from the fridge and get something else for Daisy to wear.'

'I'll get that,' Isaac says. It always shocks me, how far he'll travel for Daisy, anywhere, it seems, so she's comfortable. I know he'll make a terrific father, which is a difficult fact, considering what his own father did.

'Just a little dress or something,' I say, loving him to bits.

'I can handle it, Mom.' He's gone in time to avoid any adoring looks from me and Simon.

Jane abandons her apothecary's project in the hosta bed readily and asks permission to go in and get her purse, she has some other things she wants to buy. Simon can't hide his glee over this, and of course this undermines Jane's personhood and she has to say so.

'I've had a purse for years, Daddy. You don't even know I exist.' Then the dramatic exit from garden into the house complete with slamming screen door.

'It's the other way around, really,' he whispers to me, grazing my cheek with his lips. 'She doesn't know *I* exist.'

'Oh honestly, Simon,' I say, 'the sun rises and sets.' Jane was his first baby, and if she had her way, he'd be her only parent. The two of them sometimes seem the nucleus of the family, with Isaac, Daisy and me floating around them in the protoplasm.

'I'll open some Brouilly,' he says. 'If you hurry, there'll be a glass left when you get back! What a day!'

I squeeze his hand in apology. 'Thanks.' I can't go

into a long lie about all I had to do in Manhattan today. I leave him for the stormy indoors, where Jane is slamming around in her room, and soon locate the diaper bag and Jane's Barbie pocketbook.

'I've got it!' I call upstairs. Down she clumps in her leather sandals with heels, teary-faced, and snatches it from me.

'I was ready to leave hours ago!' she yells. 'I wouldn't have lost it if you were home when you said!'

I'm relieved to take recrimination from Jane instead of from my husband or Isaac. 'Come on,' I say gently. 'Let's get Daisy.'

'Daisy's a mess!' Jane cries. But she's resigned, and we file out. I wipe Daisy's face, hands and legs off with baby wipes. Isaac returns with a T-shirt dress he bought her that has his team emblem stencilled in orange on the front. He takes her from her happy perch on Simon's lap, stands her on the flagstone and teases her into cooperating with him. She squeals and puckers her face for kissing.

'Presto change-o,' Isaac says proudly. He carries her like a football to the car.

'What are they putting in those burgers,' Simon muses.

I leave him sitting in a lawn chair, where I know we'll find him asleep when we return.

Isaac is in the front seat. I cower in anticipation of Jane's reaction to this fact, but she doesn't put up another fuss, just installs herself grumpily beside Daisy's car seat in the back. Isaac smirks. 'Forget the steaks, Mom. Simon's not gonna deliver.'

'I know. He was sitting in his chair.'

Even Jane laughs over this. 'Daddy's really tired,' she explains. 'He kept asking us if we wanted to eat dinner. He asked us, like, five hundred times.'

'No, she doesn't exaggerate,' Isaac groans.

By now, we're back on the parkway, heading north.

'Shut up, Isaac,' Jane orders. 'You're a waste of skin.'

As horrible an image as this calls up for me, I think it's funny. 'Where did you hear that one, my darling girl?' I ask her.

'From Isaac, of course,' she says. 'He said it about me. So now I'm saying it about him. An eye for an eye, right?'

The clerk at customer service surveys me with a frown he wears like a too-tight hat, defying me to find a copy of *Jules and Jim* at any store on the planet, offering his empty palms as evidence of my ridiculous request, this from a woman carrying a child with most of one hand stuffed in her mouth. How could I possibly care about esoteric film when I'm saddled with such common responsibilities?

'What did you expect from a guy with a flat top and a fade?' Isaac whines. 'You think he's gonna know from *films*, let alone French ones?'

'I prefer not to think so categorically,' I say. *Teach them what you know*, I read somewhere. And I know that if I assume that men of twenty or so who have chosen to doctor their hair in such a manner know nothing about the films of Europe, then I am a bigot.

'Me neither,' Isaac admits, smirking. He hands me a CD of the Stones' *Goats' Head Soup*, which was popular when Pam and I were dancing around our room in ski boots, the tune of choice being 'Heartbreaker'. Jane skips up with her 10,000 Maniacs tape and one by Madonna. Then they want to go off to the Nintendo corner while I stand in line.

'Go,' I tell them. 'Destroy some cities. Solve some mysteries.' They love it when I support their every endeavor.

It is hopeless in this environment to try to hang onto the glamour of secret, good sex, but I'm in line at Sam Goody with Fowler's hands all over me, his mouth at my ear. I put our purchases on the counter, produce my Amex card, and smile mechanically at the cashier, another young man with the hairdo of our uninformed clerk. 'Get him to smile at you,' Fowler whispers. 'Do anything.'

He hands me my package and looks for the next customer. I flinch at the idea of my doing something to make him smile, then I go back into the cavernous store to locate my children, whom I find in front of two adjacent screens, both very excited over their conquests. Simon and I have not succumbed to household Nintendo, mostly because his computer wizardry provides all of the destructive and competitive options offered by a Nintendo setup.

'How goes the warfare?' I ask them.

'Level three and climbing,' Isaac reports. He won't even turn around to get horrified that I have given the stapled bag of cassettes and CDs to Daisy for safekeeping.

'I'm losing, as usual,' Jane says. I'm convinced that Nintendo was made for boys, and it infuriates me to see Jane lose heart over something so pointless.

'Let's quit while we're behind and go get some takeout,' I say, urging her with my free hand outstretched. She comes away easily, and Isaac mumbles about meeting us at the car in five minutes. We walk through heavy, humid air to our car. Jane gets in the front this time while I load Daisy into her car seat, what my mother refers to as her 'motley'. I turn on the air conditioning. After grabbing the bag from Daisy, who breaks my heart with a wail of disappointment, Jane unwraps her tape and punches it into the tape deck. I get the bag back for Daisy, who may not get over the theft for a long time, and finally sit, doors shut, and try, again unsuccessfully, to make out the profundity of the 10,000 Maniacs. But this is a group that eludes parsing. I cannot for the life of me understand what they're saying, they slur their words so.

'Janey,' I ask her.

'What?'

'Are you still mad?' As much as I hate to admit it, I do hang on the words of my children sometimes.

'I don't know.'

'Well, could you tell me when you do know?'

'Mo-om.'

I watch her mouthing the impossible lyrics, closing her eyes when a particularly sensuous moment in the music arises. I am fascinated. She's older than I thought. She's a *girl* now, not a little girl. I wonder if Simon sees it, if he can bear it, because right now I can't. Never mind how frighteningly old Isaac seems to me.

'Mom,' Jane says.

'Yes, Jane.'

'Don't be late again. I really hate it when you're late.' She watches the parking lot happenings, families loading in and out of their cars, everyone in a different mood, bound for some sort of friction, and I wonder if that's what she sees, or if she doesn't see them as I do, but simply as people going into a store to do what we've just been doing, looking and buying, leaving with something they've wanted and are now happy to have.

'I won't do it again,' I tell her.

'Deal,' she says, and in the way she has of surprising me, she throws herself on me, hangs on my neck, and starts to cry. This must be what Fowler meant when he said he couldn't bear the weight of Isaac, his perfection, the fear of holding something so beautiful in his arms. Except I bear the ache, and I cry too, for all of us, for her love of me and mine of her, for my imperfections and her disappointment, for the joy of knowing her.

'I see you two have made up,' Isaac says matter-of-factly as he gets in back.

I straighten up, embarrassed, the way I get when he notices intimate details about me these days, like the one about my looking good in Gillette's dress. 'We're fine,' I assure him. I smooth Jane's hair, and help her settle back into her seat, into the music, into our sunset ride to our favorite Chinese restaurant, then home.

'Baby?'

He has called me this forever. I've never objected, and I don't object now. I don't and have never found it corny or belittling. I have always appreciated the fact that it highlights our ten-year age difference. Furthermore, I like and revere babies, and I know that Simon doesn't mean to categorize me with them, only to point up flattering similarities: babies are beguiling and faultless, pure, honest and dependable.

I am out back being too vigilant about the steaks and too free with the wine when he calls. In no way do I feel worthy of such an endearment. That I imagine Fowler's response to hearing me referred to as 'Baby' (certainly he'd find a way to disapprove, even if he were merely jealous) confirms my unworthiness.

'Almost done,' I call back.

He's at the window above the kitchen sink, the one I frequently watch the children from during the day when they're doing their outdoor things and I'm doing dishes and planning activities for later on by telephone.

'Can you bear another salad?' he shouts.

'Anything.'

We have things under control. Daisy has been sleeping since we left the Chinese restaurant with our package of dumplings, noodles and chicken with walnuts. Jane is upstairs readying herself for camp, which starts tomorrow, and Isaac is in his room watching something loud and angry on television. Jane woke Simon when we returned. He was still outside, but the steaks were on the counter, defrosted. I got everyone fed and up to their rooms. I was terribly efficient, which is part of being guilty, I guess. I should be more careful about exhibiting too much verve. Sudden bursts of enthusiasm will draw the wrong sort of attention. Already Simon's eyes widened when I offered to start up the coals and tend to the grilling.

I turn the steaks, which look wonderful. I'm going to enjoy this meal, even though I probably shouldn't. My husband, comforted by his nap and our favorite wine, will want to talk. And I will too, not just to keep from thinking of Fowler, of myself in the youthful pose of being desired, but for reassurance: yes, we live an enviable life that must be maintained without distraction.

Simon stays in, for the ten o'clock news I'm sure. I set down the barbaric fork and lounge in his favorite chair, watching the night sky, I suddenly realize, for the first time since Jane was born. I don't know why, in the eight years we've been together, I haven't done this. It's as if someone whispered to me when I got engaged, 'Don't look up.' Or 'Stop looking.'

I like looking up, looking around, seeing. Even if it feels strange and makes my heart pound.

'Ready when you are,' Simon calls a few minutes later.

I bring in the steaks. The table is set, candles lit, wedding china, which we now use as our everyday, in place. He shuts off the news. I ask what he's heard.

'The usual,' he says, sitting. 'Fires. Highway horror. Child abuse. Border troubles. Tyranny and devastation abroad. Stop me when you've had enough.'

'Enough.' I smile. I love my husband. How could I have done what I did today? But that's the wrong question. The question, Gillette would back me on this one, is about marriage. I am beginning to suspect that I've been wrong about marriage. That it isn't and could never be, given that human beings invented it, steady and predictable. Maybe everyone strays a bit, even married people. Perhaps they don't all go to the lengths I've just gone to, although many go further. My parents are married people who live in separate apartments. As a child, I was quick to disapprove of this arrangement. It is no wonder that at times each of them looks at me sideways, as if they'd never met a bigger fool.

'Tell me about the day,' Simon says after the first few bites. 'Starting after you dropped the girls with Kirsten.'

He's not looking at me, only at his food, the perfection of angles he's achieving with his steak knife.

'I drove into the city,' I say. 'I saw Gillette.'

'What else?'

'She gave me this dress.' The dress has wilted completely, although I still like it for the freedom it offers.

'It's a great dress,' he says. Now he stares. He takes something out of his back pocket and lays it by my plate. It's Fowler's postcard. I set down my utensils.

'I met him for lunch.'

Everything slows. The eating, the sounds of suburban night. The damn seconds.

'You had lunch with that jerk?'

Simon has never been so solemn, so intent.

I don't know what to do. I turn on him. 'Lunch is pretty innocuous, as a meal,' I counter.

He looks me in the eye. Then he pushes his chair back, stands, and walks out the back door.

THREE

An hour later, when I'm doing the dishes, I imagine Fowler telling me things about myself that I'm glad rather than loath to know, apologizing, looking for my next remark, beholding my children and my house and blinking with amazement, having to sit down.

Simon, back from his fury walk, catches me talking to myself. He glares. I begin to make up a story, about trying out a new approach for the chapter we're doing, seeing how it sounds.

'Save it,' Simon tells me, leaving the kitchen for the refuge of the television. Flirting with the blank space by the fridge, I tell the imaginary Fowler that he could do better than to hang on my every word during his last year on earth.

I'm guilty of wanting distraction and getting it. I'm guilty of succumbing to boredom, frustration and vanity. I'm guilty of weakening in my resolve to provide a decent home for my children. At base level, I'm an adulteress. So I'm wondering why I don't feel worse, like a criminal, like I ought to give myself up to some authority that could dispense the proper punishment and make arrangements for our domestic life that would keep the children's best interests and Simon's above mine.

Tomorrow both Isaac and Jane start camp, Isaac as counselor and Jane as camper. I go upstairs to help with the labeling of Jane's things. On arriving, I see she has already done this. She packs her extra pair of socks, T-shirt, swimsuit and towel into a new knapsack with such precision that I'm sure she knows something terrible has happened between me and her father.

'Good work, sweetie,' I tell her.

'It's not hard, Mom,' she assures me.

Children are instinctually self-protective. They just get overpowered by disrespectful, unthinking adults.

I go back downstairs and take up my place on the sofa near Simon, who watches CNN with the stony face it deserves. Isaac resurfaces for some general advice on how to manage ten-year-olds.

'I've got twelve of them,' he complains.

'And no help?' Simon asks.

'One guy,' Isaac says. 'Garland,' he reads off an orientation sheet.

'First name?' I want to know.

'There isn't one.'

'That's ridiculous,' Simon says, gesturing for the packet. He looks. 'Sure enough: Garland.'

Our eyes meet. Mutual alarm, the only response we seem capable of sharing at present.

'Just treat them like you'd treat anybody,' I offer, and then Simon looks away, disgusted.

Daisy rolls over in the port-a-crib. Then she reaches for me with her fat little arms and breaks my heart and saves my life all in one second. If repentance were possible, if there were any way of my going back to the 'me' who hadn't done this, I would, just to avoid this one unbearable moment of need. Then Jane plods down the stairs, looking bored or sad, or both.

There is no 'worst part' of it. It's all terrible. I did what I did, and my husband knows, even though I've admitted nothing and no one has, to my knowledge, ratted on me. The thing is, I did it in full possession of my faculties. It was an honest act of will. For whatever reason, I wanted to.

'Thanks, Mom. You're a load of help,' Isaac says.

'Treat them like you should treat Jane,' Simon tells him.

'Yeah,' Jane says. 'Don't try to kill them every day.'

Until a few months ago, our life was in constant upheaval: a relatively short courtship, according to Gillette and my mother, then instant pregnancy, moving to the suburbs, Jane's birth, the process of legal adoption so that Isaac could finally start to feel like he had a father, temping here, temping there, the deaths of my remaining grandparents; then Daisy. I must have panicked without crisis and thus felt I had to create one. I must have worried, on the day of the party we had to celebrate the success of the adoption, when Rabbi Rosenthal brought his fingers to my cheek and told me I was pretty and that Simon was a lucky man, because I momentarily considered a reciprocal gesture, and thought I wouldn't have minded his tongue in my mouth, the thrill of those fingers in other places, his sudden appreciation of me. I shared my concern with Kirsten, who can be so dismissive. 'Welcome to marriage, Cinderella,' she said. 'You hear a lot about the men who are bored but not much about the women who are. Let me tell you about boring.'

She didn't need to. For one, I knew. I had wept in

the shower late the night of the party. Simon and I had made love, and it was fine, I remember thinking. But 'fine' wasn't a word I wanted to think of as adequate to our lovemaking. I just kept staring at Simon's chest, wondering if Rabbi Rosenthal's was anything like it, whether he kept himself toned the way Simon does. For two, Kirsten's husband Ted, while being the most welcoming of neighbors and the most physically appealing, is dull to a fault. He shares his amazement over the latest in lawn gadgetry with anyone who comes within walking distance of his house, as well as his dismay over crime with anyone who isn't too depressed to listen. I don't know how Kirsten can bear him, or if she really does. She admitted wanting to jump her decorator, 'but of course he's gay,' she moaned. How does everyone stand it? I wanted to ask her but did not, at the risk of sounding too ungrateful for words.

We're to sit down shortly, to another anxious dinner. Tonight's menu: spaghetti and garlic bread, Caesar salad and more of the Brouilly. Simon has been home ten minutes, just long enough to promise the older children a trip to the miniature golf course after we partake of the dinner his estranged wife has prepared. Now he's in the shower. No one has asked why he doesn't speak to me; perhaps they haven't noticed. Even Jane, whom nothing gets past, hasn't demanded an explanation from us.

'Tell me about Garland,' I tease Isaac.

'Oh, *man*,' Isaac groans.

'What?'

'I'm there five minutes, just long enough to find out where my group is meeting, and he wants my ass,' Isaac says, very matter-of-fact, as if he's given me a weather report.

'Isaac!'

'Mom!' he mimics. Then, more gently, 'Chill, Mom. He's a fag. He likes me. I'm not that desperate.'

I sit at our beautifully set table. When did my son grow up? Where was I? Why didn't someone inform me?

'I just think it's a little unorthodox for a man like that to be in charge of little boys.' No sooner is it out of my mouth than I feel like a prude. Someone should dump a bucket of orange juice on my head.

'There are little girls there too, Mom,' Isaac reasons. 'Jane goes there, remember.'

I cannot resist the notion that the world has never been so monstrous, so full of horror and violence and deviates, but who am I to subscribe to such a view? A woman who has created an extended family with such tenacity and now cannot find the strength to keep herself or it going in the only healthy manner the experts prescribe?

'I know,' I say. 'You're right. He's probably a very nice man.'

'Maybe,' Isaac says. He's flipping through channels, rejecting everything. 'He changed his name, though.'

'He told you?' My own interest isn't proportionate to the information.

'Yeah. He kinda likes to talk.'

'Tell me about him.'

'I did,' Isaac says with irritation. 'Look, when are we eating? I told the guys from the team I'd meet them at the golf course.'

'When? And when did you have time to call them?' How dare I cling to him now?

'Seven. I just called.'

'Oh. OK. Call Simon and Jane. I'll wake Daisy and put her in her chair.'

'Why don't you call them? I like to get Daisy.'

I smile at him, a sweet, tired-mom smile. 'Just this once.'

We assemble gradually, Jane bringing a book to the table and Simon bringing a hand towel that he keeps rubbing over his wet scalp. 'Wow, Mom,' Jane says. 'Is someone coming over to eat with us?'

Simon hangs his towel carefully over the rungs of his chair and sits. 'Not tonight, sweetheart,' he says. 'It's just the family tonight. But maybe your mother will have a guest for us later on in the week.'

I didn't think him capable of such indirection.

'Who?' Isaac says.

'Muk,' Daisy says.

'No one,' I tell them all, and I go out to get Daisy's milk.

'Your mother has friends we don't know about,' Simon continues without expression. 'Friends who drop in from exotic ports of call from time to time. Not necessarily to visit, you understand, just to call her away.'

'You guys have a fight?' Isaac asks.

'Not at all,' Simon tells them.

Jane looks frightened, and Isaac intrigued. I could dump the spaghetti all over Simon for bringing them into this right now, so soon, before we even know what it is we're in crisis over: my infidelity, whatever in our life has encouraged it, whatever insecurities this calls up in him, for God's sake some Jungian bit of projection if indeed he has ever betrayed me and not told me about it, maybe even some missed extramarital encounter he's kicking himself over not having seized when it came up. I don't know. But I don't approve of this sort of cruelty, if I'm allowed that observation in light of my malfeasance. Yes, I've led us into uncharted territory, but he doesn't have to drown the children in it.

I realize I haven't moved, haven't started serving the food, when Jane says, 'Mom, are you paralysed?'

Again, I go into automatic: Jane's plate, small portion, Isaac's and Simon's plates, man-sized, Daisy's bowl, noodles chopped up so she can spoon them, generally, into her mouth. I do these, then I pour us wine and them fruit punch and then I sit. I smile. Take aim, my face says to the people I love. I've double-crossed you.

'She's not eating,' Jane says. 'OK, Mom. Are you anorexic? Because if you are I know this girl at school who is and she goes to talk to a shrink about it, and now she's actually gaining weight. Now she only looks like a skeleton. Before she looked like she didn't even have bones.'

I burst out laughing. I can't help it. We have to get through this meal. I stare at Simon, try to find him somewhere in his rage, beg him with my eyes: couldn't we just *try* to communicate on this horrific subject, and in the meantime put in an appearance as parents even if one of us stinks as a mother and a wife and a citizen?

A smile flickers over his square face, then he sets his jaw again.

'It's not funny, Mom,' Jane informs me.

'Yes, it is,' I manage to get out. 'It's funny the way you said it, even if you didn't mean it to be.'

'Yes,' Simon admits. 'The notion: people without bones.' He glares at me.

'I'm outta here,' Isaac says, his spaghetti gone. He can't take tension between me and Simon. He whirls out of our sight until the storm he sees coming has passed over. This time, he hides out in his room. I can hear him above us, deciding on a place to sit.

I serve myself a healthy portion even though I have no interest in eating, haven't since I saw Fowler. The others are enjoying theirs; even Simon isn't having trouble with his appetite.

I ask Jane to tell us about her first day at camp.

'Oh God, Mom,' she says, putting down her fork and spoon, wiping her face with a napkin, gearing up. 'They have *so much* stuff to do there. It's unbelievable. Tracy and Alison are going there too, and they chose tennis and swimming like I did. It was really great, I'm telling you. I'm *so* tired, though. I'm going to bed early, after I call Tracy and Alison, if that's OK.'

'What about our golfing trip?' Simon asks her.

'Oh, no! Daddy! I completely forgot! Can we go another time? I want to stay home with Mom and Daisy.'

'You forgot?' Simon asks. 'In fifteen minutes you forgot?'

That she knew I wouldn't be going along, would not be welcome, astounds me. Simon looks crestfallen, as if Jane's sudden allegiance to me is the final straw, not my infidelity.

'That's OK, Baby,' he says. 'You do what you want.'

I take some bites of my dinner, a few sips of wine, this amounting to more than I've ingested at a sitting since before Saturday. It's all I can manage. I gather Daisy, out of the eating phase and into the throwing one, from her chair and take her into the kitchen to clean her up. Before I find a rag I sit her on the counter to behold her messy face, to test my love for her because I trust myself so little.

'You're my sweet bird,' I say.

'Mom-may,' she says.

I take time with this cleaning effort, wiping her face so gently, as if I might tear skin were I to rub any harder. In the next room, Jane is chatting up her father, coaxing him out of fury for a few seconds. Soon he and I will have to face each other. I cannot leave another hour of this to my children to fix.

We go back out to an empty dining room, all having fled for the upstairs. I set Daisy down on the living-room rug and drag over her bag of oversized Legos. I try to focus on building with Daisy, but it's no use. I'm waiting, to quote my son, for the shit to hit the fan.

Simon appears on the landing rattling change and keys and summons Isaac to miniature golf. Isaac appears, having combed his hair down with water.

'Have fun,' I say.

I can't wait for them to leave.

'Check ya later,' Isaac says, and vanishes.

Simon comes slowly down the last few stairs, every step an effort. He looks all around him before speaking.

'I expect to be back by ten o'clock,' he says. 'At that time I'd appreciate an explanation, or whatever you think might pass for one, for Saturday afternoon.' His voice shakes, and I can hear him near tears. 'In a million years, Leigh, I never thought I'd be saying these words.'

He won't wait for me to respond, just leaves quietly. I shift closer to Daisy at her work. 'Da,' she says definitely.

'Daddy,' I remind her.

'Da.'

They called her *la palatine* because she came from a region that was called the Palatinate, which is part of modern-day Germany. She married, sight unseen, the brother of Louis XIV, and her letters reveal not only the depth of this mistake but the strength she possessed to endure it. She is frank on the subjects of his infidelity, his homosexuality, his excesses. In an era of excess, she kept her head while the rest of the court indulged. She is worlds from me, but I envy her endurance, her ease with going on record, with *being* the record. As for his side of the story, it seems he didn't deserve to have one, and it strikes me as lucky that he died young.

I am ravenous for gossip, poring over these letters. I wait for her to confide any infraction of matrimonial law, but she doesn't. My daughters are sleeping. My son and husband are out whacking golfballs over a cartoon landscape. I don't want absolution, just company. I want to talk to Fowler.

I want so much more than that.

Liselotte, my seventeenth-century focus, doesn't yearn for much except the company of her aunt and one or two close friends. She is not distressed, is instead relieved, that she has no sexual inclination toward her philandering husband. I have always found Simon attractive, although I'll admit that while I sat at dinner with him tonight, no part of me filled with a yearning for sex. In fact, it wouldn't be dishonest of me to say that I rarely think about having sex with Simon, and when I do the impulse is easily thwarted by circumstance. Perhaps it is high time that I worried about this.

With Fowler, I like the whispering, the cajoling, the occasional cruel remark that requires emending. I like feeling flush in a new setting. Simon and I went to Club Med once, and I momentarily retrieved that business. But it's been years since I felt at the mercy of whatever current is loose and looking for a conduit. Fowler's postcard was all I needed to get plugged in. But I'm being ruthless now. I mustn't compare them. Simon is devoted. Fowler left me in New York City when I was eighteen years old with an infant and no income. I couldn't be sicker if I chose to run to Fowler over my husband.

Liselotte would say that the choice is not an issue, that one must be plain-speaking, true to oneself, not to others. Kirsten would shrug. 'Tell me something I don't know.' Gillette would say, 'Fuck them all,' which she does.

I have become tame to the deadening point. It can't be good for any of us.

Liselotte is under growing scrutiny for her outspokenness, for her noisy reservations about the Edict of Nantes. She has figured something out about her era and she's up a creek because of it. I look up from the thick book. Headlights stream into the driveway. Doomed, I think, because she can't handle what's been handed her — socially, I mean. What do we know about marriage before we enter into it? That it's difficult, admirable, treacherous and not for the weak of heart. We hear these things and believe none of them and only learn as we go along, bucking the confines and wanting them at the same time. *The weak of heart*. This is where I put myself tonight, in a country with the weak of heart, although mine fills at the thought of nearly everyone I know.

Isaac's triumphs abound. He was under par for every hole, the only one in the crowd. 'We're going for the real thing,' he says, breathless. 'This weekend. Simon's going to rent clubs.'

'That sounds good,' I say. I hear Simon in the kitchen, getting something to drink.

'I'm goin' up,' my son says. 'I'm really beat.'

'Sleep well.'

I had hoped for a few more minutes of him, of safety.

Simon gets a coaster for his soda can, chooses a chair and sits, elbows on knees. 'So?'

I still have the book in my lap. I close it, put it and my notebook and pen aside. This is what I summon from the miserable depths:

'On Saturday, Fowler called me. As you know, I'd had some warning of this. I met him in town. We had drinks, no food. He told me he has a year to live.'

'Why doesn't that move me?' my husband says evenly.

'I don't expect it to,' I say, in the same tone. 'I'm telling you what you've asked to hear.' He can't be the only strong one here.

'Go on.'

'We went to his apartment.'

'Even better.' He gets up, walks to the fireplace, puts a hand briefly on the mantelpiece. 'I hope you'll spare me the description of the apartment. Is there any particular reason you've done this? You still haven't made a stab at an explanation.'

What comes to me now isn't remorse, shame or a desire to be someone else, in some other century. What comes to me instead is rage, rage at marriage, at what our love has done to us, at how people who begin as lovers become friends who can be enemies at the same time. What I've done seems predictable, reasonable, given what little attention we've been able to give to ourselves, each other, while we've devoted every breathing moment to the children.

'I don't know,' I say shakily. Then, with more steam, 'I guess I wanted to.'

We wait.

'What are your plans?' he asks. Like a bullet out of nowhere.

I thought I would have to narrate the sex. I thought he'd want to know, in that way people want to know the most gruesome details of murders.

'I haven't made any.'

'You should.'

He rips a sheet of paper out of my spiral notebook, takes a pen to it and scribbles. He holds it out to me, clenching it.

'This is where I'll be for the remainder of the week, in case the children want to call. By the weekend I'll expect some notice from you as to what arrangements you've made. I cannot live with a liar.'

He goes upstairs and is back, prepacked overnight bag in hand, before I've read the scrawl. He pockets wallet and keys and is gone. I hear the healthy igniting of our decent car, and listen to it until I can't hear it any more over the softer noises of night.

Essex House, the paper says. Where we went for two nights after we were married. Both of us had to work the week following the ceremony. We had our honeymoon there. Salt in the wound I've brought on our house.

I have railed in my heart against his foresight, his belief that all can be at the ready. And now I've punished him for it. And he's punished me for that. Still, scores cannot be settled. I go in search of food. I eat cold noodles, on the kitchen floor, with my hands. They're wonderful, pasty and filling. I need them. I can't get enough of them. Even when I hear my son's heavy tread, sense his approach, feel him standing above me, I eat. Endlessly, it seems, I eat.

'Mom,' he says, his cracking voice my home, 'what are you doing?'

I douse him with assurance that I'm all right, that Simon's all right, that sometimes people just need some space so they go somewhere for a while or they get incredibly hungry so they eat like pigs, which is what has happened to the two of us, respectively.

'It's not something with Grandma Jean, is it?' Isaac hedges.

I almost laugh, his concern is so darling, so unearned. Jean is a workhorse. She blares into our life twice a year from Florida and once weekly by phone. She's always 'up to her ears' in something — visitors, bills, classes, game plans for vacations, hers and ours. She's the least absent absentee member of our family. The idea of anything taking her before she's good and ready is totally absurd.

'No, Duck. It's nothing like that.'

'OK. Good. I'll see you in the morning. Wake me up, OK?'

'Of course.' I breathe. I won't be able to put this off. Tomorrow morning I'll have to say something.

I go up and run myself yet another bath. I think about fucking. Fucking isn't even interesting enough to be a goal, I think. Not even a means to an end. Fucking is just something one does when one can, if one feels like it. Fucking Simon. Fucking Fowler. Fucking anyone. It's unreasonable to think of it as meaningful. Fucking makes so little difference, except when it leads to pregnancy. Adequate descriptions of fucking do exist, mind you, but they don't differ much, one to the next. If memory serves, marriages don't fail because of fucking or non-fucking. They fail because something else gets lost. Simon and I have lost something along our busy way. A tenderness, time to devote to each other that doesn't feel like duty. It isn't our fault. In this loss, we're blameless, just like everybody else.

'Mom?' Isaac again, whispering from the hall this time.

I jump, a roar of water threatening the tub's rim.

'Are you sure everything's OK?'

It terrifies, how much they need me, how much they depend on the structure I've set up and lost faith in.

'Yes, lovey. Get your rest. You'll need it for another day of monster control.'

'You got it,' he says, not sounding at all gratified, just faint, at the end of something.

The next morning I get out Fruit Loops for the lot of them, and our oversized Portuguese bowls. I'll give them what they want to eat while I tell them what they won't accept. By 7.30 they're assembled, perched, hungry, cheerful from a good night's sleep. This is what I tell them:

'Dad has business in Brooklyn the rest of the week, and the hours are strenuous, so he's staying in the city instead of driving two hours home. He'll call us each night to speak to everyone and he'll be back on Friday.' I bring my face up in a smile of sorts, the kind Fowler's specialist might have displayed after relating the desperate news. What I've related is a partial truth, i.e. a lie. Having related same, I fulfill my role as the liar Simon accused me of being.

This is what they tell me:

Isaac: 'Good deal.'

Jane: 'God, Mom, why do you have to be so serious. It's to cringe.'

Daisy: 'Da. Da-eee.'

We pass on to other matters: the pickup arrangements, post-camp entertainments, the dinner issue. Then last-minute gatherings and into the car to camp.

It's a brilliant day, not hot, just clear and breezy. My husband has left me, I'm sure of it. I'm afraid. We travel crisp suburban roads to the Parkway, get on, fly. There's so much cheer in our car. Even Jane's incisive summing up of Isaac's faults and his sleepy dismissal of her as subhuman is refreshing.

'You probably *like* that gay guy. All your friends have dirty hair.'

'Dog meat.'

'Moose breath.'

'At least people can see my teeth.'

This last Jane doesn't need. The day her braces were put on, the world ended. After a night of roaming the house, looking out for the dawn and drinking more wine than is good for anyone, I come to Jane's rescue and tell Isaac, 'When you're not ripping your sister to pieces with them.'

When I let them off, Jane doesn't even ask me to walk her to her group's meeting place in front of the high school cafeteria.

'You should take a nap when Daisy takes a nap, Mom,' she decides. 'You look *really* tired.'

'Thank you, Muffin,' I tell her. 'I like it when you look out for me.'

Isaac sighs goodbye, taps the door after he shuts it. 'I'll get a ride home,' he says.

'No you won't,' I say, my mind on Garland.

'You're still a kid,' Jane taunts. 'Even if you're nine feet tall.' And she's off, head down, all determination and purpose.

Isaac looks to the treetops in despair. 'Later.'

Daisy wails for a while after this, over the sudden absence of her siblings, but I coax her into a stretch of calm with the song about the beluga whale. She kicks her feet, pounding the car seat with her bare heels.

On the Parkway I pass right by our exit and take us all the way into Manhattan, by which time Daisy is fast asleep. I park at a meter on Broadway and 70th Street, take out the collapsible stroller, put Daisy in it and wheel down to Tower on 65th Street. They're my last hope before Fowler as a source for *Jules and Jim*.

Of *course* they have it, three copies, all in, and it's no trouble to join, only a dollar for membership. Sometimes I could kick myself for having moved to the suburbs. I stick the treasure in the diaper bag and head back to the car to feed the meter, to extend my escape and take advantage of Daisy's timely exhaustion. The car will put Daisy out if there are no other distractions, no matter what the time of day. I don't tell this to other mothers of one-year-olds. I don't say, 'Daisy's a dream baby. You hardly know she's there.' It just gets said to me.

I mull over visible diner opportunities, choosing 3 Guys, the cheapest. I get myself a *Times* and a window seat. Heaven. For now. I order one of the specials with eggs and try to pick out adulteresses from the passersby. I cannot tell who is one and who is not.

Nothing in the newspaper interests me. And how much coffee can one person drink, in the end?

How will we live? Who will stay and who will go? Other than the fact of his imminent death, Fowler is safe. He has only one mirror, and it doesn't accuse. He has no one to answer to, no one but himself to disappoint. It has been said that there is nothing more treacherous than a family. I've been wrong to scoff at such profundity.

I eat my breakfast, wishing I could love Simon, could love Fowler, in the easy way I love eating this meal, knowing they're good for me and are happy investments. I have loved Simon in this way, but I'm not so certain any more. I leave the diner with my sleeping baby, the envy of several retirees who seem to have no place to go to after the morning meal, frightened out of my wits: I don't know if I can call what I know of myself with men 'love'. I don't know if I have any basis for knowing what that is.

At home, I note that Catherine, of the film, hasn't got a clue either, but she's not stymied by this fact. She plows ahead, steering herself between Jules and Jim without remorse. 'Catch me,' she tells Jim, to whom she isn't married.

'She is a vision,' they each say.

'The three lunatics,' the villagers say.

'*La femme est naturelle, donc abominable*,' says Baudelaire.

I watch instead of sleeping. Simon called tonight, sounding ragged. All force and certainty he was, on leaving Monday night. Now, like me, he sees where all that gets you. We miss our routine. I dare say we miss each other. I haven't heard one word from Fowler, but that didn't come up in our conversation. He spoke to each child, then asked me about each child. He needed to hear *me* talk about them. And I needed to tell him about them.

'So you're all right, then,' he said.

I told him no, as if I had a right, and that was the end of it.

'Maybe she can't belong to just one man,' says Jim.

How dare I presume to compare myself to Catherine, to equate my level of looks to Jeanne Moreau's?

She presumes.

She dresses up like a man to rendezvous with two men.

She jumps into the Seine for effect.

She marries and has a child.

She wants the men alternately. And someone else as well. Albert somebody.

She fucks all three.

Granted, she drives off an unfinished bridge with one of them and kills herself, and him.

I don't believe we're meant to pity her, except in

recognizing where her sort of honesty gets us: to the bottom of a river.

It's another story. I'm not French, and I'm not wild. I'm watching a movie in a bedroom in New York. My children are sleeping. My husband is returning tomorrow evening to help sort things out so we don't have to drive off a bridge.

He said, 'I'll be home tomorrow night. See you then.' These are not the words of a man who accepts that his wife needs to leave him intermittently for the man who has fathered her first child.

After the call, there was an ease about the children, less irritability, less arguing. They had soft voices at bedtime. Isaac asked me to scratch his back. Even I lost some rigidity over the various rules we've set up in the house, thinking we'd perish without them. Dinner happened serially. Only I brushed my teeth. But then I had a bowl of buttery popcorn. Not the portrait of a woman about to drive herself off a precipice.

And Fowler in all this? Roaming the East Village, taking things in through a haze of death, buying the newspaper only to remember he will buy newspapers for just two or three more seasons?

I haven't called, haven't wanted to disturb the new vision of him as a man who's been tortured and wayward because I was too mind-blowing to handle. Perhaps in your thirties you're meant to run up against earlier versions of yourself, versions that no longer work, that were arrogant enough to discuss 'my life' as if this were a controllable entity not subject to whim or resurgence of the powerful past. I doubt Fowler thinks of himself in this way, as *the past* slamming into the present to wreck the future.

'You're always with me,' he said. 'You're in my head.'

For now, I will not live without him, nor he without me.

'*La femme est naturelle, donc abominable.*'

I've become difficult to wake, is this morning's complaint, direct from Jane, who can't get past my lethargy over breakfast. I keep apologizing, something that on stronger days I never do. But on stronger days I'd be bounding about the kitchen with several different taste sensations at the ready. There'd be no ground for such complaint.

'I'm sorry. I've only had a few hours' sleep.'

I stand, mid-living room, wondering how I can convince Jane that I haven't become exhausted deliberately, simply to annoy her.

'Do you miss Dad?'

'Sure.'

'No you don't.' I'm a liar, just like Simon said. 'Janey, he's coming back tonight. There's no reason to panic.'

'I'm not panicking,' she says firmly. 'I'm *hungry*.'

Isaac is on the couch, watching.

'Let's get McDonald's,' I offer cheerily. 'Come on. We can eat in the car. We won't be late for camp.'

Jane throws down her pack. 'I don't *want* McDonald's!' she yells. 'I want *real* food! Why all of a sudden aren't we eating *real food*?'

Daisy, picking up on Jane's frenzy, begins to cry, loud, exhausted wails. I had thought I had them fooled last night after Simon called, that we were easing into a new phase of family, one in which Dad and Mom can be on the outs without a general meltdown.

I kneel in front of both daughters, in front of my son. I look to each of them for a moment of help. Just one moment of openness to me, whoever I am. Daisy crawls into my lap. Isaac flips his hands, returns them to his knees. Jane keeps yelling: Why this? Why that? All of her queries circumventing the issue of her father's disappearance.

'*Janey*!' I finally shout.

It scares her into silence. She looks at me, disbelieving.

'I'm your mother,' I say. 'I'd like you to remember that.'

Jane inhales, summoning nerve.

'You don't act like my mother any more,' she says, and she takes herself to a dining-room chair where she waits for the next move from the woman who has replaced her mother in thought, word and deed.

'I'm your mother,' I repeat. 'Get in the car.'

I call Kirsten from a payphone outside the high school.

'I'm in trouble.'

'Tell me something I don't know.'

The silence on my end troubles her. 'I'll meet you at McDonald's.'

I don't even tell her I was just there. Anyway, we drove through and ate in the moving car.

'Give me a half-hour.'

I take the long road along the Hudson, passing the estates Simon likes to ogle, inventing stories about the inhabitants out of mere details.

'And these?' he said once. 'They leave home by helicopter. They can't stand highways. They gave all their cars away.'

How many cars, Daddy? Jane wanted to know, heart leaping at her daring father, at his utter lack of reserve, his bravery. I can be so much less entertaining. Witness Daisy in the back seat, once again asleep.

More coffee, and bits of Kirsten's hash browns, which are, indeed, awful.

'I figured something was going on,' Kirsten says. Her kids are grown enough to leave her home alone in the morning, free to meet her hysterical friends. 'You haven't been calling. Who is he?'

Without any prompting.

'You and Gillette are such *old hands*,' I complain.

'Yada yada. Are you going to tell me or am I eating this shit for no reason?'

She's absolutely right. It is shit, and I owe her the story.

'Isaac's father.'

She puts the remainder of the McMuffin into its paper wrapper.

'OK.' Even her cynicism can't engulf this.

'And?'

'Yes.'

'Yes?'

I keep my eyes on her. Can I say it? Can I say *it's not what you think*?

'Please,' I say. 'Please. It isn't an affair. I've known this man since I started talking about my life *as* my life. I had a child with him. I don't *feel* like an adulteress.'

'Be that as it may,' says Kirsten.

'But I *don't*!'

'*Be that as it may*,' she repeats.

'Jesus, Kirsten,' I say, and she grabs my wrist.

'This is different. This is – harder to ignore.'

She's trying to be generous, I know that. But I want to know, for whom? For whom is it harder to ignore this? Because if she's talking about Simon, if she's more worried about him than about me, then I've been rash in telling her.

'The kids,' she says, her fingers tightening. 'The kids don't hear this sort of stuff. It wrecks their world. So they make up that they hate you and love him, and then your life is over pretty much. Don't tell them. Don't tell Isaac you've seen his actual dad. Don't.'

She lets go. She's made marks on my wrist. She's in tears.

'You've done this too,' I say. 'You've told your kids.'

'Just do what I told you.' She starts to get up.

'How do you live?' I ask. 'How do you and Ted live on after it?'

She smiles. 'Who says we do?'

He's home. I continue with the tidying, arms taut, head lowered over whatever mess I'm at work on, a comical version of what I'd intended as a portrait of grace under pressure. I tried it out this afternoon, before picking up Isaac and Jane. I practiced insouciance and ease in front of Daisy, whirling about the vacuum as her favorite tune from the Fine Young Cannibals blared over its apocalyptic roar. Daisy flapped her arms and shrieked. I was putting on quite a show for her, but I stopped just short of injury after all the smashed Goldfish Crackers had been sucked up and their crackling had subsided.

He's brought the children presents. Isaac's got a new glove, Jane a new beach towel and Daisy a Sesame Street dollhouse with non-threatening pieces. He is sweet beyond words, to them.

I tell him I've waited to serve dinner, and he says he's already eaten but would be glad to sit at the table while we all eat.

So we gather.

Naturally, the talk is all about camp. Daisy sits in his lap facing him, squeezing his face in her fat hands.

'I missed you kids,' he says, as the casserole gets

considered, tried and left to its own devices. 'After dinner we're all going to sit in the living room and have a talk.'

'Daddy, can we go to the beach this weekend?' Jane pleads. 'I want to lie on my new towel and get *really* tan!'

He laughs. 'If that's what you want, Pumpkin, that's what we'll do.'

'I've got a game Saturday,' Isaac says.

'Then we'll go to the beach on Sunday.'

Jane seems agreeable to this, which she would not have been had I been in the director's seat.

They want cookies, and it just so happens Isaac has brought some, from Greenberg's, which in our household represents an extravagance. He puts them on a plate and sets it on the coffee table.

'Could you two just work out whatever it is so I can go out and shoot baskets?' Isaac asks. 'I'm really not in the mood for a powwow.'

'Just give me a few minutes,' Simon tells him.

I cradle Daisy with her bottle of milk, and Jane takes her place beside Simon. Isaac stands.

'Something has happened in our life,' Simon begins, 'that is going to change things a bit. I don't much understand it myself, so I'm going to let your mom tell you more, but I want you to know that whatever changes get made, you kids are going to help make them too, because your mom and I want what you want. *No one*,' he says tearfully, 'and I mean no one, is going to do something he or she doesn't want to do. But I have to address this new thing that's happened because I can't ignore it. I don't know how.' By this time, tears stream down his face. 'Please, Leigh. Please could you take over?'

I pull Daisy closer. I'm afraid, so afraid that I can feel my heart pounding against her. I beg him with my eyes, but he can't look at me for long.

I look at Jane, then at Isaac. I think about Kirsten's caveat. I've got no choices. I'm the criminal I said I didn't feel like.

'Mommy?' Jane says, sitting up, away from her father, more terrified by my tears than by his, it seems.

'I've seen Isaac's father,' I say to all of them, my grip on Daisy tight enough to make her squirm.

Isaac inspects the carpet.

Jane is at me again: 'Why, Mom? What do you mean?'

'I've done a thing I shouldn't have, I suppose,' I say.

'I don't think your father can forgive me for it,' I tell her.

Daisy wiggles away from me and over to Isaac's feet. He picks her up.

'How *is* the asshole?' Isaac says. He holds Daisy up for my perusal. 'Is he worth *this* to you?'

'*Isaac*!' Simon shouts, rising in rage, walking over for his daughter.

Daisy's expression has turned, and she is aware of danger. She reaches for her father, who catches her just as Isaac lets go and then slams out of the house.

'Mommy!' Jane cries. 'Mommy! What are you doing? Where's Isaac going?'

I face my husband.

'Of the two of us,' I tell him, 'it's a toss-up. You can't look me in the eye and tell me you came back here and did this out of love. So long as I bloody live, I'm not going to be convinced of that.'

I pick Jane up for the first time in months, amazed at how light she is. She is sobbing so heavily I worry for her bones. She hushes, holds on, and finally, after a quiet spell, she whispers in my ear, 'Mommy, please don't leave us.' At which point I know that my only choice is to leave. For now, anyway. But he will not take them from me. He will not.

FOUR

At three o'clock I put the suitcase back in the closet. What is a week's worth, a month's worth, of clothes? How does one imagine even a day's worth when the day promises to be blank, devoid of noise, of children? I have at times been enthralled by such a prospect, of complete self-absorption in the city: meeting Gillette, eating out, indulging in the beverage of choice, in silly plans to make money. Now the thought revolts me. It terrifies. It's unspeakable.

I do, however, know where I'm going. To my mother's — where else? I'm waiting for first light. One thing I cannot do is alarm her by arriving before dawn. She'll certainly be up, but I refuse to appear desperate.

After the dinner clean-up I imprisoned myself in the bedroom. I sat on our bed and listened to the evening rumpus. I heard Simon urge the girls toward sleep, upstairs, into their nighties, into the bathroom, back to their rooms. I froze to his slow reading of the several small books we keep by Daisy's crib. Jane I heard rooting about in her closet, which is on the other side of our wall. It sounded as if she was rearranging the shoeboxes, making room for something.

I snuck out once, to kiss them. I told Jane not to cry, she'd have her daddy for the week, the way she had me this past week when he was working, and then we'd see. When I lowered the crib rail to kiss Daisy, she was already asleep.

Isaac came in around ten, after I'd turned from the tedium of packing, given up on it altogether, and simply put two T-shirts and a set of underwear in my shoulder bag. He had brief words with Simon. The TV was on. Then he came up, used the bathroom and shut his door.

I haven't spoken in hours. I've been waiting, throat closed, eyes dry. This room of ours, this meeting place, is just a room. I've been unable to make it work for me all these hours, to put it to good use, as a library, an exercise room, an office. I haven't been resourceful, as Liselotte would have been with her letters, or Gillette, with her phone calls, or Kirsten, with her catalogues. These last five are wasted hours. Simon has done better by them, snoring away on the living-room couch. I can hear him and the television, through the closed door.

The idea that the end to this waiting is nearer cheers me.

This is the sort of scene Fowler would plunder.

'You know,' he said when we were at Hastings, before we were discovered, 'all those things you think about your parents, all that raw, awful business, will be very useful. It'll fly out of you, mutate, become something.'

He was working on a film about the tenacity of the Southern belle. He'd been taking liberties with weekend dorm duty, ignoring it completely, sneaking me off campus immediately following Saturday morning classes to the train station. We'd be in Manhattan by late afternoon, bypass my parents in favor of LaGuardia, fly to Charleston and stay overnight with his parents, J.T. and Evelyn, in their pillared house that gave onto vine- and shrub-smothered property. Fowler told her I was a film student at NYU and she smiled with vague interest.

'Jimmy always finds interesting girls,' she said.

To her I was a short, dark Northerner, possibly Jewish, another of her son's experiments, her ambitious son who needed sexual sustenance along the way to his impressive future. She was forgiving of him, but of no one else. Really, the sun rose and set on Fowler. And, I was horrified to note, he returned the obsession.

'Mama,' he'd call her, and tell her how fine she looked, how well rested, how dazzling in whatever new or revitalized outfit she'd chosen for the day. She dressed as if for cocktails every morning, late summer cocktails, my mother might have said. Whites and pastels and stockings she ordered by the dozen from Gump's or Neiman Marcus. They were hazy as summer dusk and shimmered slightly, making her legs look young and cared for. Having crested fifty, she had barely a wrinkle. She was indeed cared for. There were three or four black servants (my father would have risen up in outrage and left upon seeing them; my mother would have wrung her hands in apology and followed him out), and there was Fowler, Sr.

He was a lawyer, tall, with Irish coloring, T-square shoulders, a craggy historical face, like one of the older movie stars, O'Toole or Peck. Sometimes, when Fowler and I were making our sad love up in his boyish bedroom, I'd imagine Fowler, Sr. — J.T. — in his place. It was dangerous and exciting for me to do that, and it enhanced the actual danger in our leaving Hastings together. I'd substitute whatever Fowler said for what I thought J.T. would say to me: 'mouth' instead of 'sweet', 'Baby' instead of 'Leigh', 'come' instead of 'yes'. At the elaborate Sunday breakfast table, where the four of us lazed until well after noon when Fowler and I would have to leave to make our various connections, I could not look J.T. in the eye for the power of my imagining.

'Let me get you more coffee,' he'd say to me, and I'd bring to that, 'Let me take you', 'Let me.'

Fowler loved it. One time, while he and his mother flirted the morning away, tossing local gossip back and forth, I let J.T. get me coffee, walk me under the kudzu vines, point out types of birds and shrubbery. I had just figured out that I was pregnant, not with the help of chemicals, but on my own. I knew from the way my stomach was fluttering, from the separation and safety I felt because of it. The fluttering traveled, up into my throat, down through my thighs and knees to my feet, where I felt it telling me, 'You're different now. You're beautiful, you cannot be contained. You are too much for any one man.'

I took a bad step, into some mud. I didn't fall, just slipped in slow motion, and J.T. caught me. He had me by both elbows.

'Will we see you next weekend?' he said, as if it was easy. As if we came from two towns over.

'I hope so,' I said, looking back at him for a change.

He kissed my forehead, and we stood still for a

minute, pressed against each other in that landscape I never dreamed I'd see and which I suddenly loved because of him, not Fowler.

He said, 'You be careful, Leigh.'

I always wanted to take Isaac to him, but I didn't want to run into her. I didn't want her withering commentary anywhere near my son because he wouldn't have been able to fathom its cruelty, to ignore it.

Back we walked to the foreign civility of the house, J.T. at times guiding me by the elbow in instances of mud or steepness.

The breakfast room was empty. Fowler and Evelyn were in the sitting room. (I couldn't help loving the house, its sitting rooms, servants' wings on each of three floors.) They were going through drawers, looking at documents. Evelyn was putting papers in piles, first showing each as a treasure of family history. I learned that she was submitting Fowler's genealogical papers to several patriotic societies, which couldn't have better fed his need for nuggets for the film. His take on the Southern belle, that she was by no means a dying breed but was instead alive and biting and scratching to keep her place against any *nouvelle arrivée* daring to attempt entry into the Southern upper class, would be revealed through interviews with débutantes and their mothers, all of them unsuspecting of his purpose to render them idiotic and remote. He'd do the interviews in the summer, leaving me in a sweltering apartment for days on end. He was determined to expose how such a creature as the Southern belle could thrive in contemporary society, which seems so hostile to exclusion, the answer being: by exploiting the downtrodden, by persisting in outlandish comfort habits, by literally taming the hell out of her men.

I had one on her there. She hadn't tamed hers. But with Evelyn around, Fowler had his hands full. I may as well not have been there at all, so it was wonderful to have J.T.'s occasional focus. Every time there was polite opportunity I kissed him and he'd give me a squeeze.

Fowler said on the plane, 'J.T.'s got his eye on you.'

His amusement indicated that this was not unusual, for J.T. to take a shine to one of his women. I was more upset about J.T. walking Fowler's other women through the kudzu than I was about Fowler having them in the first place.

And Evelyn's got her eye on you, I wanted to say but couldn't. You didn't do that with Southern men, I was discovering. Maybe you didn't do that with any man, take him to task about his mother.

So I just said, 'He's a handsome man.'

'It's no wonder Mama's got her talons out.' He was looking away, entering the private tragedy that was to mutate and become something public in the film, *House Afire*, although only a few hundred college students saw it, as far as I know. He completed it the summer we lived in New York. We showcased it up and down the East Coast in the fall, shortly before I had Isaac. Because of it, because we were peddling it and not some other work of his, I always felt Evelyn was between us, pulling at him, not even entertaining the notion that he could have a true connection with another woman. If there were anyone to blame for this mess, if blame had a rightful place among the forces that have synchronized to bring us, me and my husband and my children, here, I'd put a little of it on her.

'Jimmy's got a new girl.' As long as she could keep saying this into her telephone, keep believing in the turnover, I couldn't be a threat. *Jimmy's got a new girl pregnant*! I wanted to scream. *Get over yourself*!

The film bombed. No one cared. Why would they have, watching rich debs bemoaning their loneliness and boredom, their quicksand marriages, their empty, elegant lives? But Fowler had conviction. Enough not to pay attention, to go on working and ensuring himself, through the obsession, an escape from me and his baby.

I don't think Evelyn has been told about Isaac. And since she would rely on him to ring her, she didn't have a phone number for us. She never had occasion to call and hear infant wailing in the background or wake us from desperate naps or know that I was Fowler's, that Isaac was ours, that for a brief time we had a home.

What he'd be charged about here, in my home with Simon, is the oppression, the suspension of will, the allowance of the disturbance to tyrannize rather than enliven the one who has acted in good faith to her own nature. *Rage!* he'd urge. *Go ahead. Sharpen your teeth. Find out how deep the hurt goes. Come what will.*

Fowler has always known luxury, has trusted in excess. But I have to do this my own way. Short of screaming out that I liked it, fucking Fowler, that it stirred me, moved me out of the haze that's settled between me and Simon, I can only dream of action. I can only imagine other women in my place, know that they'd behave more resolutely, more admirably. Gillette wouldn't give staying a thought. Kirsten would go on fucking Fowler in secret. Pam? Who would know any more? Catherine, I know what she'd do. She'd go find him and bring him here. She'd sleep with him in the garden.

*

Daisy's door is wide open. She's asleep on her side, her hands enmeshed in a pink blanket I knitted. I squirrel some diapers and clothes into my shoulder bag and lift her up. Her weight stuns me. She settles her head just below my chin, and I remember playing the violin as a child, having to pad the chin-rest with my father's handkerchiefs to get the instrument to fit the space offered by my long neck, struggling unsuccessfully to soften the violin, to make the whole process of my playing it enjoyable. In her heavy sleep, Daisy finds the right place for her head, the place I could never find for the violin.

Without incident, I get us out on the front porch, where the open stroller rigged with diaper bag waits, and we're out of there, walking in a cool wind to the train. You would think that a person such as myself, doing what I'm doing, would know enough not to allow herself to think of the biggest heartbreak. But I allow it, and she is everywhere, in the moving branches, the still houses, the long grey road, the hill: Jane, my Jane, my record-keeper, spine of our family. Again, unthinkable.

At the station I park us as far as is possible from a hissing radiator, something someone ought to attend to, now that it's summer. Daisy stretches luxuriously in half sleep, and I panic that she'll wake in this well-lit, unpeopled purgatory of a place, where the ticketmaster doesn't darken the door until after seven and it's up to the solitary commuter to purchase tickets in book form or just singly from the conductor once on the train and zooming into Manhattan. To anyone I do not know, it would appear I've stolen this baby.

'Waff?' she says.

Waffles. She wants waffles. I unbuckle her, draw her up.

'We'll get you waffles. When we get to Grandma's.'

I fish out half a stack of Ritz crackers from the diaper bag, then carry her to the water fountain to fill her bottle.

'Waddey.'

I drink too, with a vicious thirst, as if the more water I get down, the easier my future will be.

We settle back into our niche by the radiator. Daisy eats happily. She shakes her bottle.

'Jay?' she asks me.

I hug her. 'Yes,' I say, but no sound comes out.

I have neglected to mention Paris.

After my expulsion from Hastings, Fowler and I went there. J.T. and Evelyn had given him some money for graduate school, so we used some of that. In Paris I learned to ride trains the way I'm riding this one, aching with love for my traveling companion and with sadness for those absent, to places threatening in their decay, their beauty.

Our first train was out of the De Gaulle airport. We were sleepless, speeding on coffee, taking in as much of the whizzing in-between of suburb and city as we could. The Défense, stood out, monolithic, horrible in contrast to the miles of clay roofing of nearly all of Paris. It was June, and I was four months along with Isaac, just over the nausea, and I felt no exhaustion, only the fluttering stomach that could have been his heart beating or just anticipation of all that lay ahead: Europe, the birth, the baby, a lifetime of Fowler and joint-effort films. The only sadness was for my parents and their aging, their being out of this stage of life and having made peace with their particular estrangement.

Fowler said that the tiles of the clay roofs, long, rust-colored half-cylinders, were, before French roofing became industrialized, molded on women's thighs.

'What!' I said.

'Really!' he told me. 'The long legs of beautiful women who sat under the wet clay until it dried.'

'Beautiful, patient women,' I said.

'Yes,' said he, squeezing my hand, leaning back in his seat, exhaling satisfaction.

I had a baby with a man who could almost convince me of a story like that. I had two more with a man who would take in those roofs without making mention of them. My mistake: I love both of these men.

Riding this train, my youngest draped over me in silent wonder, the grey Hudson on our right, attempts at permanence on our left, I come to this: I have always been this person, the one I am, who sees this way, whose actions connote a vision of the world as enormous, capricious, ultimately sacrosanct. The current leavetaking alters none of this for me.

Later that morning I sat in a double bed in a pension on the Left Bank, drinking espresso and crying behind a section of *Le Monde*, willing myself to stop, failing.

Now tears darken my daughter's fuchsia sweatshirt, and I feign a coughing fit. She shifts against me, a familiar turning, as of the fetus in the later months, dragging me back. She's a perfect size for this posture, and she turns her head so that we both face the river, our cheeks aligned, and we ride into the city, watching.

Mother is upon us as I push open the door (I always carry a key), stroller on one arm, Daisy on the other. Of course, instant alarm.

'Leigh! My goodness!'

It seems to me that a woman who can manage to be in a skirt and blouse by seven in the morning and has no office to get to should be able to field an interruption like this one without so much as raising her voice. But there is the other, umbilical, consideration.

She takes Daisy, whose delight is immediate.

'I was just on my way out for the paper,' she explains frantically, 'but let me get you some coffee and breakfast. What on earth is going on. Poor Daisy, is she all right. Where are Jane and Isaac.'

In her haste over most things, Mother forgets to inflect. Statements are questions, questions statements. Discourse in general is muddled. 'Only a linguist could translate,' my father says fondly, now that he deals with this on a less regular basis.

I both adore her mania and hate it. It has given me the ability to stand apart from things and to brood to the point of cruelty.

'Mother, we're all right. I was hoping we could stay here for a little while. Simon and I are having some differences. Jane and Isaac are with him, and I have Daisy. Please don't mind.'

Out with it's been my method with Mother for a long

time. Otherwise we've got an eternity of circumlocution and non-sequitur to decode.

'Well, I couldn't *poss*ibly mind. But what about Jane, then, and Isaac. Will *he* be able to manage them. What will they do all the day?'

'They're in camp, Mother. I haven't been kidnapped. I'm still their mother. Daisy needs me more right now. And I need you to be calm.'

'Well of course I'll be calm. But you can hardly expect an unannounced visit to go un*not*iced, particularly when half the family is missing. Where on earth did you find to park at this hour.'

I tell her about the train.

'Good God. You could have taken the yellow car, Leigh, and not bothered with all that.'

Sometimes I think our differences could be summed up in the matter of nomenclature. She calls our jalopy 'the yellow car'; I call it the Mustard Bomb. She calls her arrangement with Dad 'an experiment'; I call it 'separation'. *Pas comme il faut* is her way of describing unacceptable behavior, whereas I would simply say it was crude or unacceptable. Occasionally I yearn for that gentility, but most of the time I mourn its impracticality. Still, it is easy, with Mother, to get swept up in the flourish of her idiom.

'I don't know,' I say. 'There's something about a train.'

She ignores me.

'Nama,' Daisy says, and she squeezes my mother's long cheeks, arranging her face horribly. But Mother allows it.

'You're my little fatty,' she says. Then, turning away from the glory of Daisy, 'Well, in any event, you'll need some breakfast and something to put on for a few days. And I want to hear all about this business when we're settled. Do you want your father in on it yet?'

'No.'

'He's expecting all of you on Saturday.'

'We'll be there, in some form.' I hear myself fading out, voice trailing away as it does when I'm over-whelmed. Dad loves Simon and he loathes conflict, which he considers unnecessary and luxurious given the state of our world. If I don't find some way to assure him that this is temporary, another of my aberrant responses to what is surely a paradise of a life, he'll be crushed.

I sit at the kitchen table and welcome her coffee, thick as diesel. Mother has always ignored the proportion advice as far as coffee's concerned. One heaping tablespoon of grinds for every six ounces of water is the way she does it. Daisy waits in the old high chair, the one *sans* safety strap ('Such a lot of rubbish, all these accoutrements,' Mother says of such things), for her food. Mother fixes her a boiled egg and toast dripping with butter and strawberry jam, which does nicely in lieu of waffles. She admires Daisy's appetite.

'I don't know what went wrong with Jane. She eats so poorly, always has. But look at this one!'

I know how I'm supposed to take this: you ruined her (Jane) with all that breast milk. She never got used to *other* food.

'Jane gets what she needs,' I say, horrified at the hollowness of that statement, given where I am. Mother doesn't respond, just goes on with the feeding.

Outside Macy's, where, Mother's convinced me, we'll find a few sale items for Daisy and me to tide us over, she says, 'I do think Jane ought to be with you, you know. Isaac is old enough now for a few days of this sort of thing, but Jane isn't.'

As I haven't yet told her about Fowler, I can't fathom her ability to understand what 'sort of thing' she means. All I said, over toast and eggs, was that I had some loose ends to tie up.

'Jane chooses her father.'

Mother lifts the stroller, without meaning to, and

slams it on the pavement. Daisy screams to get out. 'How can you *say* such a thing? *Of an eight-year-old?*'

The comfort of her help, of her company, gives way, and now I am helpless, a child myself, certain that the rough deal I'm facing is completely my fault. It's familiar, terrible, this certainty.

I kneel. 'I'm sorry,' I say to Daisy, but she bats me off, screaming for her Nama. I get up, defer, watch my mother gather her up, give her the Paddington rattle, shield her from me.

We pick up some playclothes and port-a-crib sheets, then move on to women's sportclothes. Mother insists on a pair of summer slacks and a skirt for me.

'You *need* things, for God's sake,' she says. 'Don't tell me you don't.'

Daisy is her phenomenally good-sport self until we get to the cash register. I leave Mother to pay, at her insistence, and head for the cafeteria to wait for her via the lavatory, where I change Daisy and fill a basin with cold water to dunk my head in.

'Wake up, asshole,' I whisper to my reflection. I'm haggard and fleshy, like a much older woman who has given up on something huge — living happily, for starters. Daisy starts into an empty stall, then backs out.

'Ick-y,' she says, smiling.

I remember that I shirked toilet repair before we left. This fact, on top of the others, fills me with grief. To have left two of my children in a house with a broken toilet . . . I imagine each of them cursing me, venting, Jane just screaming primally, Isaac doing his own sort of nonverbal damage to the doors and walls. Fist. Baseball bat.

I'm an hour away, but I may as well be in Siberia. What I've done, I just now realize, is to alter their lives, making their home unrecognizable, their parents fools. I've done the unutterable, predictable thing: exactly what my parents did to me.

Mother has found some way around the cafeteria line and to a table, probably with a graceful lie about a sick grandchild in the restroom, witness the stroller full of accoutrements for the child's recuperative period. Mother's tired beauty and her eloquence enable her to circumvent the most pedestrian of processes, which makes the fact that she's married to a Marxist all the more perplexing.

'They've got some lovely-looking soup. Vegetable, I think. Daisy loves soup. I hope it's all right with you that I ordered us some.'

'Of course,' I answer, Dad's formality creeping in. 'But isn't it a little warm for soup?'

'Oh,' Mother says, flustered. 'Now that you mention it.'

'No,' I say, softening. 'Whatever. She does like it.'

'Good. Because here it comes.'

Mother has actually gotten a server to leave her station behind the steaming chrome architecture of the kitchen to bring us three bowls of soup and two sodas.

'Here we are,' the woman says. She's about Mother's age, but thick in the middle and lavish in her gestures toward our comfort, setting us regular places with napkins and silver and asking, 'How's the baby feeling?'

I should pinch Daisy's thigh to get a proper noise out of her, but too late: she smiles cunningly, and the woman takes this as a compliment.

'See that? Rose'll make it all better.' She brings fat hands together. She's got a rich landscape of a voice, one to get lost in. 'She's a beauty.'

'Thank you, Rose,' Mother says.

Rose. It's the kind of name none of us has. We're so locked in our histories, my father, husband and son in the Old Testament, my mother, Marion Leigh Wadsworth, the girls and I on Plymouth Rock. From what I understand, neither I nor my children could ever be considered even remotely Jewish, although at Hastings I was the resident Jew.

'You ladies enjoy,' Rose says.

Mother says, 'I really think you should bring Isaac and Jane to the city. Until you get whatever it is sorted out.'

I spoon Daisy soup, then, stupidly, as I'll only have to do it again, I wipe her mouth.

'Foop,' she beams.

'I don't suppose you'd like to tell me what it is.'

'You won't believe it,' I say, looking only at Daisy.

She sighs. 'He's in town, isn't he?'

The mere mention of him brings him here, to the cafeteria in Macy's, and he's watching how we do things, what we say, a kind observer, at the ready should we drop something or forget any of our bags on leaving.

'Leigh,' she warns. 'Don't be a fool.'

'Mother, please,' I say softly. 'He had some news.'

'Of course he did.'

Fowler is in back of me, his mouth at my ear. *It's all right to tell her. Tell the planet. We make our own rules. But you know all this.*

'He's sick. I don't know what it is. He might not make it through the winter.'

Mother looks embattled. 'At this rate, Leigh, neither will you.'

I leave it. We go ahead and eat.

While Mother is at her afternoon tennis game in the park, I begin my maniac phoning.

They're not home. He must have picked them up from camp and taken them for a swim, over to Kirsten's or the neighbor's club. I can't bring myself to leave word, after listening to our recorded message, which has all of us talking at once and then Isaac saying, 'You caught us at a bad time – can we get back? Please say yes.'

Next: Kirsten.

'They're on their way over,' she says automatically.

I beg her to have them call me the minute they get there.

'You've been gone for under twelve hours, Leigh,' she says with irritation. 'Nothing's happened to them.'

'I want to talk to my children,' I tell her.

'Then *live* with them.' She hangs up.

I call her back. 'Are we really doing this?' I ask her.

'*We?*' she pleads.

My turn. I hang up.

I look around my old room, wishing for siblings. If I had siblings I could call them. They could come back to this apartment and make themselves comfortable with things to eat and pillows, and they could talk me out of this desperation. They could marvel at Daisy's chewing on the spines of my college texts in the combination desk-bookshelf-cupboard that I can remember being thrilled over acquiring. It made me feel wealthy, like one of my classmates, to have such a structure to keep all my things in. I was minus the walk-in closet, the private bath, the wraparound terrace, but I felt I was ahead in terms of the uniqueness of my parents. Not one of my classmates could brag that she had a Jewish father and a mother who didn't believe in God. (It was their one commonality, I thought, the atheism. I thought it sounded fashionable then, although it terrified me, made me feel as if I were floating in a satellite universe that was only coincidentally connected to the one everyone else was living in.)

A brother or a sister would ground me, I think.

I lie on the floor next to Daisy, who now sits over a series of inch-high plastic people, fitting them into shallow wells in a plastic school bus. I know that in minutes I'll be asleep, so I pull her over, settle her into the V of my hips, arrange the toys so she'll stay occupied while I nap. If I knew a prayer I'd say it now. I'd tell whoever it is their names, all three, and ask for help in getting us back under the same roof. And then

I'd ask whoever it is not to let Fowler die, and to flood Simon with forgiveness.

Our theory, Gillette's and mine, that glut begets immorality, holds water. In fact, given my research on the court of Louis XIV, it's irrefutable. Feigning scholarliness and singleness of purpose, I have enlisted the help of one of the librarians at the 40th Street branch, a man younger than myself, trim, elegantly dressed, who gestured dramatically, palms open to the world of European social history, when I asked for books on seventeenth-century French mores.

'My *dear*,' he swooned. 'Your chariot awaits.'

It is mid-morning. I left Daisy home with Mother. I walked forty blocks to get here despite a crashing headache and terrible fatigue. I've had six hours of sleep, in spurts of one and two hours, since I brought us to Mother's two mornings ago.

He hands me a printout of ten titles, mostly biography and collected essays, each with a long abstract.

'Tip of the iceberg, dearheart. Once I teach you the matching game, you'll be able to make your selections more expediently.'

I'm trying to be intent, but I keep wondering about this man, where he went to college. *Eliot Berman*, the nametag reads. He types in two commands and the computer lists more titles. He shows me the instructional card of prompts, and I thank him, clutching the printouts.

'You've been dear,' I say, kicking myself. Something Mother would say.

'Not really,' he says curtly. 'This is my job.'

I turn back to the screen.

'Will there be anything else?'

Almost venomous he is, all of a sudden, ill-treated servant to master, misogynist to all of womankind.

'Yes,' I say, thinking.

'Be quick, would you.' He slants his head away, eyeballing me.

'I need a book on degenerative diseases of the muscular system. Just a general text that would list them and the features of each, how each first manifests itself and progresses. If you'd be so kind. I've left my husband for a man who's dying of one of them, he hasn't told me which, and I'd like to get my bearings.'

Eliot smiles to himself, a puzzling smile, not exactly amused, not uninterested.

'Back in a jiff,' he says, only glancing my way. I know he won't be, that if he's lucky, he'll be on his lunch break or have gone home by the time I pass by the reference desk again, but I need him to know he's gotten the wrong end of the tiger this morning.

Oh, let's not do need.

I search, and find.

Dull, hardcover tomes full of dull, hardcover facts, no voices. Liselotte is my best guide. Reluctantly I jot down notes, facts, none of which has any impact. Open on the desk, Liselotte's letters drown them all out: *It is a miserable thing when people may no longer follow their own common sense but have to conform to the whims of whores and self-interested priests.*

I leave my carrel in search of a telephone.

Gillette, home, her voice huskier than usual, takes a tired tone with me.

'*You* kicked you out?'

'I suppose,' I explain, 'it's what I want. To be away. To give us room for some solution.'

'About the chapter,' she cuts me off.

I tell her about the musty old texts and that I'm inclined to go a different route with the book now, find more primary sources: letters, diaries, poetry by the women who watched as men brought home booty from war, effected royal takeovers and mergers, got rid of wives and mistresses, gained popularity.

'It's yours,' she says lightly. 'You call it.'

'Do you want to see the draft?' I ask, nervous that what I'm daring to call 'my work' has now been deemed unimportant by the only person who supports it.

'I can wait,' she says, 'until we meet with Barry.'

Barry is our garrulous editor, a classic Wasp divorcee: too smart, too jaded, too busy.

'OK. Thanks.' I feel like a teenager, fresh from a meeting with a displeased teacher, one who might have suspected the link with Fowler and who was primed for finding fault with my work, knowing it would have reason to fall short.

I call Mother.

'Sound asleep,' she says, gratified. 'All the way up Madison Avenue, after the Children's Zoo, in my arms. I even figured out how to fold up that awful stroller! But don't you think you ought to be here when she wakes up?'

'I will be,' I answer.

I race back to my desk, collect my things, leave the untrustworthy volumes, rely on Liselotte and the pounding instinct that tells me I have to get to Daisy, *now*, before she wakes up, lest all that is true about me appear in her tearful, frightened face.

I wait impatiently as the bag-checker at the exit checks bags. Someone taps my shoulder.

Amazed, I take the manila folder Eliot hands me.

'Xeroxes,' he says, 'from a medical dictionary. It's all we had.'

I'm glad he turns on his heel, doesn't wait for me to respond.

Before I reach the bag-checker I've read a description of motor neuron diseases. There are a good number of them. I close the folder until I'm in the taxi, fishtailing up Madison Avenue.

'*Amyotrophic lateral sclerosis, a.k.a. Lou Gehrig's disease,*' I read on the first page. In the top right-hand corner, penciled in tiny square letters, is 'I'm sorry.'

It's hot, and the traffic is horrendous. And Eliot Berman, who thought I was someone worth hating, has taken pity on me.

FIVE

I don't sleep. Fearful, unable to concentrate, I put reading aside and haul out two yellowing photo albums from Mother's slovenly bookshelf. I look at baby pictures of Isaac. In them, I never fully face the camera. I focus down on the baby, or away, at some off-site distraction. There are several of Fowler and Isaac sitting in the chair I sit in now, and there is one of the three of us, a momentary family, with the rock and castle background of the Delacorte Theater in Central Park. We're warmly dressed, but the ground is free of snow. It must have been March, a week or two before Fowler left me in the lurch. I show no signs of suspicion that this is about to occur.

Even in the best moments, since before the births of my children, there has been fear. I don't remember, even in the whirlwind of finding Simon, a minute without it. Mother and Daddy are edgy people, so I'm sure I became afraid at a young age. I'm not sure I knew the safety others may have known, the ones with parents glued together throughout the years, in all the Christmas photos, at the school plays and Saturday birthday parties. My parents made a career out of being different from those other parents, and they enjoyed it.

Isaac came in a flash. The labor, anything but gradual, hit me in sleep, and when Fowler and I reached St Vincent's Hospital, I had to stay in the cab on my back until he got someone with a gurney to come to me. My water had broken in the bed. I thought I'd peed, sneezed in my sleep and let loose, and then I felt the wave of pain in my lower back circle to my pelvis and down, down, through to the outside of my thighs where it got caught and I screamed. Fowler rushed, wordless, about the one large room, gathering clothes and the small bag I'd just packed with Kotex, a nightgown and the obligatory but useless tennis ball everyone said would help to ease pain if you rolled it around on your back. I couldn't stand without feeling that the baby would come out, so we crouched, both of us, and took the stairs like thieves afraid to make the boards creak.

Twenty minutes after we got to the hospital I had Isaac in my arms in a white receiving blanket with aqua balloons chasing across it. I was trying to see through what had just happened, to understand that I hadn't gone into two pieces, despite all that pressure through me and out to my thighs, my trembling feet, no end to the pain, just disbelief over it.

'You have a boy, Mrs Fowler,' the doctor, not mine but someone who was on call, said, and he shook my feeble hand and left forever.

'Seven nine,' one assistant said.

'APGAR 10,' someone else said.

I moved the blanket off his tiny, ruddy face, clamped shut except for the mouth, which was wailing the way I wanted to. Fowler was above me, at my shoulder, staring, speechless, holding his fingers out now and then to graze his son's cheek.

He'd seen me pass through, go from what I was, pregnant, eighteen, a girl who'd floated into his life, to this. I couldn't be *his* again. He wasn't prepared for this sort of damage, I guess, and I wasn't interested in damage control. If he couldn't join the party, he could hang. I finally had the most precious thing. I was leaving the sort of fear his world offered me and finding my own, more gripping one. It's this fear that has moved me through all these years of babies, work and men. It keeps me wired, on my guard, while other people sleep, my mother out cold, unaware of her radio's blaring talk show, Daisy bottom up in her enviable baby slumber.

I close the album and go back to the folder. There are several articles, some personal histories, some flat, horrifying descriptions of dystrophy and sclerosis. I picture Eliot at his monitor, commanding information for me, the harridan.

I read: causes, symptoms, treatments. I wonder, which one is it? All fatal: MD, ALS, MS, and the ones named after people. I recall Fowler's fluttering arm, his difficulty getting up from his chair. I read about motor neurons, voluntary muscle control, limb weakness, exaggerated reflexes, damage that affects speech, chewing, swallowing. ALS, the first thing I read on the bus coming home, is more prevalent among men aged 35–65. There is no known cause. It isn't hereditary. It leaves the brain, heart, bowel and sexual functions unaffected.

I am sure this is what he has. *Amyotrophic*: muscle atrophy; *lateral*: 'side' – nerve tracks run down both sides of the spinal cord; *sclerosis*: hardening – scars that remain after nerves have disintegrated. Suffocation is likely to be the cause of death, 'when muscles that control breathing cease functioning'.

I go into the drugs and apparatuses – wheelchair,

computer with wand attached to the head when all other muscle control fails, this for communication with non-sufferers. Then the personal narratives by the doomed, narratives infused with the sort of heroism unimaginable for Fowler. What like test has he ever faced? To what outrageous misfortune has he ever been enslaved?

My troubles shrivel. Until now I haven't believed in his going, in his ultimate desertion. Like my intermittent awareness of stars, *a priori*, I have counted on Fowler's being alive somewhere on the planet, bewitching women and adding to his body of remote films, out doing his Fowler thing, my first love, the father of my son. Now I am treated to preparations for his exit. How much easier my world would have been without him, and how stupid a thought that is, for, I'm quite sure, an easy world is not one I'd be comfortable in, my penchant always having been for the opposite, the sphere of dangers and surprises and absolute passion.

Ultimately I won't be put off by endlessly ringing telephones, fury or refusals. I will do as I see fit, despite the unpopularity it earns me.

By 5.30, when Mother rises, I am cheerful, prepared for coffee and conversation, for the mornings of my girlhood, busy with food and phoning and the details of home.

'Goodness, you're up early,' she says, gathering her summer robe around her. How fat she's gotten! How much more the portrait of love!

'I am my mother's daughter,' I say brightly.

Daisy whines for Raggedy (Ann), for her crocadonna (dile), her ridey toy (kiddie car).

We are starting to miss the company of our things. I tell Mother I can't believe they haven't called, three days into this odyssey.

She said, 'They're not going to behave as you want them to right now. They owe you that.'

Read: don't expect unconditional backing. You are at fault here.

We walk several long blocks west to the farmer's market. Mother buys lettuce, peaches, tomatoes and a loaf of dark raisin bread.

'It's hot as Hades out here,' she complains. 'Let's take Daisy to the sprinkler.'

Again I miss home, the little wading pool in the back, trips to Kirsten's when the heat is at its most beastly.

'I'll take her, Ma. You go home and rest.'

'I suppose I might do that,' Mother says. She squeezes Daisy. All in good fun, Daisy smacks her in the face.

'She's her own person!' Mother says. 'Not surprising!'

I stop in a deli and buy Daisy a cold box of juice with a straw and a travel pack of Fig Newtons. I turn the stroller north on Fifth Avenue. A screen above a bank entrance tells me it's 91 degrees, but I don't feel it. I've lost weight these arduous days. I move fast, planing, creating a breeze. Daisy wants faster, so I go faster, weaving in and out of sluggish pedestrians. I'm taking us to the library, not the sprinkler, to thank Eliot. It's good to know where I'm going, to be on this errand.

I ask him about lunch, if he's eaten it, if he usually eats it, and if he'd like to join us for it. Daisy wants to nosedive onto the desk, pilfer pencils and Post-its.

'You read what was in the folder, then?' He exits a file and locks his center drawer.

'Every word. I know a lot now.'

'Here.' He gives me three colored pencils and an eraser. 'These are for Herself.'

He pinches Daisy's sweaty thigh. 'Let's go somewhere arctic. I refuse to sweat in public. There's a horrible burger place a block away that's bound to be cold.'

I haven't known relief like this in a long time. I believe that lunch with Eliot will not prove harmful in any way. And this belief, relieving as it is, hurts. It informs me, as does so much right now — the heat,

Daisy's small, unfulfilled requests to be home among her things and siblings, my mother's amazed weariness — that I've been on a furious ride for years, that I've had three children in a hurry, that I've paid no heed to the smallish voice at the back of my heart, the one with the complaint that points to all the ignored wisdom of my life: *Please, Leigh, a moment of your time.*

We land in a dark, tight corner of a Burger-on-Flame. I fold up the stroller and sit Daisy on my lap.

'Infernal, isn't it,' he states, then levels his gaze at me, a woman with her life in pieces, sharing that misery with youngsters. Through the tortoiseshells, I see that his eyes are pale blue, not even blue really, and inscrutable, defiant. But somehow they take me in, they want to know.

'It's divine,' I say. 'You're divine.'

'You're mad,' he quips and grabs my wrist. 'Now *decide*. Which burger to have. I don't recommend anything with a topping. In fact, I don't recommend ever saying the word "topping". Not at all *comme il faut*. And very dicey in terms of gastrointestinal goings-on.'

Daisy dunks her fist into a glass of ice water, then smears her face with the cool of it.

'Are we as smart as Mother?' Eliot asks her.

'Much smarter,' I moan.

Eliot scowls. 'I see we're very limited on the esteem front. I, for one, only love people who hate themselves, so it stands to reason that I'm having lunch with *her*.' All of this he directs at Daisy, about me. She stares, fascinated, by the rush of words and the *à propos* gesturing.

'*Anyway*,' I throw in.

We have a waitress. 'OK!' he exclaims. He orders for me.

'I'm assuming Herself will have the fries and chocolate milk.'

I nod, laughing, losing all my stiffness to the thrill of him.

'The point is,' he says, after the waitress leaves with a similar appreciation of him, 'you're here having burgers with a person who may learn to like you despite the fact that you've completely sacked your own life. And I think it is safe to say that your clone is rather enjoying herself. So.'

'Do you always talk like this?' I say. 'Or are you doing it for the baby?'

'My dear girl,' he says, his voice sliding with disdain, as if I've been deprived of the only bit of knowledge that could possibly help me. 'I refuse to miss opportunities. And my opportunity here, as I see it, is to tell you what I see. I see someone who is, frankly, scared and friendless. It's not a state with which I'm unfamiliar. And don't think I am so obtuse that I feature myself some sort of lifesaver. But I'm intrigued here. I feel I may be looking at a Bovary or a Karenina. Except you're just smart enough to save yourself. At which point I'll become dispensable. Another state not unfamiliar to *moi*.'

I'm chilled. 'Well.'

'I thought you'd say that. Hey. Tell me your name.'

I tell him through tears, 'My name is Leigh Adelman.'

'Mama ky?' Daisy says, patting my wet cheeks.

'Mama do,' I say.

Eliot takes my hand this time. 'Mama a mess.'

I tell him about leaving, about what I did with Fowler. I am not self-editing. I'm triumphant in not boring him, in providing a tale at least on a par with the ones he's used to hearing. He takes Daisy on his lap so I can eat and reconstruct the error of my ways. He amuses her with finger games and peekaboo and smile faces on the corners of his placemat. I stop at now, at Mother's with no idea of where to go next.

'I see,' he says heavily.

'What?' It's torture. I'm on the cusp of being helped, I'm sure of it.

'Seems to me,' he says. He's good at accents.

'*What?*'

'OK,' he says. 'Here it is. You've thrown all your chips down and you're standing at the table drooling over the loss. It's unworthy of you, really, not at all dignified. I say go with what follows naturally. Blow the whole thing wide open, as they say in those idiotic movies. Introduce your son to his father before he dies. To his grandparents before they do. Let your kids know who you are. How can you hide from your own children?'

I recognize this advice. It's Catherine's. In a way, it's Liselotte's, and it might be Pam's. It's advice that cuts worse than surgery, worse than anything, because it's frightening and I know I have to follow it.

'You can't hide from your kids. Let *them* decide whether you're forgivable. They'll be honest. As for your husband, well, he has good reason to be miffed. You're not supposed to do what you did. People hate that. But who am I to pretend to know what the proper sentencing is?'

At one point in the movie, Catherine leads Jim, to whom she isn't married, into the woods by her house. 'Catch me,' she taunts. Indoors sits Jules, her husband, resigned.

I don't expect Simon to sit indoors, resigned. I didn't give any thought to what I expected him to do.

'In other words,' I venture, 'I'm already losing, why not just throw all the chips in?'

'To my way of thinking,' Eliot smiles. 'Now take this,' he says, meaning Daisy, 'and I can do violence to my GI tract with our meal here.'

I've eaten all of my burger and he's had none of his, devoting himself entirely to my cause. I put some fries aside for Daisy.

'Babba,' she says. Ketchup.

'It's *too good*!' he says after swallowing.

'What would the French say?' I revert to my need to be bleak.

'They would be horrified,' Eliot asserts, 'which is why I adore them.'

We establish our shared Francophilia during the rest of the gauche meal.

'I think you might consider taking a hint from the French,' Eliot muses. *As if I haven't already.*

On and on about lives spent in service to matters of the heart. Where does one draw the line? One is who one is, one can't help this, but is this an excuse? Am I a female Don Juan or a married woman who does the thing that doesn't get talked about: what she feels like doing?

I pay for his burger, as I said I would.

Outside, in perfectly punishing heat, he tells me I am to pass Go and collect $200. He says he must abandon me before he turns into butter at my feet. I get a pen out of the diaper bag to write on my hand.

'If you're going to be saving my life,' I say, 'I'll need your phone number.'

Which he gives me, thank the Lord.

Early the next afternoon I'm back on the train, sporting the new summer slacks and one of Mother's creased white blouses and a straw bag. I called Fowler this morning and told him of my plan to arrive at the camp at dismissal and talk to Jane and Isaac before Simon takes them home. 'You'll be all right,' he said vaguely, sounding depressed. Fearful, I guessed, of what is happening to him. 'You'll be fine. I know you.'

I've brought work, but there is no doing it. There is no doing anything but planning my speech, which a few hours' sleep and Eliot's perspective have primed me for, a sort of *mea culpa* without the self-loathing that Eliot finds so repugnant. I will tell Isaac, in the event that Simon hasn't done so already, that Fowler is his father, and that I am compelled to bring them together despite Fowler's grim news. Mother will have none of this compulsion.

'I suppose it's got more to do with your father's side of things,' she said at the breakfast table. 'That driving connection of the blood. The Wasps are so much quicker to allow a lapse, to forget about troublesome relations. But he spends half his life moaning about his rotten brother and how Mae died of disappointment in him. It goes above and beyond.'

She was referring, on her side, to some cousins who left the city to go and live on one of the Thousand Islands at the Canadian border. They never invited a soul up to visit after they moved, and this was regarded as hateful by my grandmother, who never bothered about them again once it was generally acknowledged that they'd fallen from whatever height we were all nailed to by virtue of our breeding. 'They didn't amount to much,' was the only thing I ever heard my grandmother, Pussy, say about them. This was what she said when she was pushed to the outer limits of her patience: so-and-so doesn't amount to much. With her on the one hand tamping down all emotion into such packed statements and my father's mother, Mae, on the other hand, forever threatening to die any minute, her tone a shade deeper than wistful, I developed a battery of excuses for my own confusion over things. These grandmothers, Mae, who fulfilled her threat years ago, and Pussy, whose voice I can still hear although she is three years gone (how she'd have reveled in Daisy! How horribly I miss her when we gather, anxiously, on Christmas Eve, hoping for smooth sailing through the next day, for joy over the commercial festivities), advise me alternately: stiff upper lip! rage! draw yourself up to your full height! tell them what you want!

'Grandma Mae would endorse the view that Fowler and Isaac should meet,' I ventured.

'Grandma Mae would have hired someone to take care of Fowler centuries ago,' Mother said, in an unusually light moment for this week.

'And Pussy?' I squeaked.

'Don't mention them on the same day!'

We were having fun.

'Just go and see them,' she advised. 'Forget the agenda. Jane sounds so troubled. I want her here with me.'

She didn't mention Isaac, although I heard her talking to him. She sounded very official, as I imagine did he. I told her about Eliot, the lunch Daisy and I had with him.

'A confirmed bachelor,' she said. I hadn't mentioned that I thought he was gay, but somehow she knew. This is what mothers do, I thought, know our lives in advance of our knowing them. These last few days I'd lost my knack for this sort of ESP. It was the sleep loss, the wicked distance, the total fear of being apart from Jane and Isaac. I suddenly knew the horror of what was facing me — the fact of their growing up and away from me, regardless of my behavior.

'He's a divine man,' I said of Eliot. I sounded just like Mother, just like Pussy.

'I'm sure he is,' Mother said earnestly. 'My dearest friend in the whole world, Vernon, was the same way. We drank Martinis and stayed up all night and never stopped talking. I'd never loved anyone so much in my life.'

'Ma!' The outpouring stunned me. 'When was this?'

She waved her hand dismissively. 'Way back. Way, way back. He was an awful lot of fun. Pussy didn't think he amounted to much. I brought him up for the weekend once. Dad thought he was light on his feet, and Pussy just wore her endurance smile. I was terribly disappointed.'

'Ma!' I said again, idiotically. 'How colorful!'

She looked at me. 'Don't think you've cornered the

market on the bizarre, Leigh. It's a big world, always has been. All manner of folk pass in and out of one's life. I just happened to love Vernon. And when he took up with a young man from Spain, the most beautiful creature you'd ever seen, sick, of course, not long for the world, I lost Vernon to a dying man.'

She got up and started doing the dishes. She was in tears. I shuddered, wondering if I'd be saying something similar to Daisy years hence: I lost your father to a tragedy in the making.

I'd been treating Fowler, in my impossible mind, to the luxury of health, to a comfortable seat slightly to one side of my patient family. I had some revising to do, Mother was pointing out.

Stages of city disappearing — skyscrapers, intermittent low buildings, then the trees that hide the houses of the wealthy in Riverdale, then bald lawns sloping to river. I count the minutes before arrival time, count out singles for a cab to the high school, happy that I'll be there before the 2.30 dismissal. I ache for the moment of contact, the promise of forgiveness, any vestige of their love. It's impossible not to anticipate: a tall boy, fists jammed into jeans pockets, leaning against something, a wall, a tree, one knee up, and his sister, half his height but as demanding a presence, trying on moroseness or abandon or giddiness, as the mood strikes.

I get off the train with a rare energy, one that I gained during my interview with Eliot. I must find a way to stop hurting them.

I make the error of telling the cab driver the quickest route to the high school, which he takes as an indication of hubris on my part. He is fat, with hair in a ponytail, and he sighs often. He makes turns with an energy that isn't merited, sawing at the steering wheel. He is ominous, and he sours me on my mission: I'm wrong to have come. This wasn't meant to be.

So I skimp on the tip – cause for more graceless gesture and sighing. I stand at the school entrance, two brick pillars and a plaque, beset by queasiness, thinking I shouldn't be here, this is no longer my place. How much I have erred in coming begins to be revealed when I spot Jane, a flutter of color in her pale blue and yellow shorts set, jumping up and down to emphasize something to Adrienne, in whom I'm sure she's confided everything. They're at the breezeway among some other boys and girls with neon lunchboxes and gym bags.

I start over, heart pounding, but stop just shy of the

faculty parking lot where I see Kirsten's Grand Chero-
kee. Simon is sitting in it, reading the paper, oblivious
to our daughter.

I wander over.

'Oh,' he says. 'Hi.'

'I came to talk to the children,' I say.

'You'll get no argument from me,' he says, looking
over, noticing, finally, that Jane is waiting for him.

'What kind of *talk* is that?' I ask him. He smirks, as if
I'm insane.

'That's neutral talk,' he answers. 'It's the only kind I
trust myself with these days.'

That he and Kirsten are keeping some sort of
company is apparent enough from his choice of vehicle,
but the idea of their conferring about arrangements for
my children is unnerving, to say the least.

'What has happened to our cars?' I ask him.

He slaps the paper down on the passenger seat. 'Our
cars?' he pleads. 'Our *cars*?'

'You're driving someone else's car,' I whine.

'You're fucking another man,' he says, and he pushes
the door open, hitting my shoulder, and slams it shut.

He looks thin, but healthy. She must be feeding him
well. She's a terrific cook, I'm sick to admit.

'You're fucking my best friend,' I hazard.

He stares at me in a way I've never seen, as if he's trying to figure out how I could exist and be so unjust at the same time.

'Your best friend has nothing to do with this,' he says.

'You're driving her car,' I repeat.

'Why are you here?' he demands. '*Why*?'

'I'm looking for Jane and Isaac,' I explain, appalled.

'One foot in, one foot out,' he says.

I look over at the breezeway, for Jane. I don't see her. I start to run, panicked, sure that she's taken off, having witnessed the argument. I throw open the glass door and dash down the hallway, figuring she and Adrienne are hiding in the ladies' room. But they aren't, and I don't know where they've gone. I stop to catch my breath. It is the most terrible moment of wanting I have ever known, and I sink to the linoleum in a heap, tears and sweat falling onto Mother's blouse. I think of finding Isaac, begging him to call Jane back from wherever she's gone, but my own despair exhausts me and I can't move. I can't go out into that blazing light until he is gone, until he's collected them and taken them to her house and shown them what terrible things he can do. I will stay here, I promise myself, until there is no possibility of my seeing any of them. And then I will call a cab and take myself back to Mother's.

Soon after Mother has shut her door for the evening I go in and lie down on the sofa bed by Daisy's crib. The heat has turned to rain, cooling, heavenly rain. Everything is so far from what it was when I left here this morning. I drift in and out of longing and fury and terrible need. I am afraid of sleep. I am afraid of joining the ranks of those who know scandal, create it, hope to live through it, live through it. I am totally afraid.

SIX

My father, because of his poor Polish ancestry, will brook no cost-cutting when it comes to the food for our Saturday brunches. He scowls over Mother's contribution. On his gleaming dining-room table (Mother can't abide a certain preciousness he has about his furniture: 'What true Marxist cares about the decorative arts?' she quips), she has set down two store-bought coffee rings.

'At least take them out of the boxes,' he says to her.

To me he says, 'So where are the others?'

I tell him Simon will be dropping them off.

'He's going to *shul*?'

Dad skips a beat sometimes. I have to fill in: he's surprised that Simon won't be joining us and covers his concern with the obviously wrong assumption that Simon, a non-practicing Jew, would be busy at temple on a Saturday morning. Professorship has given my father a lifetime of this sort of license. His students must feel they're in the presence of genius – or lunacy – when he omits logical connections in his lectures.

'He's going to do his own thing,' I toss off.

'Good,' Dad says, obviously hurt. 'He should have some time to himself.'

Mother has taken her usual seat in Dad's immaculate parlor, just off the dining room, where splendid sunlight dapples the oriental rug he took from their apartment.

'Leigh has some news,' she tells him. Then, apologetically to me, 'Really, dear, were you going to let it go?'

'Let what go,' he says. 'What?'

'I'm staying with Mother for a while,' I stumble. 'Daisy and I. We've been there all week.'

Dad stops arranging the glasses and platters of food, bagels, lox, onions, tomatoes. 'Tell me the rest,' he says calmly.

'There's been an interruption,' Mother says ominously.

Dad gives her a stern look. 'You'll let Leigh tell the story please, Marion.'

I see no sense in holding out. 'I saw Fowler,' I say.

Dad takes a second, then walks to the center of his sitting room so that he is directly in front of me, not six inches away. He looks into my eyes like an eye doctor would, with some idea of what he's looking for but in need of a missing detail.

'You saw that man?' he begs. 'You saw such a man and you let him have an effect on you? After all that has gone on? Please, Leigh, tell me what I'm looking at here.'

A fool, I know he wants me to say.

Daisy screams just then from the hallway. I find her flat on her tummy after a fall over the molding. I bring her back into the parlor, where Dad sits opposite Mother in a matching chair.

'I am not going to let a thing like this ruin my Saturday,' he says. 'But I will tell you right now that if you put in jeopardy your wonderful family that you have worked so hard to keep happy and healthy, you will put in jeopardy your time with me. I do not take this lightly at all. Simon is a good man, and whatever you're doing with that cheapskate from the South, and believe me, I don't want to know, Simon doesn't deserve a second of this. So you've heard from me, and now let's have some food.'

He gets up and heads for the table, pulling at the seam of his jacket the way I've only seen elderly men do. He'll be seventy in the fall, which makes my waywardness seem all the more heartless.

'Gopa,' Daisy calls to him.

He turns, takes her from me. I feel Mother at my elbow, shy away from her, then wait my turn for food I don't feel like eating, but I will eat it because that way, at least, I have something to do with my mouth other than exercise it in these obviously fruitless and destructive ways. Perhaps if I'd taken off, left New York, to have Isaac, this debt I feel to my parents wouldn't keep pulling me back to them. But it does, and, indications to the contrary, I don't take my attachment to them lightly. I believe they are good people.

We settle back in the parlor and eat on our laps quietly, until the buzzer sounds. Dad gets it, and I hear Simon's voice.

'Hi,' he blares. 'The kids are here. Shall I send them up?'

'Please,' Dad answers. 'You come too.'

'I'll be back in a couple of hours.'

'Please,' Dad begs. 'We can all help.'

Either Simon didn't hear or has chosen not to respond, because there is no further intercom communication, and two minutes later Jane and Isaac are standing in my father's foyer.

Mother is on her feet, pulling them to her, trying not to cry.

Jane hugs her stiffly. 'Hi Grandma.'

Isaac hugs his namesake and then goes directly to the food.

Jane runs to Daisy, who is squealing with happiness. There is a crushing in my chest, and I think that this is what a heart attack must feel like, a total press of pain against everything that keeps me going.

Neither child speaks to me. I approach Jane for a hug, and she turns away, fighting tears. I do the same with Isaac.

'Save it,' he warns. 'For the guy you left us for.'

I feel like screaming, telling them all to stop, please stop relying on me never to slip, never to wander, never to imagine myself differently, to make a mistake and apologize and keep on living, keep on being their mother, their daughter, their wife. And then something occurs to me, something that leaves me numb. I know that Simon is seeing Kirsten, but I'm not sure that it's in the way I accused him of outside the high school. I suddenly think he may have called upon her in a needier, more threatening way, one that may or may not involve sex, a lasting way. My leaving has given him permission to do what I've always suspected him of wanting to do, and that is helping Kirsten out of her desperate boredom with Ted. It would be too humiliating to call her, too ironic to accuse her of something sordid. I stop myself short of imagining them together, what each would say, how they would get around to touching each other.

'How is camp?' I say loudly, generally.

Everyone looks at me, even Daisy. I continue, top volume.

'I just thought I'd ask how you were doing because no one asked how I was doing. No one asked me if I'd slept any since I'd been at Grandma's, or if I missed my children, or if I thought that there was any chance I'd ever be coming back, or if it bothered me that I'm basically cast out. So I'll tell you. I'm doing lousy. I miss you. I'm having some trouble that I'm not sure how to handle, and I know I'm making big mistakes all the time. But I love you, and I don't want you to treat me like this. It makes everything even harder. You're in my head all the time. I don't even brush my teeth without thinking of you brushing yours.'

I'm looking directly at Jane, tears streaming down my face, and she is horrified, frantic.

'Mommy, please don't,' she says, so softly she sounds like a child I don't know. 'Please don't cry.'

She comes to me, and I'm shaking so hard, sobbing so

noisily, and I don't know how to stop this. I feel the family circling, retiring to the food table and peripheral seats. And I feel Jane's tears soaking me, and I will this all to be over, and I will that no further harm come to her, to Isaac, to anyone in this room.

I whisper. 'I'm going to find some things out that will help me get back to you. And in the meantime, you go to camp and have dinner with Dad and talk to me, please talk to me because there is no living without you and Isaac. Daddy and I will work something out between us that will be so much better than this you won't believe it. I promise you.'

'Mommy,' she says. 'I want you to come home. I miss Daisy.'

'I'm coming home,' I say loudly. 'Soon.'

Mother and Dad look ashen, so heartbroken I can't speak to them. But I can see that I haven't done this very well, that Daisy is bewildered and clinging to Isaac, that Jane can't let go of me, that Mother and Dad are too old to manage crises like this one, and I know what I have to do. I have to get to Fowler, to include him in the strife he and I have stirred up, to give up on doing all the damage alone. Dead or alive, he's got to start taking some of the heat.

I kiss everyone, even Mother, who stiffens. To Dad I

promise a sensible solution. To Isaac I vow better times.
Jane has my word that we will meet each Saturday until
I come home, and we'll have lunch at Dad's and shop
and be silly girls together with Daisy.

'I'm going to talk to him,' I tell them all, cards on
the table. 'Watch. Nothing bad will come of it.'

Jane waves me into the elevator, cheered, but
desperate.

It takes me exactly thirty-seven minutes to cross town by
bus and walk south to Fowler's building. I lean on the
buzzer. Nothing happens. I do it again. Then I see the
blind open above the windowbox, and his face, framed
in the window, smiling.

'Hey, you,' he says, but he doesn't get up. 'Take my
keys.'

I let myself in the building and then the apartment. I
find him sitting by the window, holding one of his arms,
trying to stop it from moving.

'I wasn't able to get up,' he explains, shrugging,
embarrassed.

I draw in a breath, and then I say, 'You have to see
him. You have to come home with me. There's nothing
else.'

'Sit,' he says, taking me in, my rush, my tone, *the*

whole catastrophe, as he was fond of saying when someone burst into his classroom at a run with a lame excuse for being late.

I do so. He subdues the flamboyant arm with the tame one, but the shaking continues, slower, weighted. There is anger in this arm, the unaffected one, and I understand it. What is happening to him is an outrage. I should apologize.

'Tell me what you want.'

I conjure Eliot. 'I want you to see Isaac.'

The shaking stops. He exhales.

'Does Isaac want to see me.' A statement.

'That's not the point.' At least I don't think it is. How would Isaac *know* if he wanted to do this or not?

'What *is* the point then?'

'You're his father,' I plead.

He lowers his head, defers to the window view, the geraniums, the benevolent sunny street. 'I haven't been his father for a long, long time.'

'Don't indulge yourself,' I tell him. No stopping me, applause from Eliot, from Gillette.

For several unbearable moments I watch as he pushes himself up from the low chair, his arms taut hoists. Standing, he gestures miserably down, at himself.

'Come here,' he says, and I go to him. He holds me, as before, as he did when we were so much younger.

'I am *so, so* sorry,' he says.

We stand, sweating, folded into each other. I feel his hand at the back of my head, cradling, the way I do with Daisy when I put her down for a nap or a diaper change. I'm charged, not unhappy, as I was two days ago when Simon and I hurled words in the parking lot.

'I'm not,' I say.

There is, I'm coming to think, a logic that is beyond us, beyond our control, into which we must somehow fit, happily or miserably, neither being of consequence. I'm not about to give over to a Higher Power, to effect the canned speech of the reborn. But until now, except for Fowler's leaving, I've directed traffic, and it has exhausted me. Now I loosen my hold on Fowler, which is to say I loosen my hold on the world, as per Eliot's instructions, and again I am grateful.

'I'll do whatever you want,' he says, and when I draw back to see if he could possibly mean it, adds, 'whatever needs doing.'

I call Mother and tell her I'm coming back to pick up Daisy and bring her down here. She objects, sighing.

'My idea is that you put your affairs in order first.

I'm happy to keep Daisy another night. It was really terrible for her when the others left with Simon.'

I ask for a description.

'Daisy wanted to go back with him, understandably. Simon was in tears. Your father was in tears. You *must* do something about all of this, dear.'

'Thank you,' I say. 'I'll see you in the morning.'

'That's fine,' she says.

I pace, my mind racing with strategies to win back Mother's approval. Futile musings these, because I've worn her out.

Fowler holds out his arms, at peace for now, for me to come and lie down. But I can't do this. I'm inclined only to act, to push things to a conclusion, ugly as it may turn out.

'I'm so far outside everything now I don't know how to act, what to do,' he begins. 'Everything I do has an echo. This may be your last time doing this, seeing that, speaking to this one, holding that one.' He shrugs. 'I'm so certain that I've been a total asshole all my life, believing I knew what was best for me, how to get it, what to say about having gotten it or not having gotten it. Anyway.'

Unable to disagree, I stare, searching for signs of the Fowler I made into legend in my mind, the one without the crippling disease, without the self-loathing. 'Join the club.'

In the morning, amazed that I've managed to sleep in his bed a full six hours, I ask for their names, the women, all of them who lasted more than a week. I'm feeling lithe from lovemaking, energetic, young. I'm thinner than I've been in years, sure of my own sexiness as I lie on my side, hip jutting up, breasts full, nipples a deep red. I actually believe I can compete with the other conquests.

He laughs, adopts a mock seriousness. 'There was a Bridget, a Sandy, a Liz. There was a Cecilia, a Martha. Not to worry.'

'Any more kids?' I'm flippant, but the prospect does horrify me.

'No, Leigh.'

I don't get any satisfaction out of knowing the names. I don't even bother with visualization.

'Do Evelyn and J.T. know?'

'They know what I've got, yes,' he says.

'I don't mean that. Do they know about Isaac?'

'They don't.'

I sit up, hunt for my underwear, find it, start getting dressed.

'I couldn't,' he protests. 'They'd have made it worse.'

I stand up very straight, a mission in underwear. 'They couldn't have,' I tell him.

I ask him when classes start, and whether he's got any money saved up.

Late August, I learn, and yes, there's money. Money from film awards and lecturing junkets and endowment grants. Professional money. The kind I don't have. Not that I have money of any other kind.

'First order of business,' I say. 'We tell them they have a grandson, and we get them to meet him. We can all fly down. They won't have to budge.'

He rolls over onto his back, studies the ceiling.

'You've got nothing to lose,' I urge.

He grips my arm without looking at me. 'But you do.'

'Really.'

'You've got a husband and three children.'

'I think my husband has sought refuge elsewhere.'

'Men do that.'

'Wrong again,' I quip, pulling him back to me, hoping to lose myself again to sex. '*People* do that.'

I call Simon after we've had some English muffins and coffee. I ask him if he can find a place to stay for a few days so I can come home and see the children. He is calm, almost pleasant. Perhaps fresh out of bed with Kirsten, or maybe still in it with her, having found something to do with the children for a couple of hours. He gives me no argument. 'That's fine,' he says. 'Jane will appreciate that. I can't speak for Isaac.'

I explain that I'll be arriving this afternoon, that he should make arrangements.

Brief silence. Then, 'As you wish.'

Now there's ice in his voice, and I don't like the insinuation of it: that what goes around comes around, that I'll get mine for the disturbances I've caused, that our house will burn, the children will turn against me, he'll win.

I put the phone back in its wall cradle in the small, bright kitchen.

'I'm going home and see my kids.'

He says he'll walk me to Mother's to get Daisy, then take us to the train.

Outside he walks steadily, lightly tapping the pavement with the rubber tip of his cane, out in front of him, like the blind do.

'Do you need that?' I ask.

'I'm not sure.' He directs this out in front of him, as if it's a cosmic question, not just something a girlfriend has asked him.

'Do you want to get a bus or a cab?'

'I want to walk,' he says.

'Of course.' We take them slowly, the long blocks west to my mother's, like tourists. Like lovers.

I ask him to wait downstairs while I go up and get Daisy. He sits on the leather couch in the lobby. Getting on the elevator, I wave nervously. He tips his hat.

Mother says she just can't bring herself to say hello today, she hopes I'll understand.

'I just can't get my mind around some of this, Leigh,' she says. 'I packed the diaper bag, but I thought I'd keep some of Daisy's things here, in the event that you need to come back.'

'Thank you, Ma.'

I've got Daisy around me like a monkey. Mother hugs us both.

'I'm glad you'll be with Jane. Honestly, to look at her yesterday, you'd have thought the world had ended.'

'She thinks it has,' I say.

'Yes,' Mother says, her eyes full. 'I guess you know that.'

'You're a good mother,' I tell her when she hands me a bag of food.

'Yes,' she says, smiling tearfully. 'I suppose I am. Now run along.'

I am so glad to have Daisy weighing me down that I wish we had more floors to travel on the elevator ride. When we get off, Fowler is standing right in front of us.

'Let's have a look,' he says, his cap off, holding out a hand for Daisy to do whatever she likes with.

'Who dat?' she says.

'That's James,' I say. I've never called him James.

'No Jay!' she shouts.

'She thinks I said "Jane",' I explain.

'Daisy,' he says reverently, 'you look just like your mama.'

The doorman gives me a look as we leave. He doesn't offer to help us find a cab. But we manage, with my various bundles, to get one at the corner, a fairly new car that gives us a smooth ride to Grand Central, near where Eliot and Daisy and I had lunch the other day.

'We were on a train once,' he says inside the station.

'More than once,' I correct.

'I was referring to the ride of the century.'

'I love you,' I say, though it isn't what I mean, exactly. I love that he says things like this, that he can be playful about a world which, by now, must seem beyond cruel.

'Ahv oo,' says Daisy. 'Oh wuh.'

'Whole world,' I translate for him. 'I love you in the whole world.'

'I love you in the whole world,' he repeats distantly.

All that I've been under is momentarily lifted by pleasantness, of company, of weather, of endeavor. If I were less shaky, more situated, I'd want to give a party, invite anyone, even Kirsten.

Daisy pulls Fowler's cap down over his face. He lifts it, offering her another opportunity, which she takes, and so on until it's time for us to get to the platform.

'You'll call,' he says.

I call the house from the station, to see where they are in their day. No one picks up, so I try Kirsten's.

When she answers, rushed, elated, I seize up.

'Kirsten,' I say, as if shocked to reach her in her own house.

'Hi.'

'Are my kids there?'

'Jane's here, but Isaac's out with a friend.'

I ask that she put Jane on.

'Hold on.'

I hear her calling outdoors, singsong. Jane's response

is muffled by outdoor noise, wind, splashing. Maybe some neighbors.

Kirsten gets back on. 'She says she knows you're coming, and she'll see you at home.'

This is enough of a promise to hold me for days.

I thank her. I can't pursue her on the subject of Simon right now, try to find out where he's made arrangements to stay. The fullness of her voice leaves me cold.

On the cab ride over I watch the passing scenery — the strip where I do my marketing, where I pick up the dry cleaning and get the gas, then the mansions where the people we don't know live, then the houses of the people we do know, the church, the home for the aged. I think I must see it as the driver does, as a stranger would.

Daisy ambles instinctively to the side door, using the Mustard Bomb for balance. I leave the bags outside. Keys out, I let Daisy in.

She is immediately at her toys in the corner of the living room we've devoted to them, the Plastic Junkheap, Simon fondly calls it.

'I'm home,' I call out insanely. I know Isaac isn't there. He's not usually home on Sunday afternoons. He goes with friends to a movie or a ball game or plays in one. Once in a while a pack of them troop down to the city to stroll in its funkier parts.

The place is immaculate, which worries me. (Has Jane applied her misery to the house? To cleanliness? Has Simon hired a cleaning woman in my absence?) I trot upstairs with a springiness I haven't felt since we moved in and the house was new to us, then experience the disappointment of empty bedrooms. My own bed looks untouched, as if it belongs in a hotel room. The bathrooms are spotless, the only evidence of life being in the children's — toothbrushes lying unrinsed on the sink, Jane's Aladdin nightgown hanging on the doorknob.

The nightgown's enough to make me stop, perch on the fuzzy blue toilet seat, take stock. A week ago, I would have cried at this moment. But now crying is out of the question. Nothing should halt the progression, should get in the way of the imminent. I have brought my first love to my home. Come what will.

I listen to the messages on our machine. One from Jane to her father about when to pick her up today. One from Isaac explaining he'll be home for dinner, which, I figure, means in a couple of hours. Then one from Kirsten, telling me that she'll bring Jane back at six. The smoothness in her voice tells me I've given everyone license to see things to their proper outcome, to do what comes most naturally, i.e. sleep with people they aren't married to. I marvel at my discomfort with this. The last message is from an unenthused, eerily familiar voice:

'Leigh Adelman? Is that your son speaking? Your husband? Or have you had a sex change? Have you had any sex *at all*? God, is this a drag or what? I'm a total *hausfrau*. It's Pam calling from Newport, shock of shocks. I haven't met anyone I like in years. Will you call me?'

Then the number, which I frantically scribble on some junk mail of Simon's.

I call Fowler right away.

'Pam Tillinghast?' he says. 'Is that so shocking?'

'Well, considering that I haven't spoken to her in seven or eight years, yes, it is shocking. I don't believe it!'

The ease of his recollection of her unnerves me. But I enjoy the relief her message offers from the gravity of our mission here.

'You haven't spoken to her in that long?' he muses.

'No!' I sound angry, which I am for some reason. 'Why is that so strange? Have you?'

'I've run into her a couple of times.'

I stand in the center of the living room, wild with confusion.

'You have?' I say. 'You've run into Pam? Why would you have run into Pam?'

I sink to crosslegs, and Daisy drags her megablock bag over to me.

'Leigh, honey,' Fowler says.

This is how he used to talk to me, how he talked to me in the car that night outside the clinic, with that posture of weary deference tinged with condescension.

'Why did you see her?'

The seconds of his inability to answer expand, hurt. Even Daisy is still.

'She showed up at a screening at Lincoln Center. I had a long talk with her afterwards. We kept up, in a way.'

This is worse for me than the thing I've constructed, with help, between Simon and Kirsten.

'You did?'

I straighten my back, lift my head. What would be most unendurable right now: to buckle under the discovery of another betrayal on his part.

'Tell me one thing,' I say. 'What has this got to do with Isaac?'

'Meaning.'

'Pam told people at Hastings I was pregnant. Remember? Do you have any recollection of that?'

'Of course I do.'

I continue unfazed, like a prosecutor. 'I never understood why she did that, why she deliberately made my life and yours a living hell.'

'She was jealous, I suppose. She was unused to being passed over.'

This has the hollow ring of theory.

'Was she?'

'Was she *what*?'

'Passed over.'

'Well, *obviously*!' he says cheerfully, too relieved for my comfort.

I can't let it go. 'Was she passed over?'

'Leigh, really. Let's move on here.'

'Was she passed over? I want to know.'

'Ultimately, yes. She was passed over.'

'Define "ultimately".'

'Please, Leigh. I don't want to invent suffering. We don't need to do that.'

For a minute I wait, willing a gentleness between us, a new past.

'Too late,' I tell him.

I hang up. I am a fool to have expected anything

different from Fowler. I will always be a fool, and he will always betray me. When he dies he will betray me again. I wander into the kitchen.

'Ope?' Daisy says, of the refrigerator. I open it and rummage, get us out an apple and some cheese and cut it all up on a plate.

Jane is dropped off by her father, who keeps the car running on the perimeter of the front lawn and waves to her several times from behind the wheel before easing away. I race downstairs from my perch at the landing window, where I have been sitting for a half-hour, Liselotte's truth open in my lap. I haven't read ten words. Instead I've dreamt a victorious reunion, the happiest of scenarios: weeping admissions of love and need on both our parts, Jane's mature acceptance of her lot, hints of a future unfettered by dysfunction.

But there's a weariness about her. She walks heavily, her gym bag slung over her shoulder, her gaze on the bricks. Something has been established in my absence, and my being here threatens it, and it has just driven away and left her here, unsafe. Things are even more different than they were on Saturday at Dad's when I made my entreaty to be heard and loved despite my indiscretions.

SEVEN

I'll have no need of advice or scolding from anyone else ever again. Jane will provide me with all I require in these departments. Gillette I will work for. My parents I'll depend on for the occasional bed and breakfast. Eliot I will call for help and venting, Fowler to satisfy wantonness and vain pursuit. Liselotte can pontificate into the future to Catherine, who will laugh back through the centuries at such earnestness as glorious men chase her through the fields of Provence. I am now seen to. I have a daughter who knows everything and will not be cowed by tawdriness.

'Mom, we have to talk.'

She stands dead center in the living room, full face to the culprit, with ample room for gesture on all sides, of which she makes good use. She and Daisy have recovered from their squealing reunion, and I have sunk into the cushions, trying to summon the hard edge I've been cultivating during my days away. It's the sound of their unknowing love that undoes me, the sound of their unbreakable love.

'Isaac and Dad and I are really mad at you, Mom,' she declares. 'We don't understand how you can do what you did. And neither does anyone else.'

I don't know why, but I look for vestiges of laughter, a smirk, an indication that she knows this speech is somehow the wrong one.

'*Who* else?' I ask.

'Only *everyone*. Adrienne, Kirsten, the kids at camp, the counselors, Grandpa, Grandma. God, Mom, it's horrible.'

'*What's* horrible?' I need to know what she knows.

'What you *did*!'

'*What* did I do?'

'You slept with that *man*. Which means you're a *slut*. That's what a *slut* does, Mom.'

She takes no delight in assigning me this term, although I do note her pride in knowing it. It's the pride one takes in a new authority, one that has been earned.

I wait a minute, for our minds to leap over details.

'Do you know who the man is?'

'Yes, I *know* who the man *is*,' she spits, in vicious mimicry. 'He's Isaac's dad, and because of him, my dad has to stay in a hotel and Isaac isn't going to live here any more.'

It is frightening to me that she doesn't think to cry as she announces these things, that she's resigned to them. I keep calm for her, and for Daisy, who's begging Jane, arms outstretched, for more relief from the floor.

'Where is Isaac going to live?' I ask.

'Like you care!' she shouts, at the same time shielding Daisy's ears from the volume.

'I do care, Jane. Now tell me where he's gone.'

'He went to stay with a guy from camp, another counselor. He says he doesn't want to see you any more.'

'Do you know the counselor's name?'

'Of course I know his name. I have to know his name. He's my counselor! But why should I tell *you*? You decided to go live with someone else too. Why shouldn't Isaac?'

'I was staying at Grandma's, Jane,' I say, 'except for one night when I didn't. When I was a slut, as you would say.'

'Only one night? Did he dump you too?'

I know who's talking here. It's not my daughter. It's Adrienne. I have never been able to understand how a mouthy kid like Adrienne could be the product of a dullard like Ted and the heretofore subtle and respectable Kirsten.

'Would you care to tell me anything else that Adrienne has decided about me?'

She does what any nine-year-old forty-year-old would do in response to a threat. She tromps upstairs and slams her door behind her. Daisy howls.

I pick her up and offer standard solace: 'It's all right. Jane's just mad at Mommy.'

'Yes,' Daisy sobs.

We end up at Jane's door, gently knocking, getting obstinate silence from within. I ply her with questions:

'Did Daddy say where he'd be tonight?'

'Should I try him over at Kirsten's?'

'Are you all right?'

'Do you want some dinner?'

'Can I come in?'

Then I hear the weeping. Deep sniffs, a high, faint whine in between. And I just barge. I'm allowed. I'm her mother. I'm allowed to do what I've always done to help her through whatever. I say this to Jane.

'But you *did* it!' she moans. 'You made all of us *so* sad! We're never going to be a *family* again!'

I'm on her bed with my back against a poster of Bon Jovi looking pained, practically eating the microphone.

'That's monstrous,' I tell her. 'We'll always be a family. Even when someone does something awful, they're still part of a family, and the family has to know that.'

'But you can't *live* here any more!' she wails.

I swallow this, unsure of its origin, hopeful that she has made it up in an attempt to order this chaos.

'I can too,' I counter. 'And I will.'

'But where's Daddy going to live?'

I hang onto her, all of us staring into the amazingly tidy center of her room, the only space of it that isn't cluttered with something pink or black to wear, pack things in or plug in.

'I can't answer that,' I say. 'Maybe here. But we don't know until we see how everyone feels after a while. May I tell you some things that I *do* know?'

She nods permission. Daisy's busy in the jewelry box, and the fact that Jane's done nothing to stop her is proof positive that things have never been worse for her.

'Sometimes grownups get just as mad and bewildered and afraid and out-of-line as children. It's not a good thing, but it happens. I'm not happy about what I did, but I did it, and I've got to keep on living despite it. I went and saw Isaac's dad, and I realized I still love him a little.'

I stop here to wait for censure, screaming,

excoriation. But she's just looking at me. I'm relieved to know that the sound of my voice, when it's level, blankets her, shields her from her own fury, and that when she lets this happen she has ceased to deny me.

'He left so soon after Isaac was born that I didn't have time to know it was over, and it really wasn't. And when I saw him I didn't think very hard about what I was doing. I was so overwhelmed. He made such a big impression. It doesn't have a lot to do with Daddy. It's very old news.'

'Adrienne says you slept with him.'

I save what I have to say about Adrienne, except for 'She's right. I did.'

'That's a bad thing to do when you're already married, Mom.'

'Yes, it is.'

'So,' she says, shifting away from our close hold, 'does this mean you don't love Daddy any more?'

'No,' I tell her. 'It doesn't mean that at all. It means that I have to do a lot of thinking to try and figure out how to resolve the problem I've created. Your dad's very angry with me, and he has reason to be. But I think I must have been a little angry with him too. We haven't paid too much attention to each other lately. That happens to people in families. You get so used to having everyone around you don't think you have to worry about them any more, and I think that's happened to us. I've stopped worrying about him, and he's stopped worrying about me. And I was the more careless.'

'Where's Isaac's dad?'

'In an apartment in the city.'

'Are you going back there?'

'I don't know. I'm not going to stay there, if that's what you mean.'

'Is he coming to see Isaac?'

'I'll have to talk to Isaac about that.'

She looks at her bedspread, pink and yellow diamonds laid edge to edge, handsewn by Simon's mother.

'Do all families have things like this happen?' she begs to know.

I hold her hands. 'No. But all families have things happen to them.'

This seems to satisfy Jane's need for logic, and she agrees to dinner, so the three of us go downstairs. Daisy makes the preparations easy by asking to go in her travel crib. We fix a cheese and onion omelette. Jane cracks the eggs and grates the cheese, and I do the sautéeing and tend to the omelette's edges with a butter knife, then fold it when it's firm and slide it onto a plate.

Daisy has passed out in a sitting position in the corner of the travel crib. We set the table for two.

'Our family's getting smaller,' Jane remarks.

'I don't know about that.' To me, the opposite seems to be true. People leaving for separate sleeping posts is something I grew up with, and our house is still standing, still central. And perhaps this thing with Fowler won't do to us what convention would have us believe.

'I want you to meet Jim,' I say.

'Why? I don't want to.'

'Because he's Isaac's father and part of who I am.'

I hate talking like this, particularly to Jane. Solid truth has a hollow ring sometimes, an unwelcome earnestness; like a candid expression of love, such truth is ill-received by people who are sharp and looking for pretense, even when they're children. But again she surprises me.

'OK, Mom. Whatever you say. But if you ever make me choose who to live with, you or Daddy, I'm going with Daddy. Because he's alone, and that's not fair.'

I want to tell her that's a choice she won't have to make, that she'll be with both of us. I want to tell her that I'm alone too, that Fowler is, as always, an impossibility lingering on the periphery. But these things, if said, will only lead to more argument.

'How's your omelette?' I ask her.

'Fine. It's not runny.'

After dinner we go driving. I have to find some more things out. Isaac would be proud of me now, if not for Fowler. I've 'chilled', as he'd say. I'm the sleek mother of three, wearing probable loss with considerable aplomb. The gas tank is full. Daisy's got Cheese Nips for dinner in the back, and Jane's wearing Adrienne's Vuarnet sunglasses, a sympathy loan, to hide signs of weeping. We're cruising to classic rock, which is to say, the music of my generation. The girls like it, and so do I. My appreciation of this music, as I recall, is the first thing I horrified my father with. Mother just listened and understood it as another form of goodbye.

'We're stopping at Adrienne's,' I tell Jane. 'Please stay in the car. I just want to ask her mom if she knows where Isaac is.'

'OK,' says Jane, too taken with herself in sunglasses, with Clapton's wailing, to object.

I park behind the jeep at 7.30, a civilized hour for visiting in this community, as it is post-prandial, a time when all has been shoved into the dishwasher and the older family members have a moment to inspect a troublesome corner of the garden or the editorial page. I find Kirsten and Ted sitting at the glass table outdoors, both reading the paper. Adrienne and her younger brother, Garrison, are visible through the bay window, immobile in front of the TV.

'Oh, hi there,' says Ted, springing up when he sees me.

We call him 'The Hidy-Ho man' at our house.

'You're alone?' Kirsten says. Ted begins to fidget verbally about iced tea or a beer, or something stronger?

'Panic not,' I say. 'The girls are in the car. We're in search of the third. Any clues?'

'I heard from Adrienne,' Kirsten says, managing to sound bored even about this, 'that he's been hanging around with Garland, who's terribly nice in the end. But Simon was beside himself about it, the sticky wicket being that Garland's gay. He's got a man living with him.'

'Do we know where he lives?' I ask.

'It's on the camp list. A building over by the river. I wouldn't worry. Adrienne says he's a nursery school teacher during the year. She doesn't think he's after Isaac.'

'Well, that's a relief,' I say, looking at Ted. He's been bobbing up and down for some time now, stopping momentarily when the gay issue cropped up.

'I'll get the camp list,' Ted says, and lopes inside.

'Are you all right?' Kirsten says. *Weary*, is what I'm getting from her. Not at all the demeanor of a woman in love.

'Fine. You?'

'*The same*. Drop over tomorrow. I just can't concentrate at this hour. It's been a wiggy week. I almost perished of overhearing Adrienne's counsel to your daughter. How's the little fatty?'

'Divine.'

Ted's back with a Post-it bearing an address and phone number.

'Whatever we can do,' he says, attempting to be doleful.

'Oh, Ted, really,' Kirsten moans. 'Let's not get divorced *for* them.'

The word startles me. I've had the nerve not to contemplate it much.

'Call,' Kirsten says.

I tell her I will. I head back to the car, where a fight is in progress. I promise them milkshakes for endurance.

It's a matter of being impervious, this returning. Just live. Let your grass grow. Let your kids yell at you, advise, hate, disown you. Let the creditors come. Let the husband who thought he loved you find out he doesn't. Whatever happens will be the truth.

At Burger King I pick up two chocolate shakes. Half of mine goes into Daisy's bottle, and westward we wend, slurping all the way.

'He's distraught,' the roommate, Travis, explains. 'He left here about an hour ago. I offered to drive him into the city, but he wanted to take the train. So Garland took him to the station and put him on the train and then we phoned your husband about arrival time.'

I hadn't expected this sort of welcome, or the fresh aesthetic of the place, very leafy, lots of wicker and shining parquet. And I hadn't expected to be treated to iced tea and cookies, now arriving on a silver tray borne by Travis, another man with, seemingly, only one name. We establish ourselves in the living room. The girls, despite the recent milkshakes, dive into the cookies, an assortment of Peek Freans and Lus.

'How's my Otter Troop leader?' Garland says to Jane, who smiles. 'You've got a beautiful family,' he tells me.

'Have more,' Travis says. 'That boy of yours should be in the movies. His eyes! They see everything. You've got to watch your step around that one!'

Mother would call Travis a dandy. Older (by a lot)

than Garland, he is more meticulous about hair and wardrobe. I learn that he works at a gallery in the city not far from Mother's apartment.

'We finally got medical coverage,' Travis sighs. 'Years of free clinics, and I want to tell you, those places are not clean, and I'm on the policy!' He raises his glass to this fact, and I, not sure if it's the right gesture, join him.

'Do you think that he would talk to me?' I venture.

'All boys want to talk to their mothers,' Travis says.

'Do you want me to speak to him about that tomorrow?' Garland offers.

'Yes,' I decide. 'Yes, would you? Would you just tell him I miss him?'

'Of course.'

'Mom, can I borrow a tape?' Jane says from the foyer. The video collection, I noticed when we arrived, in a glass cabinet, includes several we don't have.

'Did you ask our hosts?'

Travis is over there instantly, consulting with Jane about what would be best. He recommends *Bringing up Baby* and *Ghostbusters* and then puts them in a small Bloomingdale's shopping bag, the size they give out at the makeup counters. He also packages the remaining cookies in tinfoil and holds them out to Daisy.

'At some point,' I say awkwardly, 'I'll figure out how to thank you properly for your help.' I can't see how my son fits into the lives of these men, but I do know they've made room for him.

'Call,' Travis advises. 'We're here.'

It doesn't even bother me that Travis tends to speak for his mate. He's eloquent, at any rate, and I don't fear in them what Liselotte complains of so continually — an inner circle that excludes her so she won't interfere, *une cabale*.

'Can we go home now, Mom?' Jane says on the way to the car.

'We are going home.'

'Good.' She then informs me that she won't be put in the middle of me and Simon the way other kids are when their parents are fighting. Again I mentally blame Adrienne for this pronouncement.

'Can we put you in the middle when we're not fighting?' I ask.

'It's not funny, Mom.'

'Of course it isn't.'

'Mommy funny!' Daisy cackles.

Just how riotous it isn't becomes evident later when I call Simon at Essex House and he starts about the money it's costing him to stay there and about making some decisions about where everyone's going to be living. Isaac won't speak to me, so I can't get his side except through Simon, who responds flatly in the negative when I ask if Isaac will consider coming home the next day.

'I've been to see his friend from the camp,' I say. 'I don't know what else to do.'

'I can't advise you on that. What's your plan?'

'Well,' I say, furious. 'I'll make it easy for you. I'm staying in the house with whichever of my children will have me.'

'We'll see who they are,' he says, and hangs up.

I sit, stunned. Whatever people fear and loathe about infidelity sits with me on the sofa, which is now a monstrous piece of furniture that will probably have to be decided upon as well.

Monday I wake to a singing pain in my head shortly before five. Ordinarily I might make better use of this time, delve back into Liselotte's life in search of inspiring chestnuts, do laundry, sewing, letters. But instead I stand in the bathroom fingering every facet of my mouth, tortured by the pain and my inability to locate it. I can find no puffiness, and it isn't my wisdom teeth, as these were, all four, broken in my jaw and extracted when I was twenty-four. I remember weeks of mushy food and crankiness and reliance on Mother to occupy Isaac. My face was square from the swelling.

I get a cold pack from the freezer and stretch out on the couch. I tune in to World News and am treated to fires, murders, layoffs and global hopelessness. A few minutes of this, and then the notion that the pain is not in the roots of my upper eye teeth, on which I've been focusing, but in the *front* of my mouth, where my two front teeth are, the ones Fowler once remarked made me look like a small version of Carly Simon, breaks over me. I know in that seeping, inevitable way that people know they have cysts or cancer or implacable internal damage, that this dental repair is going to be major, that it will require multiple visits and definite tooth loss.

My own teeth mock and revile me. *Hag*! they cry.

I'm going to need some help with this one. I can't call Mother, because she's visiting a Smith friend on Nantucket. Daddy wouldn't understand why a situation like this would require help from anyone. Kirsten: not this time. Fowler: out of the question.

I call Eliot.

'You won't believe this,' I say.

'You don't know me,' he says, very alert.

'You were up?'

'Up?' he croaks. 'I've done Fonda, the beds and blueberry buckle. I'm about to scoot into the shower so I can get over to my cubicle for inventory.'

'*Don't!*' I shriek. 'You have to take the morning off. I'm desperate!'

'Who didn't know that?' he mutters. 'The morning off? What a novelty. But it can't happen. I'm supposed to give a week's notice.'

'Tell them you're sick.'

'Think of something better. In your case, the truth might do nicely.'

'You do love me,' I say.

'Get to it.'

'Tell them you've got this friend whose mouth is on fire with pain and she has to get to a hospital and you have to watch her kids there for her at least until lunch, that is unless surgery is warranted.'

'What's with your mouth?'

'If I knew, I might know how to handle this without calling you. Can you meet me? *Please?*'

He asks what hospital, and I tell him Lenox Hill.

'I'll meet you in the lobby in an hour,' he says.

I wake the girls and we whirl through dressing, crying, eating, soothing. I apologize more for this than I have for my entanglement with Fowler. We're in the car by seven, and Jane is even asking how I'm doing, every exit or so.

'OK. Just keep talking.'

'What do you want me to talk about?'

'Just *talk*! I don't care!' I shout. It irritates me that a child who has never been at a loss for words is now, when I'm desperate for distraction.

'OK, Mom,' she says. 'It's OK.'

At the hospital I discover that it is anything *but* OK to have this happen to your mouth early on a summer morning. The dentists on call don't respond to the page.

'Well, where *are* they all?' I demand of the receptionist, who's looking at me as if she's never witnessed such an inconvenience.

'I told you I would have the doctor beeped. You'll have to be patient. We don't get a lot of dental emergencies. Now, *please* have a seat.'

Things always have to be this way with me. I wake up to world war in my mouth and have to drive myself and my children to the emergency room for this sort of reception. I have to cheat on my husband for the first time with a man who may not last the winter. I have to fall in love for the first time and become a mother in disgrace.

'There's a man with a gun by the news-stand outside who might put you out of your misery if you ask nicely.'

It's Eliot, a miracle in khakis and pinstripes. I fall into him.

'Oh, shit,' I whisper, already crying. 'Shit, shit, shit, shit.'

'Come,' he says, guiding me to the line of connected chairs where the girls are exploring the contents of a tin with Santa and his sleigh riding across the lid. 'I'd like to introduce you to two of my women friends. They've already agreed to try my cake.'

'Mom! Look! Blueberry!' Jane is ecstatic. 'Is this your friend? He's a great cook!'

Hands splayed over my face, as if this will keep it from cracking, I try to smile through. Jane is making such an effort for me.

'This is Eliot,' I say. 'He's going to make sure we all live through this.'

Jane makes a twirling gesture by her ear to let Eliot know that I'm insane.

'You're telling me!' he says. 'Do you know that when I met your mother last week she invited me to lunch immediately just so she could plan this toothache?'

Jane screeches over this. Daisy tears apart a square of the cake.

'You are so *dear*,' I manage through my hand-web, but then I can't keep my gaze up. The toothache has gone into my forehead.

'Don't talk,' he advises. 'You talk too much.'

Having one of my front teeth ground away to a thin, gray post is a shaming experience for me, only made worse by Daisy's wandering in and out of the room where I've been sent, in the hospital's dental clinic. When she stands by the chair tugging at my shirt (she can only do this when the dentist's back is to me as he mixes his powders for this combined root canal/crown procedure), I don't know how to manage my face for her: the lower half is numb, and I'm missing most of a prominent tooth, a tooth she's used to and I'm frantic without. But Dr Peterson has assured me that this is the only solution to what he calls my 'sensitivity'.

Daisy starts to cry when she sees me without my tooth.

'Eliot!' I call out pathetically, but he's already in the room trying to coax her out.

'Where'th Jane?' I lisp, everything being out in the open. My younger daughter has seen her future as the caretaker of a toothless woman, before she puts me in the nursing home. 'Can't thee help with Daithy?'

'I've sent her across the hall for bagels,' he says. 'There's lots to eat here. They wheel the food by as often as they do the people.'

'Excuse me,' Dr Peterson says with annoyance. He's handsome, like a Ken doll, and has an obvious interest in skiing. The office walls are plastered with professionally done photographs of him and his family at the tops of mountains, fabulous vistas flanking them.

'I'll be leaving now,' Eliot announces, swooping up Daisy and raising his eyebrows at Dr Peterson's back. 'Come on, princess, let's get ourselves another breakfast. We're not wanted here.'

Nothing makes a dent in Peterson, who works at stretching a rubber sheet over the square of metal he's clamped to one of my molars. I hear Daisy crying, probably over the sight of this miniature scaffolding. I try to think pleasant thoughts of Jane and Daisy and Eliot, happy with food. I don't see how I'll ever eat again.

I'm out in two hours, a cement prosthesis in place of the offending tooth, now gone, my lower face tremendous with Novocaine. The smell of the ground tooth stays with me. Jane and Daisy cling to me, as if I've undergone life-threatening surgery and we are a family again, as if we're going home to Simon and Isaac for lunch after the disaster. And Eliot, my new friend, is behind them, trying not to avert his eyes.

'It doesn't look bad, really,' he says. 'The new one's a bit off in color, but I assume it's temporary.'

Eliot has lovely teeth, unmarred by bonding, falseness or silver. I don't dare go near a mirror.

'Eliot has some books at his house for me,' Jane brags, 'and they're worth a lot of money. He says we can have them *for free*.'

'Eliot ith a dear, dear man,' I say.

'Will ye be needin' me any more today, mum?' Eliot asks in credible brogue.

'I think I can get uth home,' I say. 'I think we'll be fine.'

'I'll call you tonight,' he says. 'And I'll want to talk to your manager about getting her those books. I've got an original Bemelmans, you'll swoon.'

We bid Eliot adieu in the hospital lobby after endless waiting by the elevator. The logistics of retrieving the car are smooth, and we ride home on an empty highway, Jane nattering on about Eliot and his jokes the entire way, Daisy taking refuge in sleep from all the novelty.

Later I talk to Simon. Of course I'm in the habit of telling him when enormous things happen to me, particularly ones that demand coverage. And, of course, I exaggerate.

'I scared Daisy. She's never seen a witch before. Never mind having to race into Manhattan with my head in a vise of pain.'

'We're falling apart,' he says.

'I just let the dentist do whatever. I didn't even care, it was so unbearable. It'll probably cost the moon.'

'Just send in the forms,' he says. 'They're under "Medical" in the file cabinet. And there are envelopes already addressed.'

I thank him, then ask how Isaac got to camp this morning.

'I put him on a train with cab money. He's going to need clean clothes, so perhaps you could drop some off at the camp before dismissal.'

I tell him I'll do that. 'What about you? Don't you need clothes?'

'I've got enough to last me. I'll be home on the weekend and we can have our discussion. The children deserve some sort of information, I think, and I'd sort of like to know where I'll be spending the rest of my life.'

'Who knows that.'

'Don't be glib about this, Leigh.'

'I'm not. I want to say how sorry I am, but it sounds despicable.'

'You might have thought of that before deciding to honor an old urge. Really, Leigh, we have people depending on us *not* to do that.'

I despair over how right he is, how difficult I've made things, how much my mouth hurts.

'Simon,' I say. 'Tell me that if wife number one came back at a low point in your life and suddenly you saw yourself a much younger man facing a world of possibility and she told you she'd be dead in a year and then came onto you like a Mack truck, tell me you'd stay your course without flinching.'

'Now I would. Now I've got kids with a woman I thought could save me from people like Carly.'

I can't say any more on my own behalf, so I don't try.

'Feel better,' he says, and hangs up.

I hurry with the clothes, some jeans and T-shirts and underwear and socks, these things I've worked to collect for Isaac. I try Fowler's number, to no avail, with the idea that I should be keeping him posted about myself. Then I make sandwiches and stick them and juice boxes, cookies and iced coffee in a Mason jar into the cooler and carry it all with Daisy out to the car. We drive over to the high school where I just left Jane, who was protesting about her own dishevelment and lack of gym bag and the ridiculous hour I saw fit to drop her off at camp. I establish us on a blanket under a tree near the breezeway and wait for a glimpse of my son at his official duty, like anyone waits for a sign of love from a child who is rightfully angry, as if my life depends on it.

EIGHT

I feed Daisy green grapes as I dial Pam's number on
the cell phone from our spot under the tree. I can't
imagine Pam will be in at two o'clock on a Monday
afternoon, and I'm right. A woman who sounds polished
enough to be her secretary takes my number and says
Pam will be glad to return the call. Then I get Gillette's
machine and tell her I want a meeting because I'm not
going to change course on the book without the
affirmative from Barry. I think Gillette will appreciate
my tone, as she likes hardball. Next I do Fowler, who is
home.

I ask him how he's feeling.

'It's not so much a question of feeling any way in
particular,' he says. 'It's a question of gradually
discovering new incapabilities. For instance, today I
haven't brushed my teeth, not because I forgot or don't
want to, but because every time I try, my hands decide

it's time to go on vacation. And right now it isn't just my hands. One of my arms has decided the same thing. I can't move it. So in answer to your question, I don't know how I'm feeling, except amazed and scared out of my fucking mind.'

'Do you want me there?'

'Another tough one,' he says angrily. 'You sound like you're calling from the Space Shuttle. It might take you years to get here.'

'The great outdoors of Ardsley,' I explain. 'Daisy and I are outside the high school in head-splitting sun. I have a new tooth. I'll come show it to you if you want.'

'I'm still thinking these moments will pass, and I won't need any help. I want to hang onto that comfort for as long as I can.'

'OK. I need to know one thing.'

'Are we back on Pam?'

'Was it when you were researching the Southern belle film? I think it must have been because a few times you went off alone, and those were the only times before you left that I wasn't with you. Was that when it happened?'

He asks me, as before, why I am doing this.

'Indulge me, please. I want information. You were my first love.'

'I know that,' he says. 'That's why talking about this
is so destructive.'

'Is that when you saw her?'

He says it was, but volunteers no more.

'How did it end?'

He says it was never enough of a thing to demand an
end. 'She was competing with you, don't you see? She
wanted to be smart and have the same things you had.'

'So you gave them to her.'

'I did *not*,' he says firmly. 'I fell into bed with her,
dead drunk, on a couple of evenings. I can't remember
much about them except that she was aggressive and I
didn't punish her for it, and now I don't feel like being
punished by talking about this for one more second.'

I push a box of saltines toward Daisy and watch her
try and open it. This frees me for more upset.

'You were my first love,' I repeat.

'And you were mine,' he says. 'That can't change, no
matter what characters have danced on the periphery
since. I wish I were with you on that blanket now. I just
haven't yet cottoned to the idea of people watching me
crawl.'

'I'm not *people*,' I say.

'I want to see you so much,' he whispers.

'I'll be there soon,' I promise. 'When you can bear it.'

As dismissal time approaches, I move us to the shade of a tree closer to the building. Isaac and Jane are among the last out. I stand with Daisy in one arm and Isaac's provisions dangling from the other. They see me right away, and Jane begins to pull him toward me, but he resists, staying on the flagstone path.

'Come *on*,' she urges.

Campers are passing on either side of us, staring and trying not to stare, and from the breezeway Garland gives me a sly wave, one that Isaac, from his statuesque position, doesn't see.

I walk straight up to him and put the bag at his feet.

'Here,' I say. 'Simon asked me to pack you some clean clothes.'

'Thanks,' he says, in his public voice.

'Do you want to spend some time before you go back to the city?'

He rolls his eyes at my idiocy. 'I'm not going back to the city, Mom. I'm staying with a friend.'

'Oh, sweetie,' I plead, second biggest mistake of the century, 'couldn't we just try a few hours together? I miss you so much, and the girls want you home too.

We could just have an early dinner, and then I'll drop you wherever you like.'

'*NO!*' he shouts. Then, much lower: 'What do you want me to tell you, Mom? You fucked up. I can't spend my life at Burger King and Toys R Us having you buy me things to make you feel better about what you did.'

He turns from me, as if it's for the last time.

'*Jesus!*' I scream. 'Where are you kids *getting* all this?'

He turns back and rests his beautiful, disappointed eyes on me, nodding, as if I've just proven the point that his mother doesn't deserve to live.

'What do you want me to *do*?' I shriek.

He comes toward me and takes my free wrist in a crushing grip. 'Put it all back where it was.'

Then he lopes off, in a rush for his ride from whomever, so that he doesn't hear me say, 'I can't do that.' He doesn't see Jane plow into me with her fists or Daisy bury her face in my neck, moaning.

Slowly, after I've shaken some temporary sense into Jane, have reminded her that hitting me won't help, I gather up our things, our blanket and food, our toys and phone, the things that are meant to comfort us because they are ours.

*

'All I want to know,' I tell Kirsten by her pool later, 'is why he was driving your car that afternoon.'

'Who *knows*,' she says. 'Who remembers.'

'Try, Kirsten, because I think it would be helpful for me to know.'

'*How*? *How* will it be helpful?'

The girls, Adrienne and her patient, are hanging by their arms from the small diving board Ted just erected. Without much spring, it offers a steady perch for them. Daisy's at the buckets and sand toys in the muddy wells by the blue wall of the pool. I've never seen her so dirty.

'I'm trying to get things straight,' I say. 'I want to know who comforts him, if anyone. I want to know how he's coping. Has he said *anything*?'

'Of course he's *said* things,' she answers, amazed. 'Who wouldn't?'

'*What*?'

She takes her long legs off the picnic bench and sits forward. 'I know what you want, Leigh. You want me to tell you he came to me a wreck and I pulled him into bed and made the whole Fowler thing bearable. You want me to tell you he was doing the same thing to you you were doing to him so you won't have to feel guilty. You want ammunition.'

'I just thought,' I say defensively, 'particularly with Ted away and me gone down the road to ruin, that —'

'It didn't happen.'

I register her genuine disappointment over this fact as she looks down at the tan flab of her legs, of which there isn't much, admittedly, 'just enough,' Simon once said.

'I lent him the jeep the morning you and Daisy took the train to your mother's. It's bigger than your wagon, and he offered to take all the kids over to camp. He called me because he thought you might be at this house.'

'Kirsten?' I say, without much humor. 'Hello?'

'I'm not going to *deny* attraction,' she blurts out. 'Who wouldn't find a faithful, intelligent man attractive? And once, yes, I'll admit, he did say something to me.'

'Such as.'

She directs a smile at the pool. 'He said it was a good thing you were around all the time and didn't travel, because it was too short a commute between our houses and he didn't think he'd have the strength to resist should an opportunity arise. He said it almost just like that. So don't sweat it. Here the opportunity arose, and he didn't take it. He just drove my car.'

'What a prince,' I finally say.

'Oh, Leigh, really,' she says.

'You'll forgive me for not thanking you for your restraint.'

She throws her Nordic head back, in despair, it seems.

'Affairs don't answer anything, Leigh. They just give you more to work out. I'd rather just think about them, actually. It's always less aesthetic when you actually have one. And yes, I've had affairs and Ted knows, and he's had them, and I know. So we just handle it in a quiet way because it's too embarrassing to talk about. Don't think his business trips are filled with longing for this fjord!'

'How can you not let it bother you?' I want to know. 'Don't you want to get rid of the trouble that makes you want other people?'

She laughs out loud at me. 'How would you suggest doing that? I don't think of it as *trouble*. It's just a fact. No one stays in love permanently, so you do other things: imagine, risk, go back, over and over. I don't know any other way to be married. Let me know if you think of one.'

I don't know whether to admire or eschew this approach. It seems clever on the one hand, lazy on the other. But what better credo have I uncovered? At least

Adrienne is still proud of her parents, untortured by them, posing as the solid one, the dispenser of ten-year-old wisdom.

Still, when the girls come to us for towels and snacks, it is with undeniable weariness that Kirsten reacts, bends down for the towels that are piled beside her, heaves her big bones up to standing and then crosses the patio to the sliding door and into the kitchen to fulfill the regular demands for iced tea, cinnamon toast and popcorn.

'Can I help?' I ask inside.

'Sure,' she says. 'You do the toast. I'll get the tea. And you can stick the fatty in the pool. Ted's cleaning it tonight.'

I am not, I hope never to be, this tired.

I read, much of that night. Liselotte's letters betray her despair, her misery, her loneliness. All in the court and on its periphery have turned against her. It strikes me that sharing is at the crux of the problems that she and I, and all people, face. No one likes to share. I should take cues from my children, the smartest people I know. Even at our most altruistic, our most generous, we worry, suspect and fear that the gift won't be acknowledged, won't be returned in kind.

I am going to have to ignore those fears. I am just

going to have to continue to take the enormous leaps my father studies, professes about and privately deplores. I call Fowler at seven, unafraid to wake him, brimming with plans.

'Can I see you today? I want to go watch boats from the South Street Seaport and eat five lunches. Daisy will be with me.'

'That sounds wonderful,' he says. 'You can carry me.'

I tell him I feel invested with superhuman strength and that this happens to me when I lose sleep. I tell him Isaac refuses to live with me.

'What about Jane?' he asks. 'Can't she come?'

'She has camp.'

He asks me to try and persuade her to join us. 'Like you,' he says, 'I'm feeling enormous. Like I have to do everything. It's one of the advantages of terminal illness.'

I promise that I'll ask her, and I go to wake them. Through our open windows I note the enormity he was referring to, of this I-contain-multitudes morning, alive with possibility. On a day like this my marriage occurs to me as a form of sleep that I've lulled myself into without much reference to the world outside it, and in my magnanimous mood I wish this sort of recognition on Simon, willing him some moments of well-being in his hotel room, some optimism he might share with

Isaac. It has to do with sleep loss, this novel appreciation of what Daddy refers to as 'it all'.

'Babies?' I call happily at the top of the stairs.

Groaning from Jane. Squeals from Daisy.

'Let's get up. We're going on an adventure!'

Fowler's standing on his stoop in white slacks and a blue blazer with matching baseball cap. He proceeds with great difficulty towards the curb, his left leg taut, the rest of him straining to compensate. I don't know enough yet not to be alarmed by this obvious degeneration in his abilities, and I gasp and bring my hand to my mouth in horror.

'God, Mom,' Jane says. 'What's wrong with him?'

'Ssssh,' I warn. 'Wait.'

Fowler leans into the car on my side and smiles at all of us.

'Hi Jane,' he says. 'I'm Jim.'

'Hi,' Jane says. She climbs over the emergency brake into the back seat and settles next to Daisy.

'Daisy!' Daisy shouts.

'Hi Daisy,' he says. Then he pulls open the passenger door and backs into the seat, arranging his stubborn legs with studied grace. He looks over at me.

'Come on, driver. Let's go look at some water. I've got a wallet full of money, and I intend to spend it all.'

In the mirror I see Jane's wide eyes, her closed mouth. I see her waiting for a signal from me, some look that will tell her she's right not to trust this man, that he's full of shit, anything to prove him unworthy of anyone's love.

'Jane,' he says as we turn onto the Bowery and head south, 'I'm honored that you skipped the day's usual activities to come out with us.' His Southern gentry voice is at its most pronounced, its most mellifluous and sugary.

'That's OK,' she says.

'I'm glad to meet you,' he says. And Jane, who has never to my knowledge uttered this word, says 'Likewise.'

I kiss him on the cheek, and he tells me to park in a garage.

'Sky's the limit,' he proclaims.

The first thing I think of is the walking, how he'll manage over to the Seaport from the garage, what challenges escalators will present. As we exit the car and assemble in the dungeon of a very pricey garage before emerging into the light of day, Jane says, 'What's wrong with your leg?'

'Well,' he says, hesitating as we hunt for an elevator without moving, 'it doesn't do the things I'd like it to do.'

'There's one!' I bark, pointing to a double yellow door that's opening for another family. I move ahead with Daisy in the stroller and let them handle the mystery together.

'Why not?' she's saying.

'It's a story,' he warns. 'Do you really want to hear it? Do you know what cells are?'

Traffic and water noise take over, but I can see it happening in just one backward glance, as Jane looks up at Fowler in profile, the way I used to. He's mesmerizing her, weaving himself into her blood and bones.

We get them pizza, balloons, plastic facsimiles of the Disney characters in vogue. Then we do T-shirts and videos and stuffed dolphins. Jane has glued herself to Fowler, as, I believe, was his intention. He's taught her about telescopes and distance, south-western weather (I now gather that he lived for some years in Tucson) and cell death. In this way of providing casual education he is not unlike Simon, who takes every waking opportunity to converse with the children about the world at large, as it confronts them. It is possible, today, for me to consider Fowler a generous man.

When he admits to the need to sit for a while, we find an umbrellaed table on a veranda, and he hands me more money to buy the obligatory coffee and some ice cream for the girls.

'We'll stay here, Mom,' Jane says, sitting by Fowler. 'You don't have to worry.'

So I go alone to the line and stand behind an elderly couple who have been watching us assemble out here.

'You have a beautiful family,' the man says.

'And look at the little one, *connehara*,' the woman sighs. She touches my elbow. 'Have more. I see all kinds of children, and some I don't say this about. Have more. They're beautiful. Don't worry your husband's tired. Mine was too! He's fifteen years older, and we have three girls and a boy.'

I thank her for the compliment.

'He's a good father, I can tell,' she continues, her eyes on Fowler as he pulls the girls' chairs close by him, his arms behaving. 'He pays attention.'

Her husband pulls at her sleeve. 'Sylvie, do you want cake?'

'When do I not want cake?' she says, annoyed.

I like them so much I want to invite them to join us,

but I don't for fear of disappointing Sylvie with the news that Fowler isn't my husband or the girls' father.

'He's a veteran, your husband?' the man asks with concern after he orders coffee and layer cake.

'Yes,' I answer automatically, because it's true, and they don't have to know who I'm talking about.

'Bless him,' the man says.

'Seymour,' the woman nudges. 'The cake?'

'You take care,' he says.

I get us coffee and brownies with ice cream on top.

'What have you learned?' I ask the girls brightly.

Very blasé, Jane says, 'That it's more fun to sail than motor. That the doldrums are when there's no wind, and that sailing is a gentle sport.'

'A gentleman's sport,' Fowler corrects, laughing. 'I was just going to get into schooners and yawls and gaff rigging, but here you are.'

I hear the noble fatigue in his tone, and I remember J.T. using it with Evelyn on a couple of occasions when he'd run out of love for her yammering: *tell about the time Jimmy sailed the Widget right up onto the beach!* she urged, although that was the whole story right there, already told. *Tell about the first time we put him out to sea on his own*. Those were her most generous moments with me, trying to get J.T. to betray family secrets, so she wouldn't have to, never using my name, never thinking to tell me the story herself.

'You look like Isaac,' Jane says to Fowler.

'I do!' he cries, feigning surprise.

'Yes,' she explains. 'You have the same eyes and nose and mouth. You must have looked like him when you were younger.'

He looks to me for verbal affirmation of this fact, but I can't speak, my throat too full of this perfect day with them, my girls and this man they've taken in to make me happy. Instead, I open my arms to them.

In the car, Fowler apologizes. 'I'm afraid I'm going to need an escort when we get back to my place. Any takers?'

'No sweat,' Jane says, a phrase she's taken from Isaac.

'Friend for life,' I tell him.

He looks spent, wan. It's hard to come down off this day, for me too.

'I've read a lot,' I say. 'But we don't have to talk about it.' My home schooling in neurodegenerative diseases, provided me via folder by Eliot, is something I don't want to keep from him.

'We will,' he says quietly. 'Just not now.'

'Will you just tell me when you found out?'

'A couple of years ago. I couldn't get my hotel door open. I mean, I couldn't turn the key in the lock. Thank God they've invented those Braille-like cards that you just insert! Should I ever need to be in a hotel room again.'

This is the beginning: a key that won't work. And the end? Suffocation. He's right. It is too horrible to talk about.

'This was a good day,' I say.

'It was,' he says.

I let him get himself out of the car and ease around with the cane and one hand on the hood. Then he puts his arms around me, and we walk slowly to the stoop and up the steps. To anyone else, it will look like we are tired lovers reluctant to part. It won't look like most of his weight is on me, or that I'm bearing it well.

'I'll go in with you. I can see them through the glass,' I say at the door.

'No. It's all right.'

'But the key! What if you can't turn it in the lock?'

'I left it open.'

He sets the cane against the building wall and takes my face in both hands and kisses me with such force that I fall back, down one step. Then he picks up the cane and leans into the door to get himself through.

In the car Jane says, 'He's nice, Mom.' And she starts about all the things we did, and all the things he told her. And when she's run out of that to talk about and we're on the highway yet again she says, 'Is he going to die soon?'

'Yes,' I say.

'When?'

'Maybe in the winter.'

'Why?'

'He's got a disease there's no cure for, and it's getting worse, and I think the winter will be too hard.'

I go on, about what I've learned. I say the words I now know, try to get used to the sound of them, tell her what the disease is called in our country (ALS) and what it's called in Britain (motor neurone disease), that it's very rare, that no one is sure where Fowler got it because it's not in his family but that the nerve cells in his spine, arms and legs are dying because transporter proteins have been lost and can't clean up glutamate blockage. I sound logical and calm, establishing an order to the event of Fowler's going, but the only thing I really know is that he will die in the winter. I just know this, and then . . . then what? Then there will be other voices to listen to, other things to say. Part of my life will be over as well.

'I can see why you love him,' Jane says.

Pam calls that night. I'm relieved to find out she had no notion of Fowler's illness.

'Are you still in love?' she says in her husky, forgivable way.

'Yes.' I don't bother with *Are you?*

'Is this going to kill you?'

'I think so.'

'I've wanted to call you for years, you know.'

'I know.'

'I was a real jerk back then,' she says, then adds, laughing, 'Still am!'

I'm softening on her, on everyone. 'My son Isaac,' I say. 'It would freak you out how much he looks like Fowler. He's so beautiful. We are *so lucky* we don't have to go to school with him!'

Pam says she misses me, she's still never met anyone like me, or him, for that matter. 'You guys were quite a duo!'

I agree, and then we make the inevitable vague plan to meet in the fall, just us, she'll come into Manhattan, we'll take an afternoon, etc. It saddens me to hang up, to feel yet another dead certainty — that a life in which Pam would be a close friend is now impossible, given our stations. After I check on the girls I fly to my room, strip to nothing and dive into bed. There's nothing on earth that can keep me from sleep now, not even the fact that I don't know where my son is sleeping. I trust he is in good, local hands or with Simon and that I'd have heard about it if he wasn't.

Early Friday a cab pulls into the driveway and Isaac and Simon get out, slamming doors the way men seem to do, not in anger or haste, just for punctuation's sake. We crowd the foyer to receive them. I watch Isaac just as I watched Jane a week ago, searching for signs, but he heads for the front door neutrally, out of habit, not committed to any mood I can discern. He drags the duffel I gave him in front of the high school, which has to be full of dirty clothes for me to wash.

'I'm out the door,' I assure them when they enter. I've arranged to meet Gillette and Barry for lunch, and Simon agreed this would give him some time with the girls before we all sit down for a powwow later. 'You have a good day, and I'll see you for dinner.'

I busy myself with accessories — pocketbook, briefcase, umbrella. Then I look up at Simon, who looks puzzled, as if there's supposed to be some evidence of a change in me that will dictate our future. I return his gaze, then toss my hands outward in question. 'What? I'm going to work. *Really.*'

'Good,' he says. 'We'll talk tonight. I'll take care of things here.'

'Good,' I say, and out I go to walk to the train, one of my smoothest exits ever, so thrilled with Simon are the girls. I took in Isaac's beeline for his sisters, his avoidance of me, and I didn't address it.

Gillette has finally given up on fronting the work I've done for Barry. She told me this morning, on the phone, after my finest sleep in weeks, that she saw no reason for her to pose for Barry any more, what had she been thinking? She was far more interested in the marketing end of things, she said, and she was going to tell him she could no longer support both sorts of efforts and that the book on cults had actually been written by me with her editorial input. I didn't bother her about the other trash we've put together. Finally having a clear line to Barry would be enough, I thought. Already I'm walking more legitimately.

'You're mellowing,' I said to her. It's as if we've switched places, and she's lost her hard edge to Latin love while I've absorbed that edge to negotiate the tough spots.

'Maybe so,' she admitted. 'I like rolls and coffee

brought to me in the morning and movies I don't have to watch alone. And there's the perk of traveling with someone who can speak four languages.'

My brief view of Pasquale hadn't allowed for the language proficiency. I congratulated her.

I spread my work out over three seats on the train, admiring my refinement of plans for the book. I think Barry will appreciate what I've done. The idea of economic glut as a precondition for moral collapse is compelling, but it seems obvious now and not enough of a statement. Instead, I'm proposing a collection of personal commentary by royal and aristocratic women who have found themselves on the cusp of such collapse. Liselotte will be one of them, but her view will occur rather late in the book. I'll require time and funding, and I'll put all of this to Barry and see what he says. I've got nothing to lose.

The way I remember Barry — loud, portly, opinionated — is not at all the way he appears now. He's slim and suntanned, and he gestures generously at the empty seat after Gillette and I have done the hugging and exclaiming over this and that. I only met Barry once, at a party at Gillette's after the book on cults came out. My dislike for him was affirmed within the hour. He began a conversation with me and left in the middle of it for the bar and someone in a backless dress who had left modeling for writing and Barry's editorial tutelage. The minute I'd told him where I lived and that I was working out of my home (I'd been instructed by Gillette not to let on what the nature of that work was), he'd glazed over.

Now he's drinking iced tea, as is Gillette. We sit, and Gillette resumes the serious face she had on when I arrived. The French place is way west on 43rd Street, Barry's idea. Everything – the music, the menu, the Provençal décor – is understated, I'm relieved to see.

I order iced coffee and the same entrée that they're both getting, and then, like a Renaissance king in his battle tent, I lay out the plans before them, more interested in the perfect logic of my strategy than in what they think of it.

'I'll go back to the Ancient Greeks,' I inform them, after a preliminary overview. 'I'll have to find out if there's any documentation on the wives of the Greek leaders. So far all I know is that Sappho's writing survives only in snippets and that there were certain strictures that women were meant to observe in the time of Homer. But if Penelope is any indication, there were ways around some of those stringencies.'

Barry looks at me, amused. 'Go on.'

'There's more on Egypt, of course, and I'm thinking Hatshepsut would be my best representative, as she was, in fact, a king.'

Gillette is wearing a long face, losing focus, her mind, I feel sure, on Pasquale. I am, comparatively, in tremendous command, which is probably why Barry, as we begin our upscale warmed salads, invites me to talk further with him at his office after lunch. Gillette applauds the idea.

'I've got to get back uptown anyway,' she says. 'I'll drop you.'

We have *crème brûlée* and espresso, and I change the subject to the food, which I absolutely love. When Barry excuses himself to take care of the check, Gillette says, 'Go for it! He's totally into it. When have you had time to do all this?'

'So easy,' I lie. 'I give up a few nights' sleep per week, power nap when the kids are in front of the tube, and get the work done.'

'And you've got time? With all that's going on with Simon and Fowler?'

'And Isaac and Daisy and Jane!' I laugh out loud, drawing the irritated stares of some business types. 'The thing about two men,' I say with authority, 'is that it gives you all kinds of time. You're really not with either of them, so you've got the same kind of time you have when you're alone.'

Gillette shudders. She's too far from being alone now to see that it's bearable.

'More power,' she says. 'You're a rock.'

She drops us on a corner in the West 50s, and Barry leads me to his office in a building full of offices devoted to like causes – agents, publishers. I sit in a red leather chair while he sifts through papers to find a sheet of standard criteria for me to follow when I write up a formal book proposal, a 'query', as he's calling it.

'Frankly, I'm glad you've revised the first idea,' he says. 'It lacked punch, that dialectical stuff – peace begets crisis begets peace, etc. Get me the new proposal as soon as you can and I'll push it. They'll probably make an offer, and you'll tell me what you want to do.'

We shake on this, and I thank him for the lunch.

'Thank *you*,' he says. 'Gillette seemed pretty unenthused about the project. I'd rather see someone who's charged take it on. Here's my card. Be in touch.'

Outside I walk south in drizzle to the library to peek in on Eliot and get more books.

'You're a sight better,' he says. 'Where are my women?'

'With their father. I came for more books.'

'Are we doing France or medicine?'

'Neither. Greece. Antiquity. Aristocratic life.'

'You got it.'

He keys in commands, and the printer spews out titles. As it does so, Eliot asks about Fowler. I tell him about going to the Seaport.

'Can you handle this?' he says. 'I know whereof I speak.'

'Do I have a choice?'

'No,' he says. 'It's just such a long way down. Further down, maybe, than you've ever been.'

'I don't know about that,' I say.

At home I find Simon out in the garden with Jane. Daisy's asleep in her travel crib on the porch. Isaac, I gather, is out with a friend.

Jane says she's tired of weeding and asks if it's all right if she goes in and watches TV. I tell her to go ahead.

'Have you seen him?' Simon asks as we sit at the picnic table.

'Yesterday.'

'Is this likely to continue?'

'What? Is what likely to continue?'

'The *contact*.'

For once he's talking to me without doing a second thing, flipping through a computer magazine or wielding a hoe.

'Yes,' I say. 'Until he dies.'

'And do you expect me to wait until that happens and then return to being the man in your life?'

'No.'

'What *do* you expect?'

I mull this over. 'I don't expect anything, really, except that we continue to be available for the children. I don't think I *can* expect much, do you? I'm not sure that *expecting* is all that wise of a thing to do in general, anyway. You set yourself up.'

'Yes, you do,' he says. 'But the children expect things. They expect their parents to live under the same roof. We're disappointing them.'

'I don't know if that can always be the ultimate consideration,' I say.

'You've always bemoaned the fact that your parents didn't live under the same roof. Now you seem to condone it because it suits your whim.'

'I know that's how it seems,' I say, 'but I think I've been misguided in criticizing them. They've pointed that out to me for years. They live as they think they have to.'

'I can't afford a hotel any more,' he says. 'And I'd like some time in my house as well.'

'Simon,' I tell him. 'Sleeping arrangements can be made. For God's sake, I'll go to Mother's at night if it's too unspeakable to be in separate rooms for a while.'

'For a *while*? You act as if you made a small, forgivable error! As if you dented a fender or broke a glass!'

'I don't feel as you do. I can't help that.'

'We have to make a plan!'

'All right. I say we continue to share in the household duties, and if you want a week alone here I'll make myself scarce, but if you don't mind, I'll continue to live and work here and be your wife and the children's mother.'

He looks at the back of his hands, flattened on the table. 'As if nothing is different.'

'No,' I insist. 'As if we know everything is and we can manage it. As if it isn't so awful. How awful can it *be*, for God's sake?'

Of course, my mind is on Fowler, his legs and arms betraying him.

Simon tells me he'll take the porch, as he likes

sleeping out there in the summer. He asks that I confine my Fowler visits to times when they will not be obvious to the children. He says that as far as he's concerned, this is a temporary arrangement, until one of us takes up residence elsewhere.

'All arrangements are temporary,' I remind him.

'That is only as you would have it,' he says.

We go inside to see to the girls and dinner.

NINE

In summer in Ancient Greece industry slowed, men lay about, recovering from the cooler months' labor, the manufacture of battle gear, battle itself, and agricultural duties. Women, according to one of my sources, 'grew soft and languorous'. But during other seasons the women were as industrious as the men and as free to be at large outside the manor house as their husbands. Granted, they kept separate quarters within the house, and visits to the husbands' quarters would occur upon invitation, as it was customary for the men to have concubines as well. The women took separate meals, but they joined their husbands and male guests in the great hall, the *megaron*, at banquet's end and often presided over the conversation and entertainment.

For my part, separate sleeping quarters and meals don't seem uncivilized customs, and I mention this to Simon while he's making up the cot out on the porch.

'A convenient philosophy for some,' he mutters. 'However, you aren't taking into account that these privations were balanced by a reward system I don't think even *you* would approve of.'

'Meaning.'

'First of all,' he explains (Simon has read far more than I have on Ancient Greece, having studied the great mathematicians for most of his educational life), 'you'd have to be willing to spare a maid to answer the door when my concubines came to call, you'd have to forget about Fowler and external work, and you'd have to spend a good share of your time at the loom and in preparation of side dishes for me and my friends. You wouldn't be permitted to cook the meat.'

'Let's talk about whom you'd invite,' I say playfully.

He tries hard not to smile at this suggestion. 'Let's put our efforts toward a more elevated purpose. Like who's going to go driving around and find Isaac. It's after eleven.'

'Let me,' I say.

'That wouldn't be allowed in BCE Athens.'

'You made your point,' I say. 'A hundred times.'

'Do me a favor,' he snaps, 'and don't expect business as usual.' He sits down on the squeaky cot, disgusted.

'I don't. That isn't what I want.'

Again I'm out in the car in search of my son, first over to Garland's, where there's no answer when I buzz up, then to the Burger King he frequents with his baseball pals, then to the movie theater, where the 9.30 showing of *Speed* is about to let out. I stand under the marquee for a while, but the night is so sluggish and thick with humidity that I go ahead in and buy a coffee and sit on the carpeted stairs in the air conditioning, grateful not to be confined to housewifely duties.

When the doors finally open I see Isaac, his arm draped over the very tan shoulder of a dark-haired girl who is as tall as he is. I stay, frozen, in my seat on the stairs leading to the upstairs theater.

As soon as our eyes lock, he nudges her in the direction of the exit furthest from me. She hasn't taken any of this in, intent as she's been on telling him something private, close, right in his ear. Her smooth, tan face framed by long straight hair, animated by the secret she's told him, is prettier than any girl's face I've seen at Hastings or in movies or in Manhattan's most glamorous shopping districts. They leave the theater for the hot outdoors, and I watch them climb into a royal blue Miata parked in the first row, her car, I'm assuming, as she's the driver.

Nothing — not Kirsten's longing for Simon, Fowler's

mild pursuit of Pam, Adrienne's poisoning my daughter against me — has prepared me for this.

'Ma'am?' a sweet voice behind me says.

The creamy-faced girl who sold me the coffee stands alone in the lobby, carpet-sweeper in hand.

'We're closing,' she says apologetically. 'I'm going to have to ask you to leave.'

'I'm sorry.' I expel myself into the hateful heat, desperate not to admit the jealous rage I've been denying my husband, fighting to keep the composure, the nobility of a woman who knows (and reveres) her place. But this vision, of Isaac with a girl, doesn't fit with any I've ever had of him. I am incredulous. My son has a girlfriend. It's an outrage.

At home Simon is at the computer, typing up some sort of an announcement.

'Did you know that Isaac has a girlfriend?' I ask.

'I had that sense.'

'Has he said anything to you?'

'He's said plenty. But not about that.'

'I just saw them leaving the movie theater together.'

'Really.' I can't tell if this bothers him.

'What are you doing?' I say.

'Writing up something for the temple. I volunteered

to do it. They wanted someone with good graphics capability.'

I stand still as an animal threatened by headlights. 'Oh,' I say. 'I didn't know we were doing that.'

'I took Jane and Isaac on the Saturday you were indisposed in the city. They have a program for kids, I heard. Turns out it's more for Daisy's age.'

We've never taken them either place, church or temple.

'While Leigh errs, Simon straightens.'

He hits one of the keys hard. 'Oh cut the crap, Leigh. You're way out on this one.'

I redirect, away from the betrayal.

'Who is this girl? She's absolutely stunning,' I say. 'Drives a blue Miata. I'm not sure if I should have followed them or what.'

He stops typing. 'What would that have achieved?'

I can't think straight on this. 'Shouldn't I be concerned here? He's *fourteen*, for Christ's sake. And she, clearly, is older, since she's driving that sexy car. Is this what fourteen-year-old boys do? Find women who can drive them places? Two minutes ago he was hitting grounders in little league. I just can't get my mind around this.'

I sound just like Mother, without the grace.

'Around what?' Simon laughs. '*This* is precisely what you've given him permission to do!'

'You seem relieved about this! Doesn't it bother you at *all*? Don't you feel any compulsion to go out and find him?'

Simon turns back to the computer and effects the involved process of turning it off – screen, printer, monitor, an order he has taught me not to violate, as I could 'blow the mother board' or commit countless other computer atrocities.

'Leigh,' he says, as if it's the last word in the language he wants to have to say, 'I have learned, pretty recently, that however bothered or upset I am about anything that happens has no impact on the event or its perpetrators. I have learned that what I feel and think doesn't matter. How am I supposed to get upset about Isaac riding around in a car with a beautiful girl?'

How like my father he is, with all his wisdom.

'I guess you can't.'

'It wouldn't help anybody.'

'So I should just let him stay out all night.'

'I have met the girl. Her father had me put in a system at their house. I took Isaac along. He also knows her from camp, where she's working in the office, not that she needs to work. Her father also owns the camp.

We've talked. So unless you want to involve the police, we need to trust him to come home or stay there. If you like, I'll call her father. I'm glad you saw him with her. We can take shelter in the fact that no crime is being committed.'

'Do you think *I've* committed a crime?'

He sits forward, his face gentler than I've seen it since before the crime.

'I'm too tired to think about it at this point. All I want to know is how we're going to live. I'm not sure this cot thing is going to work out. I can't pretend like you can. And I don't know if I can forgive you. You've reminded me that we see things differently, and that troubles me. And as harsh as it sounds, I don't think it's fair that you get to stay in this house when you've threatened the very life inside it.'

'A lot of things aren't fair,' I say. 'It isn't fair that Isaac's dad left him when he was four months old, or that people get lonely enough to have affairs to begin with.'

'I think that's too easy,' he says.

'Do you want me to pretend I haven't been lonely? You say I'm so good at pretending – I'm not. I like having a man look at me when he's talking to me.'

'I'm looking at you.'

'But the gears are working against that,' I burst out. 'You're thinking of the next thing, the next project or task or event, so what you're seeing isn't me at all, but tomorrow. *Or*, if you do see me, you just see some person you have kids and a house with.'

'And when you look at me, what do *you* see?'

'I see rules. I see structure. I see love in its standard definition. I see the end of me.'

'You see someone to complain about.'

'I guess so.'

'That's not so good, is it?'

'I guess not.'

Instead of moving into rage, he rolls toward me on the chair we fought about buying at Staples last month.

'Do you think he'll give you back the beginning of you? Do you really think he can do that?'

'He's pointed some things out,' I say. 'Without meaning to, he's shown me a part of myself that I've buried in duty, and it's a part that I like.'

'And you no longer think I'm capable of doing that.'

'I didn't say that.'

'But you're in love with him, so of course it appears that way. It's hard to believe I'm capable of doing anything for you when you're in love with him, isn't that true?'

'Yes, that's true! But I don't see any reason, outside of anger and pride, to abandon the life we've made because of this. I just don't see the reason! I haven't done this to hurt or spite you! And I don't blame you for feeling anything you may feel about anything! But I can't leave my house and children because I love, in whatever ways I do, two men. I can't. You'll have to get the authorities to drag me out of here. I'm not going.'

Simon laughs again. 'I'm not going to do that.' He leans back in the contrary chair and flips a pencil he's been turning in his hands over his shoulder.

'What, then?' I say.

'I'm not sleeping on this cot.'

'OK, then I will.'

I lie down on it, as if I'm testing its firmness and durability. 'It's fine. You take the bed.'

'No,' he tells me, moving from the chair over to me. 'No, that won't do either.'

He kisses my ear, cheek, jaw, then my mouth, chin, neck and down the center of my chest to my navel. He looks up briefly.

'Stop?' he asks.

'It's OK.'

'Are you here with me?' he says. *Or him?* I know he means to ask.

'Yes,' I say, amazed.

He makes me come with his tongue, and I cry out again and again, too loud for this house, for all of us, the cot groaning beneath me.

'Are you with me?' he asks again as we lie on our sides afterwards, thin people facing each other.

I tell him I am.

'Let's sleep here. Let's say you're the concubine and my wife is upstairs asleep among her maids in antique splendor. You don't even have to dress and sneak out of here before dawn. One of my grooms will take you home.'

'What's my name?'

'Connie.'

'Connie?'

'Connie the Concubine. Connie Lingus. Connie, short for Constance.'

As tired as we are, we roar over this.

'Where does Connie live?' I ask.

'Wherever she wants,' he says, drifting. 'Some women do that.'

While he sleeps I listen for cars, for Isaac being driven home by his concubine. But there are no cars. No raccoon fights or cats in heat. No snoring or humming fridge. My ears are full all the same, and it's deafening, the change in this house.

'Who slept on the cot?' Jane calls as I'm getting out cereal.

'We did,' I call back.

She appears in the kitchen, as if by magic.

'You and Daddy?'

'Daddy and I.'

'You're sleeping with Daddy again?' she pants.

'Jane, honestly.' I turn my back on her to get Daisy into the highchair and get her bib and spoon.

'Mo-om!'

I face her, lean against the counter, sipping coffee with cream, utterly satisfied.

'Are you and Daddy getting back together?'

'It appears so.'

'Oh my *God*!' she screams. 'Adrienne's going to take a fit!'

I stop her right there. 'Here's the deal,' I say. 'Adrienne doesn't know everything. There are things occurring on the face of this earth this very minute that Adrienne has no notion of and could never process or judge. Do me a favor, and don't believe everything Adrienne tells you.'

'Where is he?'

'Where is who?' I'm thinking of Isaac, who didn't come home last night.

'Daddy.'

'At the store. We're out of jam. And I thought we needed croissants.'

It's actually true that I have a craving for croissants, but she lets it slide. 'Is Isaac up yet?' She's so animated, so delighted that we're under one roof, that I don't want to tell her he isn't.

'Probably.'

'Did you guys talk? Is he talking to you?'

'Not yet.'

'Are you driving us to Grandpa's for brunch today?'

'Yes.'

'Oh God, I'm so happy!' She hugs me swiftly, then sits for Honey Nut Cheerios.

'Hap-py!' Daisy bangs out with her spoon.

'Mom, you're gaining weight,' Jane warns.

I look down. I'm in shorts, which isn't usual for me. My legs do look fat today. Sometimes after sex they look that way, wide and wiggly.

'I'll bear that in mind.'

'It's OK, Mom,' Jane says. 'You can be fat. As long as you're *here*, you can be fat or thin. I don't care.'

'Thanks.'

'If you get really fat, though, you should see someone about it. It means you're depressed. And people might talk.'

'They're already talking.'

She laughs, and I get more coffee, which I shouldn't have, as it will make me hungry later, and then fatter when I honor the hunger. I join them at their breakfast, Beethoven is on the classical station where my kitchen radio dial rests. Before the sonata concludes, I hear the front doorknob turn. I force myself to remain seated. Isaac walks into the kitchen and looks at each of us without speaking.

'Hi,' I say.

'Hi,' says he.

'Do you want some breakfast?'

'Yeah,' he says.

'What would you like?'

'I'll have that.' He points to the Cheerios.

'Where *were* you?' Jane says. 'You look like shit.'

I put the bowl and spoon down in front of him.

'Out,' he says. 'You look like shit, too.'

'Do you two mind?' I say. 'There's a civilized baby present.'

'Out where?' Jane says.

'Wherever.' He starts shoveling.

'Did you stay out *all night*?' she says.

'Pretty much,' he says. He shoots me a triumphant, fuck-you look.

'Aren't you *tired*?' she begs.

'I slept.'

'That's nice,' I say. 'Then you'll come with us to Grandpa's today.'

'Sure.'

He's too smooth, too easy, too pleased. He's had sex with that beautiful girl, and that's that. Mostly it's been me dishing out truth for other people to swallow. Now it's my turn to swallow it.

The four of us ride into Manhattan in a glaring haze, the air conditioning on high, a new tape of Isaac's by M.C. Hammer playing at an intolerable volume. Simon's meeting us there after an errand to the computer wholesaler. I wish he were here, just to turn down the tape deck.

'Turn it down, Mom!' Jane shouts into my ear.

'No problem,' says Isaac. Downright jaunty, he is. Agreeable, interested and in my face.

'Do I get to meet her?' I ask.

'Am I meeting him?'

'Sure.'

'What if I don't want to?'

'Then you won't. But he'd like to meet you – again.'

'Well, she doesn't want to meet you, Mom. Sorry.'

'May I know her name?'

'Her name is Alex. Alexandra.'

'She sounds like a snob,' Jane injects.

'Like you'd know anything about snobs,' Isaac retorts.

'Alexandra *what*?' Jane demands.

'Alexandra Aidinoff.'

'Aidinoff,' I repeat. My mind reels. A name like mine. Jewish, maybe. They'll make him convert.

'Where'd you meet her?'

'Camp,' he says coolly. 'She's helping in the office. Her dad owns the camp.'

'How old is she?'

'Jesus, Mom. How old is *he*?'

'Forty-seven. How old is she?'

'Nineteen. Does it matter?'

'I think it matters to you. It means she can take you places in the car.'

'Did you *sleep* with her?' Jane asks, thrilled.

'Put a sock in it, Jane,' Isaac orders with disgust. But I catch him smiling into his shirt.

'What does she look like?' I can't help it. I want to hear him describe her.

'Like you, Mom. She looks just like you.'

'Except she's nine feet tall and looks like Brooke Shields,' Jane cackles.

'Just one thing,' I say, feeling horribly dwarfed. 'You call. You call and tell me you're at a friend's house and you'll be out all night. And then you let me talk to one of her parents. Only so I'll know you're not dead.'

'No problem,' he says.

'Mom and Daddy are back together,' Jane announces. 'In case you were wondering.'

'Hallelujah. She's back together with all of our fathers.'

I pull over, once we're in striking distance of Daddy's apartment, into a metered spot. I grab the front of his shirt so hard he doesn't even attempt to fight me.

'You listen to me carefully. I had you when I was younger than your new friend, and I don't need to go into what a total party it was raising you when I had no husband, no money and just about nothing to recommend me. But I'm your only mother, I'm it, and I'm not going to take this shit from you for one more minute. Have your girlfriend! I won't stop you! But mouth off to me like you just did ever again and I'll get in touch with her parents faster than *yesterday* and tell them she's sleeping with my fourteen-year-old boy who doesn't use birth control. I'll make sure you never leave your room again, in addition. You got me?'

He stares, frozen, at the dashboard.

'*You got me?*' I yell.

'Yes,' he murmurs.

'*What?*'

'*Yes!*' he shouts back.

'Good! Now take your sisters upstairs. I have to get a coffee ring.'

He gets out, slams the door as I expect him to and stands on the curb while I get Daisy out. Jane, frightened, looks up at him and slips her hand into his. I give him the baby, who clings to his neck like a chimpanzee.

'Don't drop her,' I tell him.

I get a pecan ring at the bakery, practice deep breathing in the elevator to prepare to hold my temper at Daddy's, and give the doorbell a good punch. I don't expect a warm greeting, and I don't get one.

Daddy's handing out frosted theme cookies, Miss Piggy for Daisy and Power Rangers for Jane and Isaac. 'The children are well,' he says finally. 'All in order, I see.'

'All in order,' say I.

'Good to know. Your mother should be here soon.'

'She's back?' I'm surprised. Usually she stays on when she goes to Nantucket.

'She called yesterday. Apparently things weren't so easy up there, and she decided to return.'

Today it annoys me that my father always speaks as if he's reading from a book.

'What went wrong? I thought Amanda was very spry still.'

'Oh, Amanda's very spry. Your mother wasn't visiting Amanda. She went to Vineyard Haven to visit an old flame who's had a stroke and can't get around too well. Add that difficulty to his homosexuality – your mother has never seemed to mind that fact – and I suppose you've got an even more remote chance of a good visit!' Tickled, Daddy begins to fuss over the table, adding my pecan ring to the mix of bagels, cream cheese and chives, lox, onions and sliced tomato.

'Sounds like he has a few strikes against him,' I say, furious.

'It's a nice ring you've brought,' he says.

Vernon. She went to visit Vernon. She still knows him!

'Daddy,' I say.

'Yes,' he says in his what-is-it tone.

'Simon's coming.'

'Yes? Good.'

'And Isaac has a girlfriend.'

Isaac looks up from the antique music box he's been winding up for Daisy.

'And why shouldn't he?' Daddy says, walking over and cupping the back of Isaac's dark head. 'A boy like this?'

'And I've got a book contract, I think. Or I'll know by the end of the month, probably. And we're all just fine, except for Fowler, who's got Lou Gehrig's. But we're all here, and I think we're fine.'

'Lou Gehrig's?' my father says. 'Fowler's got Lou Gehrig's?'

'Yes.'

'What's that?' Isaac says.

'A degenerative disease of the spine and musculature,' I explain.

'Your mother didn't say anything about Lou Gehrig's,' Daddy says. 'Why would she not have mentioned a thing like that?'

'I didn't tell her what he had because I didn't know until recently. I only knew that he wasn't well.'

'*What are you talking about?*' Isaac shouts, now on his feet.

'He's *dying*,' Jane says. 'He walks with a cane, and his legs and arms don't work always. But he gives people things anyway. It's like he knows he's dying, so he wants to do everything he can before he dies. He looks just like you, Isaac. And he's a nice man, right, Daze?'

Daisy looks up, then back into the music box to try and figure out why it has stopped playing.

'Is this true, Leigh?' Daddy asks.

I nod, not taking my face from Isaac's, which is full of hatred.

'All of it.'

'Halloo!' Mother calls from the hallway, having let herself in. She finds us all clumped around the ugly facts. 'Halloo, family! I'm sorry I'm so late. Isn't anyone going to have anything to eat?'

For the first time in weeks all five of us are in one car. We left Daddy and Mother mulling over the Movie Clock in the 'Weekend' section. All three children are asleep in the back seat.

'My guess is that they end up at the Merchant and Ivory.'

'Daddy hates Merchant and Ivory.'

'Really? I'd have thought just the opposite. I'd have thought the European settings, the classic plots, the sophisticated company, would be right up his alley. Nothing to foment over, no contemporary angst to ridicule.'

'He can't stand the way people leave the theater whispering "How wonderful" after those films. That's what he hates.'

Simon smiles. 'I've underestimated him.'

'Oh, they're fairly colorful, my parents. Mother was up on the Vineyard visiting her first love, who happens to be gay. Daddy couldn't have been more pleased.'

'No threat there,' Simon reminds me.

'That's not why he was amused, I don't think. I think he just finds everything human amusing, or at least intriguing. He has an ability to see everything from a distance, to apply Hegel's dialectic to a cocktail party. And Mother supplies the party for him to analyse.'

'Is that why they separated?'

'I guess it wasn't enough of a party, just the three of us in one house,' I say. '*In the absence of conflict we create it*,' I boom out, in Daddy's lecturing voice.

'Is that what's happened with us? It's not enough of a party for you any more?'

'A *party*?' I demand. 'Jesus fucking Christ, Simon!'

Simon raises his voice to meet mine, despite the sleeping children.

'Have you thought about him dying?'

'Yes,' I say, taking it down. 'Party's over.'

We drive on in silence until Simon breaks in again.

'You know that Isaac wants to meet him.'

'That's not what Isaac told me. All Isaac wants, it seems to me, is an easy formula for matricide. Why? Did he say something to you?'

'He doesn't need to. And he wouldn't anyway. He probably thinks that by wanting to meet his real father, he'd be shutting me out in some way. I've heard it said that we can have no notion of our parents at all and still spend our lives longing for them. So here's a request from his adoptive father.'

'OK.'

'Please don't let that meeting take place without my knowledge. I'm not planning to recede into the darkness because Fowler has surfaced, and I don't think Isaac should think I will. Fowler, well or sick, is big on the meteoric appearance, but that isn't going to be a totally great thing for Isaac. For any of us, really. I've got legal claim here, and I don't want to be forced into calling upon it. So let's do this thing right. I'm saying: you consult me.'

I agree to this. Then I ask to make a request.

'Shoot.'

'Talk to him about Alexandra. Just arm him with some information. They're too young. Take it from someone who knows.'

'I've already talked to him. He did this one night last week. He spent the night on the floor of her room. It's an enormous house. I told you. I installed a system over there a week ago, and believe me, that girl is not bad news. She's a sweet kid, and her father is aware of Isaac. He even knows about Isaac being there overnight. He and I were on the phone about it.'

'So you pretended not to know where he was going.'

'I was a little angry.'

'You let me believe my son was out impregnating the local population at the age of fourteen.'

'She's hardly a "local" girl. And think of what you've allowed me to believe lately.'

I didn't want to have to *like* this girl. 'So, are you telling me we'll have to meet these people and talk it over or something?'

Simon bursts out laughing. We slow for the toll after Dyckman Street. He flips the token into the basket.

'It might be nice for Isaac to see that we approve of her, providing they approve of him. Then he wouldn't have to sneak around.'

'I think that's the part of it he likes the most.'

I lie back, and the next thing I know we're in the Toys Я Us parking lot. Half asleep, I look to Simon for an explanation.

'I thought we all could use a lift.'

'Whoa!' Isaac says, waking. 'What's our limit?'

'Twenty each, not a penny more.'

Jane and Isaac tear like wild horses out of the back seat, and Daisy's hands dance furiously at the prospect of this store, which she knows almost as well as Shop-Rite.

I stop Simon at the entrance. 'This was a good idea,' I say.

'Yes, I think so. Try and center things a little.'

I tell him I have to shop for food, there's nothing in the house, and he says we have time for all that. Then he puts a hand under my chin.

'Open,' he says. When I do, he looks perplexed. 'That tooth doesn't match your other ones *at all*. We've got to call that dentist.'

'It's temporary.'

He isn't satisfied. 'Well, make sure you get a good look at the permanent one before he puts it in. They'll have to break it in your head to get it out if it's wrong. Look.'

He shows me his first molars on the bottom, the two crowns I've inspected for him before. 'These were properly stained. I was lucky.'

'Could we get out of our mouths now?' I beg him. 'It's time to buy some toys.'

What is available to know about Sappho is representative, I'm starting to find out, of what is available to know about many aristocratic women of antiquity – precious little. That she was married to a wealthy man, that she had a daughter and plotted against a tyrant which earned her banishment to Sicily are undisputed rumors, as is the notion that on Lesbos in the seventh century BCE aristocratic women met informally to write and read poetry. Sappho apparently led one of these societies, but all that remains of her ten books of lyric and elegiac poetry are the fragments for which she has been lauded and denounced through the millenia.

I read this one to Barry:

'Leave Crete,
Aphrodite,
and come to this
sacred place
encircled by apple trees,
fragrant with offered smoke.'

'Put that in,' he says. 'The tone is what you want. It's urgent and strong. It says what you're saying. Have you done the proposal?'

'In the mail.'

'Good,' he says. 'Keep working.' He clicks off.

What I've come to value in Barry is efficiency. Now that he's on the wagon Barry runs a tight ship. It's inspiring. And Sappho is inspiring, lifting the sensual above where our current world would have it, challenging those who have put non-standard love in the gutter to leave their unholy places and venture into her holy one.

'Tell me, beloved, what you want of me —
I am love, who am filled with the all.
What you want,
we want, beloved —
tell us your desire nakedly.'

'Mom?' Isaac calls from the bottom of the staircase.
'What?'
'I'm going out for a while,' he says. 'OK?'
'OK.'
'Not all night,' he says. 'Chill.'
'OK.'
He starts out the door.
'Isaac,' I say.
He turns around, about to lose patience, when I say, 'She can pick you up here, you know. There's no sense in waiting on street corners.'
'Right, Mom,' he says. And goes.

TEN

The last week of August Barry makes me an offer for the book. I go numb. I don't leap up off the couch, toss the cordless joyously ceiling-ward, dance atop the folded sheets and trousers. The elation I'd planned to feel were something as unimaginable as this ever to happen to me eludes me. There will be money, apparently. And more work. But it fixes nothing. My children wish to disown me, my husband works overtime to avoid killing me, and I seem, for the moment, to have run out of old friends, so I scramble around after new ones.

I accept, of course, and thank Barry in as graceful a tone as a women folding laundry in front of a talk show can muster. Then I return Fowler's call, dragging my heels, afraid of what will be asked of me next.

'The fact is,' he says, 'I need a wheelchair. Do you know anyone who could take me wheelchair shopping?'

I ask if tomorrow will be soon enough. I haven't seen him since our day at the Seaport and have only permitted myself occasional daydreams, lapses in attention when I'm alone with Daisy. What I dream is always the same – the two of us at a table, staring off, desperate for the next moment of contact and afraid to let it occur because we know these moments are numbered.

He says his doctor has recommended a place midtown, if I wouldn't mind picking him up. Without consulting Simon, I tell him I'll be there at nine.

'How are you?' he asks suddenly.

'I think I'm all right. I really do.'

'I have some things I'd like to talk about.' His speech is slow, as if he speaks another language and is translating from it. 'Will you have the day?'

'Yes,' I say, already arranging it in my head: older kids at camp for the final day, Simon at work, Daisy with me. 'I'll work it out.'

Simon calls from his post at the computer out on the porch, 'I take it that was Himself.'

'He needs a wheelchair.'

'And you're going.'

'Tomorrow morning.' I wait for the *éclat*.

'Do you know where to get a wheelchair?'

'No, but he does.'

'Are you taking the car?' he asks, without hostility.

'Of course not!' I go into a spin about the train, the subway, a cab to the medical supplies outlet, a cab back to Fowler's and home on the train.

'I'll take the kids to camp,' he says, 'and then figure out something to do with Daisy. You'll be home for dinner?'

Again, of course, a million times of course.

'How's he getting along then?'

'I guess not very well. If he's needing the wheelchair.'

'Well, didn't you ask? A guy who has no wheelchair and needs one must be in pretty desperate straits. Did you ask him if he'd fallen and couldn't get up? This strikes me as fairly serious.'

His aggression grates on me, but I treat it as concern all the same. 'I'm sure things have gotten pretty bad. He wouldn't have called otherwise.'

'Bodes ill for the course he's slated to teach, doesn't it?'

It occurs to me that we're gossiping.

'People can do all sorts of things in wheelchairs,' I say.

'Please, Leigh,' he sighs. 'Spare me those details.'

Simon and I have had more sex over the last two

weeks than we've had in two years, it seems, and when we get to bed tonight I begin it, wanting to try something different, if there's anything left. I'm on top, rocking on his mouth and then over to the side, my back to him. I try to think of where I am, with which man, but sometimes Fowler's face and long, white body dominate and sometimes Simon's mouth and hands do, and once or twice I just see myself in the company of the women I know and read about, caressing, being caressed and feeling, ultimately, the peace of having come in the presence of them. So when, afterwards, Simon starts to comment on what seems an unusual interest on my part, I hush him. 'Sleep,' I say.

'Sleep,' he says, smiling, eyes closed.

The unburdened, untenanted look of Fowler's apartment, as I originally saw it, has been overwhelmed by newspapers, clothing, books and dirty dishes. I decide to straighten, despite pleas to the contrary, despite the limit placed on our time by the hours kept by the medical supplier and the message I left with Barry, that I'd stop by in the early afternoon to give him a more detailed outline.

Fowler has managed to dress himself in the usual

classic gear, and he sits at the butcher block table on a stool.

'Isn't there a better chair for you?' A man who is at the mercy of his own limbs should be wary of sitting on anything backless, I'm thinking.

'I'm all right. You clean,' he teases. The coffee and croissants I brought stay, untouched, on the table.

'Do you want some help with that?'

'I'll have a sip of coffee, yes,' he says.

'How have you been managing with food?'

'Another challenge,' he says, effecting boredom.

He takes sips of the coffee as I offer it. The croissant he can handle for the moment. I separate the tasks, collecting dishes first, to put into a sink of soapy water, then clothing, to soak in the bathroom sink piece by piece, piling up books and newspapers. I make the bed, take a broom to the floors and water the flowers in the windowbox. Then I rinse dishes, pile them in the drainer, and drain the clothes, to hang in the shower to dry. I'm aware of my efficiency, of his watching me bustle about, moving from room to room in Gillette's dress, single of purpose, a professional housekeeper.

'You look great,' he says.

I try to stay straight about what I'm doing.

'It appears, sometimes,' he says in the new, studied way, 'that I've thrown my life away.'

'I thought that for a while,' I say. 'About myself. But it doesn't help to think along those lines.'

I sit down on the other stool and open my coffee.

'You're going to need more help. You have to start living with that. A wheelchair is only part of it.'

He brushes crumbs off his pants with a gentle sweep of the back of one hand, and I sweep again.

'There's no way to get a wheelchair up those steps outside. Have you spoken to the landlord?'

'It was a lot just to call you,' he says distantly. 'It's as far as I've gotten.'

'What about the course? Can you still teach the course? Does the college know?'

'They know. I'm going to give it my best shot. It's just screenwriting. I only have to sit in a chair and talk.'

'You have to get there. You have to feel up to it.'

He raises a hand, but I don't stop.

'You're going to need a ramp outside,' I posit. 'And rails for the bathroom.'

'And probably a hundred other unspeakable things,' he says angrily. 'Let's just get the wheelchair done today.'

'Fine. But I have some questions.'

'You've gotten inquisitive.'

I remind him that I'm rearranging my world for him, in spite of the past, and that he must indulge my curiosity. I ask him about treatment, clusters, likely causes, the acceleration of the disease itself. 'Because if I'm going to be your help, if I'm going to be with you while you die, I need to know what to expect. I need to know how to behave! It's a lot, for you *and* for me.'

'There's no cause,' he says, as if I'm ridiculous for wanting to know. 'It is not hereditary. The clusters, of which you've obviously read, have been cited in Berkeley, LA, Guam, and among teammates of the '49ers. And there's the case of the famous baseball player, as you know. All the information sits there and there's no conclusion. You'd think a man like Stephen Hawking, who's got it, would be able to come up with a known cause and a cure. Some people say toxins cause it, some say dormant viruses in the nerves. There might be a drug, but there might not. I don't think about these details any more. I'm just living it. Your reading will supply you with all the facts you'll need.'

'What about J.T. and Evelyn? Don't they want to be part of this? Don't they want to help?'

'Yes, they want to help. But Mama likes a manageable world where weakness only comes to the back door and never sets foot in the house. This is an ugly thing that's happened to me. She can't fathom it.'

This much I believe. 'And J.T.? Can't he fathom it?'

'He lives with Mama.'

'Jesus Christ.'

'Look, unless you want me to get someone else, we should get going so I don't keep you all day.'

I throw the trash from breakfast into the garbage can, tie up the plastic bag and take it outside, where I wait for him to join me. I have read about the football players and the isolated cases, but I'm not living this yet. I'm still with the facts he's got past. I'm part of the ugliness Evelyn wouldn't invite in through the back door.

'I'm sorry,' I tell him in the cab. 'I'm not being fun.' I rest my head on his chest.

'We're going to buy furniture,' he says. 'Let's enjoy it!'

'I almost made you lose your humor.'

'Not even you,' he says with confidence, and kisses the top of my head.

'You're so *small*,' he says. 'How could I love a woman so *small*?'

He has said this before, but I can't remember when.

It must have been at Hastings because I remember feeling I'd triumphed over the larger, fairer Pam. I remember liking his amused attention and thinking that this was as perfect an expression of love as any other. I love this man. I don't want him to die, and I'm not sure I can bear for him to live. Those are the facts.

At the medical supplier we listen raptly but not distracted from the ludicrousness of our mission. We accept the offer of coffee from our salesperson, an older man with glasses, even though we've just had some. He brings out a binder containing pictures and descriptions of wheelchairs, manual and mechanized, for us to peruse.

'Would you both like to look at this?'

'I think so. Yes,' Fowler says.

I scooch over in my chair and consider the grim offerings.

'Do you think they'll have this in a blue?' Fowler asks me, of an elaborate, multi-functional tan chair that I cannot imagine him sitting in, never mind operating.

'We can get that for you in blue,' the man says, coming around the desk to inspect Fowler's choice. 'It's a cobalt, if that suits you.'

'Cobalt is nice,' Fowler says, not quite pleased. 'But I prefer navy. Unless there's a cerulean option.'

'Would you like a test drive?' the man asks. 'We have one in the stock room.'

'In cerulean?'

'In sand,' the man says.

'I'm game,' Fowler says.

The man calls the back of the store and then goes to hurry the retrieval along. When Mother and I picked out Pussy's tombstone, there was a similar tone to our dealing — a let's-pretend-we're-talking-about-the-weather levity that Mother just ate up and I was tortured by.

'You can't very well sulk over the choices,' she counseled, as we came away from the place in Pussy's rattly Mercedes, which Pussy had been driving the day before and in which she'd left some crumpled towelettes and a half-eaten pack of candies.

'He didn't have to be so fucking chipper,' I complained.

'You won't succeed in offending him by using that language *now*,' Mother said. 'If you felt so antagonized, maybe you should have used it in the shop.'

I ask Fowler if he's offended.

'Sand is a pretty offensive name for a color,' he says.

'I suppose I'm offended. Deeply offended, now that you mention it.'

When the salesman returns, we're laughing so hard he waits a few paces off for us to stop before introducing the chair. The steel shines so brutally in store light that I have to turn away for a second.

'Let's dance,' Fowler says, and he holds out an arm for me to help move him out of the stationary chair into the mobile one. The salesman goes at the buttons and levers to demonstrate the chair's versatility, and then he wheels Fowler out into the cavernous store. Fowler sails off and returns an eternity later, sweating.

'It's a keeper,' he beams. 'I won't need you any more, Florence. I can go anywhere in this thing. How does it do on the highway, Sherman?'

'Maybe you should keep her around for the highway,' Sherman says. 'Is there anything else I can help you with today, assuming, that is, that you'll take it in sand?'

Fowler defers to me, and I talk quietly about rails and a ramp for the steps outside.

'That the building should take care of, but this is New York. I'll see what I've got. The rails I can send you home with today.'

We get it all, rails, wheelchair, a huge pair of tongs for picking things up, which Fowler refers to as 'grabbers', and a wristband with an electronic button that will signal the local ambulance service, in an emergency. We thank the salesman, and we cab back to the apartment in horrendous heat, no apology from the driver, who didn't warn us in advance about the broken air conditioning, who probably figures that helping us to his trunk for the bulk items is all that should be required of him.

We're back by 11.30, time enough for me to get to Barry before he goes to lunch.

'We did well,' I say to Fowler, as if we've driven a hard bargain.

He slumps on the couch, the wheelchair facing him, positioned for any need that might arise.

'I can't tell you how I hate this,' he says. His face is red, and I'm sure he will cry, so I join him on the couch and whisper how lucky we are that the 'sexual function remains unaffected', and then I do with him what I did with Simon twelve hours ago.

I catch Barry at one, on his way to lunch, and he insists that I join him for Indian food.

'You look flushed,' he says in the elevator.

'It's hot. I've been running errands.' I hand him the outline for a chapter about Hadewijch of Antwerp, a

Flemish woman of the thirteenth century, who relinquished private life for a community of the spirit.

'I'll review it later. You'll be happy to know your proposal was accepted without issue, and they're talking about a first printing of 20,000,' Barry says as we leave the building. 'Frankly, I'm surprised. This is unusual, this sort of interest in a book on centuries of complaint!'

He's teasing me, I know. I wish I was more in the mood for it. I'm greedy for importance, but not diminished importance.

'Are you all right?' he asks me in the restaurant.

'What?' I can't settle. I can't seem to *be* here.

'You seem distracted. I thought you'd be ecstatic over this news.'

'Oh, I *am*,' I croon. 'I *am*. Please don't think I'm not. I'm thrilled. I'll take a while to believe it, that's all.'

'Believe it,' Barry says kindly. 'People are impressed with you. You work like a bear.'

'I apologize if I seem ungrateful.'

'Not at all. Let's see if I can recommend something to eat. What's your pleasure?'

'I think I might just have an appetizer and a coffee. I'm not very hungry.'

Barry hits himself in the forehead with his menu.

'Forgive me. I'm a boor. I didn't even ask you if you *wanted* lunch. Listen, we don't have to stay here. Or we can stay and I'll eat fast. Or I can just skip lunch in favor of a walk back to the office.'

'It's fine. I'll have an iced coffee. I don't know any boors.'

I'll go no further with Barry. While his charm is overwhelming, I'm not crossing the line with him.

'So . . . Hadewijch?'

'Hadewijch,' I say. And we go back to that.

'He's not *in pain*,' I tell Simon, whose interest is bizarre but I don't think distasteful. 'Physical pain isn't part of this. It's the loss of control that's so agonizing.'

For the second time today I stop myself from going into detail, realizing that in doing so I save myself a little, from having to consider Fowler so ill.

'You look exhausted,' he says. 'Why don't you go upstairs and take a nap.'

I know I need a nap, but I can't imagine taking one. There's too much to do, to think about and prepare.

'What is there to do? I'll get the dinner going. You've been running around *all* day. You should take advantage of Daisy being asleep and *lie down*.'

I look around me, at the straightened rooms, at Daisy,

rump-high in the travel crib, at Simon, whence cometh my help.

'Really, Leigh. You're doing so much. Take an hour.'

'All right. OK. Are Jane and Isaac —?'

'They're fine. Adrienne. Ball practice.'

'Ball practice? On a Friday?'

'Game Sunday. Sleep.'

Upstairs in our quiet bedroom I open every window to the dead heat and lie down. The bed seems huge, edgeless, a flat warm place for me to rest in the open air as people have done in centuries past.

I wake to a happy racket below, in the kitchen, the noise of dinner preparations and the older children returning. I smell garlic and butter, and when I arrive, stiff and bleary-eyed, in the kitchen, Simon has three things going at once — the food processor, the pan with the sautéed garlic and onions and the water boiling in the lobster kettle for pasta. Daisy's emptied the pasta box on the floor and is breaking each stick, and Jane, in an apron, is manning the food processing operation, holding green peppers and tomato chunks cavalierly above the wretched thing, happily sending them to their doom.

'What's going on?' I say.

'We're celebrating,' Simon answers. 'I thought the book was worth an Italian meal, at least.'

'You're going to be rich, Mom!' Jane says. 'It's *so* cool!'

'I didn't think it was *that* much money,' I say offhandedly. In fact, I've spent it in my mind already, on piano and ballet lessons for Jane, on private college tuition for Isaac, on a vacation for all of us, on clothes.

'It's *enormous* money!' Simon announces. 'Have this outside in a chair. I'll be out in a minute.'

He hands me a glass of our favorite wine and the *Times*.

'Jane and Daisy can come out with me if that would be easier.'

'I'm busy, Mom,' Jane says. 'And Daisy has to finish breaking all the noodles.'

'*Go*,' Simon orders.

Mother's Day in August. That's what it feels like. I'm half expecting Isaac to appear at the edge of the garden with a torch of Tropicana roses and a promise of lifelong loyalty and forgiveness.

Instead, I read my paper in suburban splendor, unbothered by the heat. Sweating and disheveled and drunk am I after several sips of wine, and this is the mother who greets Isaac when he actually does appear at the screen door with his friend, the Alexandra of camp fortune and Miata fame, a girl whose beautiful languor, even as seen through wire mesh, can't be disputed.

'Mom, this is Alex,' he says. 'Is it OK if she stays for dinner?'

I adopt the casual pose of a person in the midst of a routine sit in the sun. I shield my eyes, draw a hand loosely through my tangled hair. I am wearing a wrinkled dress, and my breath is bad from iced coffee and Indian hors d'oeuvres and sleep. I must appear at the very least slovenly, possibly insane.

'Of course it is, dear. Hello, Alex.'

'Hi, Mrs Kaufman,' she says, nectar in words.

'I'm just reading my paper for a while, then I'll be in,' I sing. I conjure a much more attractive setting for Mrs Aidinoff at her reading, a solarium with glass tables and white cast-iron sofas with floral print cushions.

I take about a half-hour to read an uplifting article about teaching in the Bronx and to finish the wine. Then Simon comes out with the cordless.

'Fowler,' he says. 'Dinner in five.'

I remember Mother handing me the telephone when a boyfriend would call out on Fire Island. She'd be in her apron, her hands floury from covering swordfish steaks or making fritters of some sort, and she'd bring the phone out to me on the small deck of our rental, stretching its white coil to maximum length and announcing the name of the caller in the same bored, can't-be-helped way.

'Hello,' I say, with the muted anticipation I reserved for those summer boys, whoever they were.

'I'm calling to report some successes,' he declares. 'The ramp will be put down Monday morning, the rails are going up as we speak. And I've got a new lease on life because of my new wheels. I've just been to the deli. Thank you.'

Under the cheer I hear something else: yearning, I suppose, for company.

'You're welcome.'

He says he has yet another favor to ask, if I can bear it, and that is for me to arrange a meeting between him and Isaac, 'before too long'.

'I'll see what I can do.'

'Soon,' he reiterates. I know why. He doesn't want his son to see him for the first time later on, in the advanced stages of which I've read too much. I know it has to be soon, for everyone's sake.

Simon and the girls are fixing six places at the table.

'Where's Isaac?'

'Upstairs, listening to CDs. Alex is staying for

dinner,' Jane says. The challenge of adapting has become attractive to her. A cool acceptance of whatever gets dealt out here may mean victory over it.

'Evidently.' I sound wounded.

'Mom, *you* said she could stay,' Jane reminds me.

'Yes, I did.'

'So don't act so pissed off.'

I direct my attention to the only one of us with a clean mouth. She's happy to have me join her at piling up the animals and fencing from her Fisher Price farm. For her I remain blameless and heavenly.

'What's the news?' Simon asks. He's barreled in with the sauce and noodles all in one bowl.

'He wants to see Isaac,' I report. 'Before things get unspeakable.'

'Then he should.'

Simon disappears for the salad and bread, then adds, 'And I should meet him. I'd sort of like to see what all the fuss is about.'

'I'll talk to Isaac later, when he's not so indisposed.'

Outside Isaac's room I pause and listen for talking under the music. At Hastings there was a door-open, one-foot-on-the-floor rule during coed visiting hours. I thought it was funny that a person like Fowler was assigned proctoring duties and had to enforce such safeguards against promiscuity.

I rap loudly on the door. 'Dinner.'

Then I hurry to the shower, shed my slept-in dress, soap, rinse and towel off, planning a youngish outfit all the while. I put on jeans and an ironed blouse, high-heeled huarache sandals and I pin my hair back in a clip.

'Wow, Mom, you look pretty,' Jane says. 'Doesn't she look pretty, guys?'

Simon says, 'Yes, she does,' and Isaac looks for salvation from us all in his lap. Alex has risen from her chair to shake my hand. She towers above me, and her extended arm, sunned, *sans* hair or moles or extra flesh, is that of a ballerina and yet puts me in mind of God reaching down from the apex of the Sistine Chapel to desperate, adoring underlings.

After dinner I'm on the phone calling our friends. The kids want a party, a barbecue. During dinner we made up the guest list. So far everyone's coming — Eliot, Garland and Travis, Fowler. I suggested Fowler's coming to Isaac's final ball game, and Isaac shrugged, 'Whatever.' We sent him and Alex over to her house with an invitation, and we await word.

'I don't get it,' Kirsten says when I call her.

'It's a party,' I explain. 'To have fun. After Isaac's last game of the season. Fowler wants to see him play.'

'Hold on,' she says, covering the phone for a muffled consultation.

She returns with, 'I don't think so. It might not be good for Adrienne and Garrison. Ted thinks they might get depressed.'

'Not *good*?' I whine. 'For *Adrienne*? I thought she'd jump at the chance to be close to someone who's actually *dying*.'

I hang up, shaking. Their selfishness has sent chills all over me.

'I won't be able to help with the shopping,' I tell Simon.

'You'll be *doing* the shopping,' he says.

'What about Fowler? He can't get here by train or bus, not in that chair. He'll only have had it a day.'

'I'll pick him up.'

'Oh no, Simon, really. That's above and beyond.'

'Everything about this is above and beyond, so why make distinctions? Why draw lines? If you've taken him on, I have too. Let's not try to be discerning at this point. *I* am going to get him.'

I worry about this, naturally. 'Just don't kill him.'

Simon laughs. 'I don't have to do that.'

'Simon!'

'I mean, that isn't on my mind. I'm not entirely without scruples, you know.'

'I know. You have many, many scruples. I've met you before.'

'I'm taking Isaac with me. It isn't a good idea to have a first meeting occur at a public sporting event. First we'll go to a diner, Isaac and I, and then pick up Fowler — could I call him by his other name? It's too preppy for me, this last-name-as-first-name business.'

'Call him Jim.'

'I'll do that.'

'I'll let him know you're picking him up, in that case.'

At one point, when she is married to Jules, Cathcrine drives to pick Jim up at the train when he comes to visit her and Jules and their daughter, Sabine, on the Rhine. She has dressed up for him, and Jim has the impression that all is not right for her in her life with Jules and Sabine. In the village, they become known as 'the three lunatics'.

Simon is sparing me the extra melancholy here. Perhaps I won't have to drive myself and one of them off an unfinished bridge.

At Shop-Rite I decide to put everything on a card

instead of using the cash Simon took out last night. A hundred dollars isn't going to suffice, in the end. I send Jane off with a list she can fulfill in one half of the store, with her own cart, and Daisy and I work on meats, beverages and deli salads. By the end of our separate foraging we stand at the checkout with two carts piled over capacity, and the bill totals just under two hundred dollars.

'That's nothing for us now,' Jane says proudly.

We load in, assembly-line style, Jane as middleman between me and the cart, Daisy in the driver's seat of the Mustard Bomb. I'm grateful for this project; all morning I've been thinking of the other car, its volatile cargo, its bizarre destiny. As we are meeting them at the field — Isaac left in uniform, cleats and all — I will have no idea what to expect on arrival.

'Stop worrying, Mom. You'll get wrinkles,' Jane advises.

'I've already got wrinkles.'

'You'll get more!'

Anyway, we have much ahead of us before game time, which is twelve o'clock — arranging the outdoor furniture, the bar, transferring the food into more appealing conveyers, providing a general welcome for our guests, a welcome that has so much riding on it.

From our camp behind home plate I have a clear view of the wagon when it pulls in. Isaac is the first out, and he opens the trunk where Simon joins him to help with the chair. Fowler's head appears on the far side of the car and then disappears, as they help him into the chair. Simon walks ahead, purposefully, with a folder of colored pages in one hand. Isaac pushes. I wave madly until they see us and start heading over.

'How was the *ride*?' I holler before they reach us, a real Mother question, a pleasantry that eludes answer, inane, idiotic.

Fowler's got Daisy's favorite cap on, and he tries to acknowledge me by tipping it, but the arm can't manage the arc up. Isaac releases one hand from the chair and gives a thumbs-up.

'I've got coffee in the thermos. Does anyone want?'

Now I'm Daddy, focusing on the food to steer through tension. But the tension is my own.

'He wouldn't let me show off,' Fowler says. 'He had to push.'

'Take the help,' Isaac teases, just like Simon does with me when I play Iron Lady and insist I can do everything myself.

I'm stuck on the two faces, identical, one above the

other. Simon occupies the girls with some bakery cookies, then attends to the straightening of the stack of papers in the folder, half an inch high, mint green.

'She brought all the stuff you like, Dad,' Jane says, forever smoothing. 'We have milk in a carton, sugar, hot cups, coffee, juice and croissants. Even jam. And you should see what there is for the party. We set it all up, all the tables and chairs and the ice and sodas. Mom's *really* nervous.'

Some of Isaac's teammates are gathering in front of the fence.

'I've gotta go,' he says to Fowler. 'Warm-up time. My bag's in the car.'

'Can I walk you?' I ask, dying for information.

'No, Mom. It's OK.'

'It's open,' Simon tells him. 'Coffee, Jim? I'm starting on my second breakfast here.'

'Great. It's not too hot for coffee.'

In fact, the weather is turning. A cool enough breeze, occasional clouds: September weather a couple of weeks early. I don't think we could have asked for a nicer day. The two men remind me, minus the wheelchair, the mammoth effort on Simon's part, of golfers, squinting into the challenges of the course, with good will.

*

After the coffee, Fowler suggests we move nearer the bleachers between home plate and first base.

'We'll be over shortly,' Simon decides. 'The girls and I need to do a little more eating, I think.'

'You go on and find us a spot,' I tell Fowler, remembering that he may want a chance to motor on his own.

'You bet,' he says. He works the gadgets with ease, turns the chair and charges off.

'What's all that?' I point to the flyers.

'Tot Shabbat,' he says. 'For after the game. See if we can drum up some interest.'

'Nearer my God to thee,' I mutter.

Deadpan, he tells me, 'Just because you've left the earth, don't expect us all to follow.'

I look at the gathered families.

'I think he's very impressed,' I offer, remembering my place on the undistinguished periphery.

'I don't give a shit about that,' Simon retorts.

The crowd cheers as our team fills the field, Isaac taking up the enviable outfield.

'What I meant is,' I apologize, 'I don't see how you get to it, how you know that this is the thing to do.' I point to the folder.

'At one point,' Simon says casually, 'I might have had some interest in talking to you about this.'

He starts over to the bleachers, but I catch his sleeve. 'Please. Just tell me how it went.'

'It went,' Simon pauses, 'quietly. Jim was all ready to go. He took a good long look while Isaac stood there taking a good long look, and then we were all laughing for some reason — nerves, probably — and the rest was logistics.'

'Hm.' I'm actually jealous, wishing I'd been there.

'What else can I tell you? He's a man seeing his son for the first time in fourteen years. I can't blame him for wanting a front-row seat.'

'We can all have a front-row seat,' I say.

'You go. I'm letting them have their day.'

I join Fowler as Isaac's team, having kept Ardsley at zero during the first inning, comes in for a turn.

'Come here,' Fowler says, holding out a hand. I perch on a few inches of metal bench beside one of the Ardsley mothers. I keep Fowler's hand between my two. Isaac's team huddles and erupts with a team howl, bringing their fists high; then Isaac breaks away to start the batting.

His signature walk to bat involves the habitual downward focus and a few thumps on the earth with the bat, a flirtatious glance at the field, several shifts in weight from one long leg to the other, then the utter sobriety he brings to lifting the bat gracefully up behind him in defiant readiness. It happens to be true that he rarely fouls, has never struck out in a formal game, and can be counted on to hit a ground ball through the infield at least once per game. The outfielders run, stumble, scoop up the ball and throw it just too late to third or home plate, and Isaac, if he's come in, strides neutrally back to the bench, as if any acknowledgement of his success will detract from it, will mortify his teammates and the spectators, always a small crowd.

The pitch comes in down the middle, fast, and Isaac smacks it, hurls the bat and bolts for first and beyond.

'He's got it!' Fowler shouts, rising from his chair, rocking it, falling back.

The Ardsley fellows do their sorry dance as Isaac lopes around the field and tags home. He catches his breath, doubled over, hands on his knees, by the swearing catcher. Then he looks straight at me and Fowler and laughs skyward, his arms open in the wild questioning gesture my father is famous for, as if to say, 'You were expecting something less?'

'IZ-ZY! IZ-ZY!' his teammates chant.

'That's a kid-and-a-half!' Fowler says, grinning. 'He plays ball like a pro!'

'He does?' I ask, because, in fact, I don't know this.

Fowler looks at me, disappointed. 'Open your eyes, Mom. He's God out there. He's where everyone's looking.'

Of course, Fowler would notice this. I have always looked only at Isaac on the field, letting the other players drift, helpfully or drastically, in and out of my vision, their names and heights and hair color sliding away with their actions. It's Fowler's first time out, his first time looking at the only thing worth looking at, that being his own child.

To my left, in a clump of mothers and dads, is my husband, gingerly offering the printed news of the temple, his place of refuge from me.

The victory, over the Ardsley team, subtle and well played by both sides, is cause for further celebration. Garland and Travis, who caught the final inning, are our first arrivals. I steal Travis away for a conference and some help in the kitchen.

'You didn't tell me Isaac was such a Romeo,' I scold.

'Fool. This is just the beginning of the nightmare. But you don't need to worry with her, darling. The car's a total deception. She's a *doll*. It's like she just came out of her house for the first time this summer. I'm surprised they didn't home-school her. She's a five-year-old with breasts. And speaking of the Aidinoffs —'

He pulls me over so I can peer out the window at a couple older than ourselves, standing at the edge of it all, with Alex. Mrs Aidinoff has on muted madras trousers and an ivory blouse, an outfit I might be seen in ten years hence, and her husband, like Simon, wears pressed jeans, loafers and a tennis shirt.

'I think it might be a good idea if you went out there,' Travis says. 'Garland's beating you out for the big shmooze. Here's to arranged marriages!' He raises a cup of iced tea. 'I'll stay here and remove Clingfilm. You go on, get out there, before Garland takes over.'

'Hard to believe, of a guy who never says anything!'

Eliot sweeps in, studies me, then Travis, trying to discern the cause of the laughter.

'Is she being wicked?' he says sweetly. 'Pay no attention to her, Travis. She's the world's most ungrateful woman!'

He's got a canvas bag of books for me and two bottles of Chardonnay. 'I brought the Bemelmans books for their majesties. It's a loaner, though.'

Travis relieves Eliot of both packages.

'Eliot, Travis. Travis, Eliot.'

'She *is* a bitch,' Travis says. 'Come help me with these barbaric salads. You'd think there wasn't enough mayonnaise on earth. Have they ever heard of oil and vinegar?'

'Yes, ma'am,' Eliot says, laughing.

'Men,' I cluck. 'Hello!' I shout from the doorway.

'I'm Ruth,' Mrs Aidinoff says and holds out her hand in the same graceful, pitying way that Alex did last night.

'This is my dad,' Alex says, one arm around the tall man.

'Seth,' he says pleasantly.

'We love your boy,' his wife says. 'He's so polite, such a gentleman.'

I try to hide my dismay in disclaimers, but it doesn't work.

'Really!' she assures me. 'But all children are different at home!'

We're joined by Fowler and Isaac, still ushering, as if he's been hired as an attendant.

'Hi, everyone,' Isaac says. 'I'd like you to meet my dad.'

Fowler lifts a hand in greeting. There's no question that arm control is now a thing of the past.

'Good to meet you.'

'Spitting image,' Seth remarks.

'Jim, this is Alex,' Isaac says.

'A pleasure,' Fowler says. Alex approaches Fowler, on this our sacred ground, and rests her hand on top of his.

'Isaac says you make movies,' she says. 'I'd really like to see some.'

Jane, who's been spying from the side, grimaces and trods off to join her abandoned father at the grill. Even in the grave, I believe, Fowler will possess a magnetism. Something on the tombstone, or in the landscape where it stands, that lush, foreign landscape, will work as an invitation and a warm welcome, will draw the women to him.

Isaac and I sit in bumper-to-bumper on Broadway, after dropping Fowler home.

'This sucks.'

I try to defend my choice of this route over the clogged parkway. He says we should have taken the highway.

'There was a game,' I remind him. Yankee Stadium will be emptying in a few minutes.

'How'd it go today? Before the game?'

'God, Mom, give it a rest.'

He's right, so I give it a rest, and we listen to the glum traffic reports and inch along in the dark.

'Just tell me one thing,' Isaac says finally. 'Tell me what you did that made him leave.'

Ever the hero, Fowler.

'I had you.'

Isaac guffaws, unbelieving. 'Had to be something worse than that, Mom.'

'No, I don't think so,' I say firmly. 'He just didn't want to deal.'

Isaac looks straight at me. 'As long as I live, I'll never believe that.'

I get us over into the passing lane, not that any passing is possible. 'And I'll never believe that while you sit there listing my crimes, you manage to forget that I was the one who *didn't* leave.'

ELEVEN

Fall is always a hard season, asking for so much smoothing over, assurance, happiness through change. We do our errands for fall clothes, our back-to-school cut-rate shopping at the stationer's, our pre-school trips to the school for sign-ups, book purchases and scheduling. I've put Daisy in nursery school two mornings a week; even Daisy requires a shoebox full of supplies in the event of rain or a cold snap. Simon faces a load of work, as early fall is the panic season in the schools, when none of the scheduling software behaves as promised by the manufacturers, and he makes double overtime, by his own standards, to troubleshoot. Isaac has remained silent on the subject of Alex, packed off to Brandeis three weeks ago, focusing instead on private weekly visits with Fowler. I don't know what they do other than eat dinner, which I supply in a picnic basket, and when I drop Isaac at the apartment, I'm not permitted to go in and say hello. Jane, in heaven because she and Adrienne have been assigned to the same homeroom, is my slightest worry.

I see Fowler on Wednesdays, when Daisy and I come in to help with the shopping and the work for his class. He can't stop thanking me and boasting about his son as we have our lunch in the living room.

I drive and work. I wait for a signal to stop and rest to stop and rest from one of them, one of my boys or one of my girls, but they are content to have me on the periphery making sure things go smoothly and working quietly on this book about mythical women who actually lived, these prolix angels who did not believe in the public worth of their words, words that are now cause for Barry's delighted surprise. I work early in the morning and late at night.

'You're burning the candle,' Simon tells me, day after day. 'You need sleep. It's going to catch up with you.'

'I've never been a good sleeper.'

It's Simon's way, this concern over sleep, of letting me know I've brought enough to this household. We speak only of the details now, not of the disease or the person it has afflicted or the inevitable outcome.

Until one night in late September when Isaac comes

out of Fowler's building to the car, where I'm waiting with coffee and reading, and he is crying.

'You should go in there, Mom,' he says. He draws his forearm across his face.

I expect to find Fowler compromised in some specific new way that can't be helped by our summer attempts to rig his apartment with mechanical aids. He is in front of the TV; the remote rests on the arm of the wheelchair, and his fingers dance over the buttons. Images flash and vanish, flash and vanish. The sound is off. Fowler glares at the set, his chin low, supported by his sloping chest. For all his original height, he looks tiny this way, further diminished by the trance the rapid channel fire has him under.

'What are you doing?' I ask him.

'I'm watching television,' he says neutrally.

I snatch the remote from him and shut off the set. 'How *dare* you?'

He presses a button on the chair and spins to face me. 'I beg your pardon?'

'I've got a crying boy outside in my car who could be home studying now but has chosen instead to bring you dinner. Maybe you could have saved this performance for later, after he's left.' My voice is a contained scream.

'Maybe these efforts are a little wasted on me now,'

he says. He's so slumped in his chair I can't help thinking it's intentional, a posture meant to inspire pity.

I wait a beat, to head off a furious outburst.

'That may be. But I'd prefer that you take that up with me privately. Isaac's a child, and he doesn't know from his own wasted efforts yet. You're the *last* person on earth who should be informing him about same.'

'Spare me the random insult, Leigh.'

'No. You spare *me*. Don't allow Isaac to feel that his efforts in your direction are wasted. He's never put himself so far into an effort before, and considering what you dealt him, I think it's pretty extraordinary.'

I pick up the picnic basket and slam out of the apartment. On the ride home I ask Isaac, through rage, 'How long was he doing that?'

'The whole time I was there.'

'The whole hour and a half I was outside in the car? Why didn't you come out sooner?'

'I thought he'd stop. Then I thought he was going crazy.'

'He just sat there like that for an hour and a half? Did he say anything at all?'

'He said he can't lift his head. I said we should take a walk and he just laughed. He said why go for a walk if all he can see is his lap.'

I keep talking, but I'm running out of schemes. I'm running out of ways to look at this thing and reasons for dragging my husband and children through it with me.

I'm back at Fowler's the next day, after a midnight call, in apology and admission of the need for more help. It's late morning, and again he hasn't eaten. His teeth and hair want brushing, but somehow he's dressed himself and begun reading the student manuscripts that have accumulated over the first month of the course. The pages he's read lie at his feet in the nightmarish arrangement some of the Hastings teachers got us to imagine when they described their methods of evaluation. 'Whatever lands on the top stair gets the A.'

'Which means,' Pam said, 'that I have a chance of passing.'

'How are they?'

'Pretty demonic. Such attractive people, and all of them with murder and sexual abuse on the brain. At least they've steered clear of terminal illness.'

'I called Sherman at the warehouse. He says he's got a neck brace and head support that we can attach to the chair. I thought we'd go get it and then I could take you to lunch.'

I'm crouching, picking up the pages and ordering

them, sparing myself the actual reading. This way he can see me and not be reduced to talking to my feet. Daisy's glued to *Barney*.

'You're going to need a sweater. And a comb.' I find a navy pullover in his bottom drawer and bring out the comb and toothbrush and a cup of water.

First we do hair. I draw the comb through, without incident.

'Later you'll give me the honor of washing this.'

'Heaven.'

Then we do teeth. I scrape around, remembering, in horror, Dr Peterson's drilling. He drains the cup and spits back into it, disgusted. 'I'm impossible. How can you bear me?'

'Good question.'

I put the sweater over his head, smooth his long arms through it, stay with my hands on his chest, my head resting next to his. 'It'll be good, to get the brace. Looking at the ground all day sucks.'

'I love your optimism, Jolly Hockey-Sticks.'

I ask about the bathroom, but he says he can manage on his own. 'Thanks to our elaborate restroom rigging.'

'It'll save you, that humor.'

'So I've heard. Say, did you read about the guy who

was afraid to laugh because he might literally laugh his own head off?'

'It was one of the first articles Eliot found for me.'

'You've done good work.'

'Meaning.'

'You've always managed to surround yourself with decent people. How have you done that?'

'I don't know. Certainly not by being decent myself!'

He smiles into his lap, then motors into the bathroom. On screen the big purple dinosaur is gathering children under his short arms and mouthing the words to the famous song that Daisy has memorized and that cynics like Isaac and Jane ape. *Won't you say you love me too?* Barney and his entourage wonder. Jane and Isaac have made up violent replacement lyrics, and we've laughed and laughed. But here we are, as odd an assortment of creatures as that on the set, trying to gather our spirits into one common effort. Who are we to deny Barney?

I try to take comfort later from the letters of Hadewijch: *Try and remain inwardly detached in all that happens to you; when you are troubled and when you enjoy peace of mind.* She was a Beguine; she chose to give up material wealth in service to communal peace. Of my situation she might have said that to react personally to hardship is to behave selfishly, to ignore the divine. But I am not a religious woman — how could I be? — and tonight the words of my wise women don't comfort me. I look past them at the specifics: at my dutiful, aloof husband, at my distressed son, defiant daughter, wondering parents and at my baby, forgiveness incarnate. Then at Fowler, who cannot continue on his own, no matter what his mind has made up.

I join Simon at the dining-room table, where he's doing his accounts.

'Today I got Fowler a neck brace and head support. I'm not sure he can manage much more by himself.'

'Of course he can't.' Simon records some numbers on a slip of paper, accounts he'll enter into his computer later.

'I may have to stay there.'

Simon puts the pen down. 'We spoke about that.'

'Yes, but under the circumstances —' I begin.

'There are no circumstances that dictate your living with him. Bring him here if you have to. We'll set him up on the porch. We know it can't be forever.'

'That's insane. That's a totally bizarre idea.'

'Leigh, we're not dealing with ideas here. A lot of this, for me anyway, has become a matter of function.'

'So you're telling me it's OK to bring him here.'

'I'm telling you that is the only way for you to continue to help him and stay married to me. You are *my* family, not his. You live with *me*, and when he dies you stay with *me*. Wherever your mind is most of the time, your body lives here. There's no other way I can look at any of this and stomach it.'

'Fowler says that I'm a lucky woman.'

'He was probably referring to your good fortune in having known *him*.'

We stop at this. The past tense, creeping into his speech like that, stops us.

'Talk to the children,' he says. 'And it may be time to reintroduce yourself to those enormously helpful parents of his who seem to think nothing of luxuriating in Southern splendor while their son fades out in a cold climate.'

'I love you.'

'I know you do. I keep praying that will be enough.'

He takes his bath and goes to bed, and I look over his books. He's been making money. I spend it on bridge tolls and on take-out for Fowler, on books, clothes and sundries for the children, groceries for the household, and Simon rakes it in, privately, seeing that there's enough for me to spend. Hadewijch writes: *When Love*

first spoke to me of love — How I laughed at her in return!
There's a love of happening, of connection, of image, of
learning that Simon is asking me to notice and heed over
the love of Fowler, the love of myself with Fowler. He
is giving me what I've been asking from him since
Fowler came back, what I'd begun to doubt: a request
that I stay. An unabashed statement of need.

The following Wednesday, Eliot and I have dinner in a
coffee shop across the street from the building where
Fowler holds his class.

'You always take me to the most elegant places,' Eliot
moans as we pore over the menus. 'You'll forever
remind me of hamburgers.'

'You love hamburgers.'

At the barbecue, Eliot ate two of them, smothered
with onion and ketchup, 'a real train wreck,' Travis
commented when he saw the plate. 'Let's watch him eat
it.'

'You look fabulous,' Eliot tells me. 'Whatever misery
you're laying claim to, it suits you. You're so *svelte*, and
that is not a word I lavish often on people of your
height. The man must keep you jumping, chair and all.'

'What about you?' I ask. '*Is* there anyone?'

'I'm keeping quiet, for the present.'

'The present is lasting a while.'

'Suitable mourning has not been concluded,' he says.

I ask who it was, when mourning commenced. I'm anticipating, trying to learn what will be required of me, what limits I can reasonably impose on grief.

'He was Michael Peter Osborne, of Stratford, England. He was a dilettante with an inheritance. He died in his sleep in our apartment two years ago, at the age of forty-nine. He believed in nothing except me, and the same was true for me.'

'And now?'

'Now I'm keeping quiet, as I said.'

'Are you waiting for someone else?'

Eliot rests his head on the heel of one hand. 'There isn't anybody else.'

'Nonsense,' I quip, as my grandmother Pussy did in response to any unbearable notion. 'What about Travis?'

'Too old and too married. Who's the stiff anyway? Could we get a haircut?'

He refers to Garland so hatefully, I think he must be interested in Travis. 'You let me know if you want me to have another barbecue. In the meantime, Fowler is coming to live with us.'

'Oh?' Eliot says, still in the realm of the dead Michael Peter Osborne. 'I thought he already was.'

*

I wait outside the classroom to collect Fowler and drive him back to his apartment. Again my mind is on the details — on the outfitting we've done for the place, only to find it wasn't enough, on the commuting and the storage and the informing we'll have to do, on all the sorting and re-rigging that will have to go on *chez nous*.

I hear the respectful tones of serious discussion, the occasional polite laughter that occurs in professional exchange. I peer through a murky window at the faces of his few students, poised in a semicircle around his chair. I want to know what he's saying, how he's engaging them, charging them to be more honest, more raw, less vitriolic and didactic. There's a girl in the middle who doesn't take her eyes off him. She's not stunning looking, just put together, short brown hair and tortoiseshell glasses, a button-down man's shirt, blue jeans and boots, a yellow sweater thrown over the shoulders. Minus the boots, she looks a little like my mother did in a photograph taken of her when she was an undergraduate at Smith. But my mother was always laughing, or on the verge of doing so in those pictures. This girl looks suspicious, not entirely willing to go Fowler's distance, believe what he says. Still, there's no denying fascination and surprise. She uncrosses her thin legs and bends over a notebook to jot something down.

Were I this girl I'd wonder how it is that a man in a wheelchair can pull me in like this, whether it's the strength of mere words that draws me, whether there's wisdom in them, and what has gone on in this man's life to get him here? I'd stare too, at the inscrutable tension in his face, and want to be closer, to have him trust me, only me, with his story, and look at me with mutual fear and longing.

Suddenly the girl looks up and catches me looking at her. She levels her intelligent gaze on me, angry for the intrusion. I gasp, recede quickly into the shadows of this wide, empty hall, a hall where, quite frankly, rape wouldn't be out of the question. How dare I presume to know what this girl is thinking? Perhaps she is even bored by what Fowler is telling them in his new, halting way. Perhaps she was jotting down a grocery list or notes for her own work, which she might consider far superior to any that has been submitted.

I suppose I want to continue to see Fowler as a man whom no woman can resist because it keeps him further from death and closer to me. And because, naturally, I don't want him to be so sick and to need me so much that I cease to be the lover and become the nurse, the mother, the friend.

But these are selfish musings, and when the students

finally file out and I walk in and start taking things up for him and he watches me, his head at an angle in its stiff brace, I realize I am all of those things and that in his gray, frightened eyes is more love than I've ever thought him capable of having for me. For the second time in half an hour I'm mortified. Fowler loves me, he actually does love me, and it isn't a response I've procured by design. It just happens that over time and distance Fowler has had one woman in his heart, and she's been me.

I gather their work, slide it into his worn leather case that has been everywhere. Then I lay it in his lap, slowly, lovingly, like an offering.

'I thought I'd write to Evelyn and tell her you'll be staying with us for a while,' I say, facing him, lying close on the couch.

'I called her today. I told her.'

'She still doesn't know it's me, does she?'

'She will,' he says. His fingers slide along the inside of my arm. 'She will.'

We decide on Rosh Hashanah for Fowler's arrival.

'Why not?' Simon said. 'Start him off on the new year.'

I pick Mother up at the train station. I've been up since four writing and cleaning and drinking far too much coffee, and I may very well have forgotten to brush my teeth.

'Heavens,' Mother says when she gets a look at me.

'Sorry. I've been cleaning. I've never seen so much dirt.'

Fowler might say I've inherited some of Mother's resourcefulness.

'Can I do some of it for you?' she suggests.

'No, you just watch the kids. You can take them out for breakfast.'

'On Rosh Hashanah? Your father wouldn't *hear* of it!'

'He won't know. Please take them. They're bored out of their minds. Daisy loves IHOP — you can take them there.'

'Fine. And is there any shopping I can do for you. Do you need anything?'

'We have most of the stuff he needs at the apartment. We had to get a hospital bed for the porch — don't be horrified.'

Lord, but I'm reeling from the coffee and the fact of his coming.

'You're sure of all this, dear?' Mother asks gently. 'I

mean, you know where it's leading and you still want to do it?'

I haven't really thought about *wanting* to do it.

'I'm sure.'

'You're very brave, you know.'

I clench the steering wheel, unable to understand why such a comment might cause me to cry. But I don't cry. I'm too busy, too wired.

'What time is dinner?'

'You should *ask* such a question?' my mother teases, inflecting as my father does, as if she comes from the Old World too and can target such foolishness the way he does.

'OK. Sundown. And he knows Fowler's coming?'

'He knows,' she says. 'How is Isaac?'

'He's wonderful,' I say.

'Really.'

She doesn't believe me. She's disapproved of the reunion from the start. But she will see the change in him, the new purpose, the possessiveness and pride in every gesture.

'He's finally got his father,' I tell her. 'It's what he's always wanted.'

In the driveway she waits to get out.

'I just hope he can bear to have had a father for such a short time.'

'I don't expect him to bear it,' I assure her.

'Always with the answer,' she says, again mimicking Daddy. 'You sound *so old* sometimes, I can't get over it.'

'Someone's got to be old, Mother. Someone's got to manage. I don't have points glamorous to run to when it all comes crashing down. I don't have my own apartment to hide in.'

'Oh really, Leigh, if you only knew how unfair that is.'

'Why don't you tell me how unfair it is? I grew up when I was ten, when you and Daddy decided you needed two playgrounds because you didn't like to share.'

'I didn't go to the Vineyard to escape,' she explains. 'I went to say goodbye to an old friend.'

'An old *boy*friend, Mother. Let's be precise.'

'As you wish. An old, *gay* boyfriend who's had a stroke and can't talk or feed or clean himself. I may not always say exactly what you want me to say or be exactly where you want me to be, but I'm here now, so don't accuse me of frolicking while the world around me falls on its ass.'

She settles back into the seat from which she's come unglued while raving.

'I'm sorry. I didn't know he was that sick.'

'No one knows how sick *any*one is until they start living with them. Now let's go in. They'll think we're having an argument.'

'We are having an argument, Ma,' I say.

'Thank you for telling me.' She gets out.

The minute they see Grandma the children leave off with their morning bickering. We announce the IHOP plan.

'Are you letting Grandma drive?' Isaac says.

'I'm the only one who's old enough,' my mother says. 'And I'm a damn good driver.'

'But you never drive,' he argues.

'You'll have your license soon enough,' she says. 'Then we'll buy you that Miata or whatever it is.'

He raises his fists high above him, in rigorous approval of the idea. 'You may not need to,' he says, grinning. 'And I want a Porsche.'

The boy has such faith! He believes that a girl he hasn't heard from in six weeks still has him in mind, that she'll someday just give him her car.

'Go,' I say. 'There's always a line there on a Saturday.'

After they drive off, I do the floors under the couches and the windowsills and then go out to make up the hospital bed we rented from Sherman. It's got an awful mint-green mattress that's creased from use, even when flat. I plug it in to test its various functions. Then I lie down to feel it peak at my knees and collapse, raise the head for an imaginary feeding, level the thing, then lower and elevate it as I lie flat, as if my arms, legs and head can no longer move. I make myself stay flat like this for several minutes, wanting to scream, wanting to pray, but I don't know who to scream for or pray to. I've got no notion of God, and this frightens me. Without God I am just something on a bed, something that can make noise and not be heard.

'What are you doing?'

Simon stands in the doorway, at the end of patience.

I sit up, embarrassed. 'I don't know. I suppose I'm getting ready.'

Simon and I drop Mother and the kids, all scrubbed and changed into holiday best, outside Daddy's building. They go in empty-handed — Daddy said he's always taken care of the holiday food, why should things change now? Simon insists on coming inside with me at Fowler's. On the stoop I stumble and fall, tearing my dress and stockings at one knee. Simon pulls me up with one hand.

'Get a hold of yourself,' he says sternly.

I use the set of keys I had made for myself and Isaac a month ago, when it became clear that Fowler couldn't answer the door, and let us in. Fowler's waiting in the living room, a packed bag on either side of the chair, his tweed jacket over his knees.

'Hello, couple.'

'Hi, Jim,' Simon says gruffly. I can only think that Simon's instant offer to check around for anything left unlocked or untidy is nervous compensation for his horror at seeing Fowler so shrunken, a concave man with a lolling head. I get Fowler in the car while Simon loads the trunk.

'We can always come back if you need anything,' I say. As the apartment is not sublet, the furniture and books stay.

'Everyone in?' Simon asks, out of habit.

'Fine. Thank you,' Fowler says, with his verbal leisure. He's in front, where there's more leg room, and I'm shoved in between Daisy's car seat and the folded chair. Somehow we'll get the chair in the trunk so we can all fit in for the ride home.

*

Mother does her big-deal greeting, somehow making sure that Fowler feels he's forgiven although this is not necessarily the case. She takes over the wheelchair and brings him in to reintroduce him to Daddy, who's got Daisy on his lap with some playing cards, trying to teach her her numbers.

Daddy puts Daisy aside and stands reverently, his hands clasped, as if in the presence of an esteemed scholar.

'I'm glad you're here,' he says, touching Fowler's arm. 'Come. I'll explain the dinner. It isn't religious. I consider myself a cultural Jew —'

'Blah, blah, blah,' my mother whispers to me.

'Isn't it terrific the way he can move that chair on his own?' she says aloud.

'Of course he can!' Isaac snaps. 'He can do pretty much everything.'

Mother shoots me a look, in gratitude for such treatment. 'I have a few things left to learn about all of this,' she says. 'You'll do me the favor of indulging me my ignorance.'

I join Daddy at the table where he's pointing out the chopped liver, stuffed eggs, apples and honey.

'You eat the apple with the honey so you should have a sweet year,' he says.

Fowler smiles wryly. 'The year is almost over.'

'Not for the Jews,' my father continues. 'This is the start of a new year, thus the celebration.'

'I like that idea,' Fowler says.

'Come. Look,' Daddy says. He takes a slice of apple, dips it in the honey and brings it, cupped with the other hand so it won't spill on Fowler's trousers, and he feeds it to Fowler, who accepts it and nods several times after swallowing.

'L'chaim,' my father says, turning tearfully to all of us who have gathered around the table. To life.

'L'chaim,' we echo.

TWELVE

Adrienne has begun calling our home 'the hospital'.
'It's horrible here now, Mom,' Jane says. 'No
one will come here.'

'No one *ever* comes here,' I say carelessly, desperate
for levity.

'Adrienne said to only call her after he dies.'

'I think that gives you a lifelong excuse not to bother
with Adrienne. Don't you think she's mean, Jane?'

'You're mean, Mom. For making us live with him.
He should be in a hospital.'

'According to Adrienne, he is.'

She storms out of the bathroom, slamming the door
so its wind rips through my bubbles, decreasing them by
half.

It's a duration we are living, a dark period that will
blend in with others long after it is over. Over? I

prevent its being over, delay his dying by having him here. And he lets me do it.

I haven't had time to see Kirsten, despite requests to meet here and there, at the local eateries, so she can hear what's really going on in the hospital and not depend on the vicious speculation of her daughter. I have volunteered, on the telephone, that we are frantically busy trying to make Fowler comfortable, to get him to his doctors and his classes and to places he can enjoy with Isaac, movies mostly, an occasional trip to a museum.

'How's Simon?' she asked.

'Fine,' I chirped, although that is always, no matter what situation it applies to, a lie of a word. The truth is we're engaged in a project that doesn't allow me to think in such terms, that is, as Simon said, more easily described as 'a matter of function'.

Fowler's gotten so much worse over October, he needs so much help, that much of my energy goes to arranging care: I get Isaac, Jane and Daisy up early so that they can use the space I need for readying Fowler for the day *before* he gets up. We've cordoned off the porch, his bedroom, but now the nights are getting too cool for him to sleep out there and there is talk of bringing him inside, apportioning a corner of the dining room and setting up a screen around the bed. As it is, the hectic look of the house would turn any visitor away. In the evenings, after Isaac has done his schoolwork and Fowler isn't too tired, they play detective games on the computer. Simon bought a wand that attaches to a headband, and he's angled the laptop so that Fowler can, with a swift flicking movement, the only movement his head is still capable of, punch the keys and play. The laptop stays on top of the dining-room table, so Fowler can go there to type any time, and during dinner, which we all eat together, he can use it to take part in the conversation.

Dinners are *not* weird. It is generally acknowledged that the important connection, the reason for Fowler's staying with us, is the one between him and Isaac, not between him and me. The sexual element my older children were so quick to excoriate me for has receded into the realm of the ridiculous for them. Fowler is properly unsexed in their eyes. I cannot say the same for myself. I cannot say that the man who has drawn me to him all these years has disappeared. I think of this affliction, this monstrous insult to his beauty, as temporary still, and at night when Simon and I are in bed, our lovemaking is an effort for me, and I've stopped him, in favor of sleep, too many times.

Last night, when I did so, he said, 'You and he aren't still . . . ?'

'You're insane,' I said.

'Any man in my position would have to be.'

But Fowler is still capable. Some mornings when Daisy's at the nursery school and we've spread our work across the dining-room table, we ignore it. Afterwards we go for a walk in the neighborhood. I think of those French villagers in the movie who nicknamed Catherine, Jules and Jim 'the three lunatics'.

This morning I'm stripping the garden. We had frost last night. I toss green tomatoes into a tall wicker basket, set the ripe ones aside, snap the eggplant off and pull up the basil. The yard is brown. We can see through to next door's garage, but the ground, when I sit to rest, is surprisingly warm. I hear the screen door slam, then the squeak of the chair as it descends the ramp.

Irritated that this, probably my sole moment of peace for the day, has to be disturbed, I go to see what he wants.

He points to the garden, says, 'Please.'

I push him to the garden's rocky edge. Simon handpicked these large, white oval stones one night on a Massachusetts beach. We filled the trunk of the car, so that when our week there was up, the luggage had to ride on the roof.

He points to the ground.

I gather him to me in the way we do for the bath, from one side of the chair, under the arms. I lower us and settle his head on my bunched-up sweatshirt so he can look up at my devastation, the garden in sunny ruin. I start to pull away to finish the harvest, but he keeps a hold on me with one urgent hand.

'Stay.'

There is only one way to do this, with us now. I straddle his chest, put a hand on him while I unbutton my shirt with the free one. He's already hard when I dip down, give him each breast, fill his mouth with my tongue. Then I take care of my lower half, graceless as it is to take off boots and jeans when you're kneeling. Above him I watch for signs of release, hope, anything, from his stymied state, and when I'm wet enough to lower myself onto him, the muscles in his jaw, around his eyes, constrict and slacken, constrict again, slacken, over and over until we're done. Only when he hushes me do I know I've cried out, who knows how much, a naked woman in her garden, making love, again, to a man not her husband. But I don't care. I don't care. It's too hard, all of it, and it's the last time. I can't bear it any more. I lie on top of him, my knees, elbows, even my mouth, filmy with earth. I fasten his lank arms around me, feel them recede, and then I sob loudly, an awful, ugly, animal sob. And Fowler shifts under me, sideways, away from my noise.

'I'll leave soon,' he manages to say, at that painful pace.

'Good,' I say.

That night I call Evelyn. 'The course meets four more times. He wants to finish it.'

'Leigh,' she says, still cool, still busy. 'Are you the Leigh we knew so many years ago?'

'I am.'

'Oh, I can't believe he didn't mention that to me. When he said he was staying with an old friend and her family, I had no idea he meant you. Somehow a family didn't fit with my image of you when we met.'

'I was sixteen then,' I tell her.

'Of course you were. And you've been so good to him. Can I talk to him myself?'

'Well, that's sort of a problem because he can't manage too many words at once. He does most of his communicating by computer now.'

For once she waits to respond and when she does

speak her voice is colorless. 'Thank you. Can you tell me when he'll be returning?'

'Within the month,' I say. 'We'll let you know the details as they become available.'

'Before you hang up,' she rushes to say. 'How is he?'

'He's very ill. He would like to come home. He hasn't got a lot of time.'

To move the bed into the dining room we have to take it apart. Simon gets out his toolbox, and Isaac hauls up the yellowed, peeling Japanese screen from the basement and makes a show of cleaning it with a damp cloth and Wood Preen for the joints. Fowler tells him, 'Thank you.'

'Sure thing.'

When we get it all done, when our dining room is a bedroom too, I point to myself in question – does Fowler want my help getting ready for bed?

'That's OK, Mom,' Isaac jumps in. 'Man's work.'

Barry makes a sleeping pill recommendation.

'I sleep fine, just not enough.'

'You don't have to work *so* hard,' he jokes. 'You've got one check. There's no threat to the second.'

My advance, contracted to be made in two payments, is a gift, not a worry. I tell Barry as much, squeeze his large, freckled hand. 'You've been a huge help these last two months. I like having work.'

'Good! You've needed a little help! Maybe when you finish the book, you should take a vacation.'

I smile. I should tell him some things, just to be clear, honest. But I can't. I can't verbalize to strangers these days, say how things are snowballing for all of us, moving toward a monumental place, how it's impossible to think in terms of normal needs, sleep, food, routine. I've been reading Mirabai, the Indian prophetess.

'*I have felt the swaying of the elephant's shoulders; and now/you want me to climb on a jackass? Try to be serious*,' I say to Barry.

'You don't have to live their lives,' Barry says affectionately. 'You don't have to suffer what they've suffered.'

'I'm not,' I say.

I meet Pam at Sarabeth's and we gobble the tomato soup. She can't stop talking about how good I look, which strikes me as preposterous and indulgent, coming from her. She's the one who is and always has been beautiful, and she's wearing the clothes and jewelry to up that ante, to draw the stares of other lady lunchers just aching to find a flaw. They want us to be surfacey or gay or just plain stupid.

'So where do you actually *live*?' I ask, in that slidey voice we had at Hastings.

'In Providence. In a big, honking brownstone. Dave's an architect.'

'I know. I read it in the bulletin.' I remarked, then, on Pam's marrying someone who might not have money. But she could have married any fortune-seeker.

'Show me the kids,' I say.

She takes out her leather case of wallet photos and shows me the girls, replicas of herself at Hastings, tall, blonde, seriously beautiful, on an expanse of lawn leading to water.

'Where was that taken?'

'In Maine. At Dave's parents' house. This one's Eloise, and that's Madeline.'

'You didn't!'

'I did. The only books I ever liked. Now my turn.'

I get out my laminated photos that float in my bag, all done at Sears.

'There he is,' she says, stopping over Isaac's. 'Big as life. God, it's incredible. They're clones.'

'Almost as if I had nothing to do with it!'

She looks up, confused.

'Sorry. I'm letting myself say things.'

She sips Pellegrino. 'No. Go ahead. Don't let me stop you.'

'Fowler's going home next week. His doctors say he's in the advanced stage. It's happened faster than usual with him, although there really is no usual. Some people can last decades. Some go in three years. The point is, you're not going to get to see him. He's really too sick.'

'What makes you think I want to see him?'

'History.'

'Look, I'm going to let you go,' Pam says. 'I know you've got a lot to do. And I'm only in town until tomorrow. I'm going to hit the museums and Bloomie's this afternoon. And Bianca has the world coming for drinks tonight. Here's twenty. That should cover it.'

I should apologize, but I can't. I watch her shroud herself in a camel-hair cape.

'Ciao,' she says.

'Ciao.'

I can't do it, the lunches and the Biancas and the museums, now. I only came to tell her off, after all this time.

It's the beginning of November, cold, brilliantly sunny, the sort of weather that's perfect for a city. The pleasure the chill affords me flares and is consumed by the next thing, the next plan, an afternoon of taxiing, from the house to the schools to pick up Jane, then Isaac. Then later, back into the city for Fowler's class, God willing he's up to it.

Simon and Fowler are at the computer. Daisy claws the air for me. I throw my briefcase and coat on the couch.

'Come, baby.'

Daisy stumbles to me, whimpering. Jane comes out of the kitchen after checking the fridge.

'There's nothing for *dinner*, Mom. What are we supposed to *eat*?'

'I'm getting to it.'

'I'm hungry *now*.'

'We'll get Chinese.'

'That'll be the third time this week,' Simon reminds me.

'McDonald's it is,' I say. 'I'll go with Daisy. Any requests?'

'That we not get McDonald's,' Isaac bellows from the stairs.

'OK,' I agree. 'You all figure something out.'

Simon stands. 'There will be a moratorium on McDonald's until further notice is given.' He sits down.

Fowler and he continue with their game, Sleuth, I think it's called.

'Then what are we going to *eat*?' Jane screams at Simon.

'We'll improvise,' I say, trying to keep peace.

'I've done all the improvising I can,' Simon shouts, giving up on the game, getting on his jacket, leaving by the back door.

Fowler gets himself out of the game with painstaking punches of the keys. Then he types me a message. 'Soon,' it says.

Sometimes an exalted life, whether it's full of bravery and self-sacrifice or sin and degradation, isn't glamorous. Sometimes what you get is just a group of people in a room screaming about hamburgers.

Fowler and I leave at seven, after grazing on peanut butter and crackers. When we get to the classroom the students barely acknowledge the shift in personnel, as if they've expected me all along. They wait while I plug in the laptop and angle it for his convenience.

'Jim has asked me to help with some of the commentary here,' I explain a little too apologetically, as if I've got no business dealing with the written word at this level of its use.

Some smile out of obligation; others just gaze at me blankly.

'Do you want manuscripts?' one young man asks.

Fowler gives me a 'yes' with his eyes, and I collect them.

'There's a good chance this will be Professor Fowler's last meeting with you,' I inform them, 'which would mean that I will be substituting for him for the remaining meetings.'

I look directly at the girl who reminds me of myself, waiting for her to fire off an objection.

'Does that mean you'll be giving us our grades?' she asks impatiently.

Here I improvise because Fowler looks panicked. I tell her that the work turned in this evening should provide Professor Fowler with all the material he'll need for a final evaluation.

'Can't you let *him* tell us?' she asks snidely, gesturing toward the laptop.

My response to bad manners has never been graceful, but in light of my behavior toward Pam this noon, I keep quiet, except to say, 'All right.'

They move in close, to witness the results of the laborious typing.

'A*maz*ing,' a large, wrestler-type says.

'Totally,' says the one who asked about turning in manuscripts.

We discuss, verbally and by laptop, two unpromising dream sequences chosen by Fowler because of their coincidental use of dream, not their lack of promise. We go over ways in which they might be rooted to some context and thus improved, ways in which the dreamer and the dreamed could communicate more credibly. Then, of course, the matter of credibility as crucial comes into question, and references to Fellini and Buñuel abound. I like the informality of it, of Fowler typing in direction here and there, but not overwhelming the talk. I begin to see what is fun about this, which is the surprise in it, the fact that you don't know what you'll get when eight people sit down in a circle to talk. I see why he's done it, the teaching, all his life, in addition to the films. It's anything but safe.

On the way home I vainly ask how I did.

'They – loved – you,' he manages.

'They loved me because they love you. Already!'

He expels air, not letting himself laugh, for fear, I know, of losing head control.

'I don't know how you've done it,' I say.

'Mm?'

'I don't know how you've kept doing it while all this happens to you. It's totally amazing.'

Again, a semi-laugh. 'How — you — talk.'

Then I laugh. I haven't laughed, it seems, in months.

'I was about to call you,' Eliot says when I call him at work. 'I'm going to do it. I want the number.'

'What number?'

'Travis's number. I shouldn't, I know. But that guy with the hair isn't going to last with him, trust me. So I'm just going to call. I'll need the work number.'

I tell him I only have the home number.

'Then I'll call there and tell the stiff I'm an artist. Etcetera.'

I get the number.

'Now tell me what's wrong.'

'I just called the airline,' I say softly. I'm upstairs, away from Fowler, having a bad morning about it, not wanting him to know.

'Oh, God. It starts.'

'Eliot,' I say. 'How does a person do this?'

'Do what, dear,' he says, although he knows very well what I'm asking.

'This. This death thing. It feels like it's taking so long, and then you call an airline and it feels like there hasn't been any time. I'm way out there, Eliot. I'm looking down at my house, at this big mess I made, as if I've just decided to get out and leave it to get better on its own. This is horrible.'

'Do you need me? Can I come out there, take him for a walk? I can tell them there's an emergency, like the day with your tooth.'

'No. No. I'm just having a bad moment or two. You don't have to come.'

'You call me after he leaves. You do that.'

'All right.'

I go back downstairs and sit across from Fowler at the table. He's tired of his reading, and we've already eaten and walked and started in on the packing. He's leaving. I'm staying. This is not so unfamiliar for us. It should be easier than it is.

It's after two when I hear the 'Marseillaise,' at casual volume, through the screen door. Eliot blows in shortly, encumbered with a shopping bag and a bouquet of apricot roses.

'Knock, knock, who's here!'

I'm halfway through the second soup feeding of the day. I made tomato soup from our final tomatoes, even the green ones, and put Daisy to sleep with a bowl of it first. Eliot takes a brief look at Fowler and turns to me, probably done in by the bib I draped over Fowler's chest.

'I don't know who looks worse!' he cried. 'For God's sake, friend o' mine, fix thyself!'

It's true that I cry out for attention, my jeans and crew-neck sweater in their third wearing, my hair flat and greasy. 'I will shower,' I promise Eliot. 'Soon.'

Fowler backs his wheelchair off from lunch, upset by the intrusion even though he's admitted to liking Eliot.

'I'd hug you, but I might put you off your tea. You'll want tea, won't you?'

'Need you ask. It was frigid walking from the cab to the back door. I'm a popsicle. Lots of milk and sugar, and don't feel pressured to open the madeleines.'

He sets the tin that once delighted Daisy and Jane in the Lenox Hill waiting room on our table.

'You made madeleines?'

'Well, you can't buy them anywhere near the library! I figured it was the perfect dessert for a Francophile such as *vous-même*.'

'Oh my God.' They're piled, six per row, and they're so spongy and sweet I feel I shouldn't even have the one I'm eating. I hold one in front of Fowler, but he shakes his head, slowly, side to side, then motors to the other end of the table where the remaining pages of the last student manuscript are propped up on two cookbook stands that Simon's mother gave me when we got married.

'The train was dreamy, since you asked,' Eliot continues. 'So nice and smooth, and above ground! And then an enormous creature drove me over here for a small fee, so *voilà*, feast your eyes. I'm on holiday.'

Because he's so nervous, I start to wish he hadn't come, even though the pastries are to die for.

'How about a walk?' he asks generally, unable to question Fowler directly.

Fowler types something out with the wand. 'You two go,' it reads. 'Daisy will sleep.'

Eliot and I step outside. 'He's self-conscious,' I explain.

Eliot puts his arm around me. 'No he isn't. I am. And it's making him angry.'

'It is?'

He stops and leans against the house, covers his face for a second. 'I should go.'

'You just got here! Let me at least get your tea.'

'Can you drive me? To the station? I'll have the tea in the car.'

I get the tea and join him in the cracked front seat of the Mustard Bomb. 'It's bad, isn't it?'

He wastes no time in saying, 'It's over. When it gets so that you're worse off than the sick one, it's over. You are so lucky he's leaving, you have no idea.'

'Of course I don't!' I shout. 'How could I?'

Eliot sniffs, sips. 'You couldn't,' he says.

On Isaac's birthday Simon drives up in a rented minivan and honks shamelessly until we're assembled in front. I've got a picnic I know no one will want to eat, blankets and cameras. I convinced Isaac, when he complained of our family's lack of flair in terms of birthdays, that apple-picking was an original party idea, that we'd go to the orchards and get messy, then come home and make stuff with the apples for the rest of the weekend: caramel apples, pies, chutney, what-have-you. We could even think about selling it, I told him.

'You're trying to make up for Hallowe'en, aren't you, Mom?' he said.

'Maybe.' I don't see how a trip to Salinger's Orchard could compensate for my inattention on Hallowe'en, Jane explaining to the trick-or-treaters that her idiot mother hadn't had the decency to buy so much as an M&M.

I must say I have never ridden in so smooth and roomy a vehicle, and that the fact of our all fitting in without issue, with the wheelchair, is cause enough for a party. Simon and Fowler take the front thrones, Jane and Isaac the middle, then Daisy and I in back. I open the Cheetos and we roll.

'Brady Bunch on the road,' Isaac scoffs. I flinch at the Brady reference, thinking of the Brady Bill on gun control, but Isaac doesn't bother with the news, thank God. It's hard enough with Jane and her bandwagons.

'Mama sad?' Daisy asks, because I'm making some sort of face about it.

'No, sweetie pie. Mama happy.'

'Happy Bewfday?'

'Happy Birthday. Isaac's birthday.'

Daisy laughs crazily. I want to take her out of that motley and squeeze her.

We're impossibly cheerful as a crew, and I think it's because Fowler leaves tomorrow, and we have to be. Mother keeps calling, worried. She's sure I can't handle what's about to hit me. But I've told her, over and over, it's been hitting me since June. 'Still,' she says ominously.

We're driving him to LaGuardia tomorrow. Evelyn has been notified. He'll be flying alone.

From where I sit I can't see him. His minivan throne hides him entirely. I do catch Simon looking over now and then, asking Fowler if he's all right, if he needs anything. Simon should have been the doctor, not Carly.

'Mom, I want those maple sugar men and ladies that come in the little white boxes,' Jane says.

'Fine.'

'They'll get stuck in your rig,' Isaac says, taking more aim at Jane's braces.

'Drop dead,' Jane says, which sends me into a complete frenzy until I detect laughter in the front, he's letting himself laugh, and Simon's got an arm out for support.

'Nice one, Brainless. Any other choice phrases you'd like to spit through all that metal?'

'Enough, you two,' I warn. 'Enough about teeth.'

'Yeah, Mom. Are you ever going to get that tooth fixed? You have one white tooth and the rest are brown.'

'Thank you, Jane.'

Simon glances over at Fowler. 'Jim, I'd like you to meet your new family.'

At home, Mother and Daddy greet us at the door and help with the bags of apples. They give Isaac his presents right away, a handknit sweater and a check. 'Put it toward your Porsche,' Mother says. At which point, Alex steps out of the front hall closet, all in black, having somehow avoided gaining the Freshman Ten: the traditional ten pounds put on in the first year at college.

'Your dad called me last month,' she tells Isaac, who is red with embarrassment.

Isaac's eyes dart between Simon and Fowler, unsure.

'Happy Birthday!' my father shouts. 'Come on! Let's have some cake. There's coffee, Leigh. Your mother made fresh.'

'Now you're only three years younger than I am,' Alex says adorably. She holds out a present done up in tasteful plaid wrap. 'Happy Birthday.'

I stay in the hall with Fowler for a minute.

'You called Alex? At college?'

His eyes assent, closing with pleasure, as Isaac's did, for the short embrace.

'You're a smart man,' I say. 'You gave him exactly what he wanted.'

He points inside, where the cake is being brought, dots of fire in the darkened dining room.

'You're not a bad father, either,' I add.

*

After the cake, Daddy asks for a word with me. 'Would you like me to drive the young lady home?'

'That's OK, Dad.'

'I don't think she should spend the night.'

'Neither do we, Daddy. Give us some credit.'

My father smiles. 'I give you much credit,' he says. 'I don't know of anyone doing such a wonderful thing as you have done here.'

I break away from the dishes for a second. 'I guess I'm not the fool you took me for.'

'I'm the fool,' Daddy says, 'if I ever thought you were.'

Mother pokes her head in. 'We've got a train in half an hour,' she alerts my father.

'I'll have just enough time,' Daddy says. 'I'll tell her her chariot awaits.'

'You haven't driven in years.'

'Oh, let him have his little thing,' Mother says.

We follow him into the living room.

'I'm taking Alex home,' he tells Isaac. 'You can come along.'

'Conference time,' Isaac says. We go back in the kitchen. 'Why can't she stay?'

'Because she can't.'

'But I've stayed there.'

Fowler drops something in the next room. We find his wand on the floor. I pick it up, and he starts typing.

'Take her home,' he types.

'Why?' Isaac types back.

'Because your mother told you to.'

The next morning Simon brings in croissants, butter and jam. Jane holds Fowler's coffee for him, which he sips through a straw. I've been up packing Fowler's things and making a list for Evelyn, of ways to take care of him. I put Isaac's baseball photo, in its frame, in Fowler's carry-on. One unmarked box stays by the bed.

'What is it?' I ask him.

He types: *For you and Isaac.*

I take off the top, which indicates that there's Xerox paper inside. I find film reels instead, at least thirty canisters, all labeled with the titles of his films. In the presence of my family I say, 'I love you. I have always, always loved you.'

After the food we suit up. Simon packs the car. Then he kneels by the chair before lifting Fowler in. 'God speed.'

I go to my husband, as he takes up the sidelines again. I know I will cry if I tell him, just now, that he has held all of us up, that he's the best person I know, that I don't deserve him. So I reach for his hand, which he gives for me to press to my cheek. He gives my hand a tight squeeze. 'You'll be late,' he says. 'Go.'

'Mom, you forgot his hat!' Jane yells, rushing out to place it carefully on Fowler's head, to her sister's immediate chagrin. It *is* Daisy's favorite hat. 'Don't let anyone feed you who doesn't know what you have,' she counsels. 'Bye.' She offers her cheek for a kiss, which he gives, then backs away.

I don't look at them. I have Isaac hold my coffee until we're on the highway. He hands it to me without my asking, a good thing, as I don't dare speak.

Airports are grisly places, generally, too functional, too full of departure. It's hard to say which task is more onerous: parking, baggage check, the detailing of Fowler's particular needs to the clerk behind the desk who says we'll have to repeat this to the flight attendant anyway. The announcement for pre-boarding is made as soon as we've checked Fowler in and gotten his boarding pass.

I sink down and face him, holding onto the chair. Isaac is behind me, both hands on my shoulders. Fowler's hands cover my own.

'Mom,' Isaac says. 'Mom.'

I don't know what to do. I don't know what to do, so I stand up. Isaac is taking up Fowler's carry-on and assuming the post behind the chair. Fowler smiles — I know he is smiling, eyes narrow, lips pressed into an effort. He pushes the brake lever and pulls a slip of paper from his sleeve on which are typed the words *Every day*.

I take his hands, press my cheek to his, and kiss his lazy mouth. I draw back.

Isaac stands expressionless as a Buckingham Palace guard. Then Fowler flips the brakes off and they go, into the conveyor to the plane, and I am left to the long avenue of chairs and carpet at the gate.

'No!' I say, loud enough to startle myself. 'No!' Like a deranged person, over and over again until I gain the sense to direct myself to a stable piece of furniture, in this case a railing, and just hang onto it and look at it and hang on and look until my son returns.

And when he does come back, free of luggage, free of that beaten man he's learned to care for, he is weeping so uncontrollably that I have no choice but to let go of my rail, my help, and be his.

'Oh my sweet, sweet boy.'

'Mom,' he cries. 'Mom, help me. I didn't want to do that. I didn't want to put him on the plane. I had to tell them how to do everything for him. I didn't want to do that.'

'I didn't want you to have to,' I say, folding him into my arms as naturally as the first time he was given to me.

We walk, away from the engine blast. We walk out of the terminal, out of the airport, to the lot, our arms locked. We drive home.

A week later I hear from Evelyn by mail, the same day I receive Gillette's wedding invitation. First I attend to Gillette via the answering machine. 'Rue the day,' I say. 'Of course we'll be there. Bells on.'

Then I open Evelyn's letter.

> *Dear Leigh,*
>
> *I have first to thank you for sending Jim home with this marvelous computer and all the instructions for his care typed out so very helpfully. We have been in constant touch with his New York doctors, who have established us with local specialists, and I do believe he is growing used to his old home again, as doddering as his parents are, and we are trying to give him everything he needs. You have been good to him, good to us.*
>
> *Thank you also for the photograph of this beautiful child, who, as I understand it, is our grandson. I think I*

have seen this face before, in the younger version of his father. I wept upon seeing it. All the years you managed on your own must have been trying indeed. I wish we had been told before now about Isaac, whom I would like to meet.

Of course, this is a desperate time for me and for J.T. and, more so, for Jim. I trust you'll understand my reluctance to overwhelm myself with meeting Isaac right now. J.T. and I feel pressed to spend every minute with our son, who, we understand, will not see the new year. I fear our next communication with you will not be a cheerful one. But hear from us you will, and again, our thanks to you and your family for taking care of our boy.

Yours,

Evelyn Fowler

I roar through the end of the class, the end of the book. I find Kirsten at our booth in the diner.

'Oh, love,' she says. 'I'm so sorry. You don't deserve this.'

'Deserve this!' I howl. 'I deserve every second of this, and then some!'

She ignores me. 'I ordered for us. I want you and Simon to go away for a weekend. I'll take the kids.' She slides a flyer, from a Catskill lodge, in front of me.

'I can't leave my kids for a second these days without weeping. A weekend would kill me. When I drop Jane at school, she tells *me* I'll be OK.'

Kirsten smiles. 'It's OK not to be OK, so Adrienne tells me.'

'Our daughters. They should go into practice together. But Adrienne needs to be a little easier on the terminally ill.'

'She's a kid,' Kirsten scolds. 'Now, eat. You're too thin.'

I shovel in a tuna melt, fries and coffee while Kirsten talks just to let me know she's still around and that these meetings are still available on request. I've resisted her; she's been such a wench. I've wanted to stay away from everyone because meeting and talking means there's something to get over. He's not even dead yet. But I can no longer hear him. I cannot call his face clearly to mind. It does seem I've lost something. I know what he meant: *Every day*. He was never fully gone from me, as he is now, into that foreign, kudzu-smothered place. Nor was I, I see, gone from him.

I thank her, drive home and throw up.

The call from the South comes two days before Christmas, very early, after an hour of snowfall, when it's just Daisy and me playing on the floor beside the tree, where we set up a small village and the electric menorah.

It's J.T., with the news.

'When?'

'Four-thirty.'

I'd woken up! I'd woken up to see the clock, to wonder why I was up and Simon wasn't. And then I'd drifted back.

'Evelyn couldn't call. She's overwhelmed.'

'How did he go?' I so very much want it to have been peaceful.

'There was a fair amount of coughing,' J.T. says. 'It was a difficult end.'

'Oh no,' I say. 'Oh, I wish that weren't true.'

'I do too, Leigh.'

We are both crying, listening to the other. It's permissible. There are no rules in death.

'I'm going to write you a very long letter,' he says. 'Will that be all right with you?'

'That would be most welcome.'

'All right then.'

He says that he'll be in touch about the funeral, and that if it's too much for me, I shouldn't strain myself to come, but they would like to see me at some point, me and Isaac.

I leave Daisy at the base of the tree and climb the stairs. Through Isaac's slightly open door I see he's awake, staring up, waiting for me to pass into his line of vision.

'I heard, Mom.'

I sit on the bed, dry my face with the end of the bedspread. Isaac doesn't cry. He rakes his fingers through that hair.

'Mom, you're fine. I'm fine. We're all fine.' He swings his legs past me, to standing. 'It's like you said. It's the winter. He wasn't supposed to live longer than the winter. He was too sick! We have to go downstairs now, Mom, and eat something. Where's Simon? Is Jane up? What have you done with Daisy? Let's go, Mom. *Now*. Come on. Get up.'

Lord, but the life anyone leads can bring them to their knees.

He takes me by the hand, leads me through the house as he hollers, 'Breakfast! Get up, punks! Let's eat! Waffles! Pancakes! Syrup!' Sounding the alarums, raising Cain, summoning the living and the angels in our house, Isaac, my answered prayer, Isaac, who has come to me this time.